WAGONS WEST

by

Glorianne Weigand

Happy Trails
Glorianne Weigand

Dedication
To my mother,
Louise Roufs Chandler,
With Love

Cover Photo by Paul Tremaine

Wagons West

By
Glorianne Weigand

ISBN# 0-9644141-6-3

Copyright © 2000 Glorianne Weigand

All rights reserved. No part of the material protected by this copyright notice may be reproduced or utilized in any form or by any means, electronic, or mechanical, including photocopying, recording or by an informational storage and retrieval without written permission from the copyright owner. Printed in the United States of America.

Publisher
101 Ranch
Route 2 Box 31
Adin, California 96006
Fax & Phone 530-299-3465
www.dustytrails101.com
Email: weigand@hdo.net

Printed by
GRAPHIC PRESS
651 Market Street
Klamath Falls, OR 97601
541.884.4193 • 1.800.241.3441

Forward

Fort Sage: The Land Of Sheep, Cattle and Rustling, tells the story of Pike Garnier. The range war between the cattlemen and the sheepmen in Oregon was a troublesome time. The age-old fight and belief that the two kinds of stockmen did not get along and hated each other was true. Such was the case with Emmanuel, Pike's father. The cattlemen would shoot the sheep and shoot at the sheepmen.

In 1903 they headed to California where they had heard of the wide-open spaces at Fort Sage near Doyle. Fort Sage never did materialize as a Fort because while it was being built the Calvary had to go on an assignment and in their absence the Indians burned the Fort down.

One year it was so dry they could not put up any hay and had to drive their cattle 100 miles to Adin where hay was purchased to feed them through the winter.

Rustling of cattle was very prevalent on the desert near Fort Sage. Not too many years ago forty head were stolen. The brand inspector had watched cowboys working cattle and loading them into stock trailers, but just thought Pike was moving to another pasture. The cattle were never recovered.

The Swiss Families Of Sierra Valley is the story of the Lombardi and Dotta families. Coming from Switzerland to New York they traveled across the land to San Francisco, P.J. Lombardi found small jobs. He finally found work in dairies where he taught the art of making Swiss Cheese. Later moving to Sierra Valley he milked cows, made cheese and with his team and cart operated a milk route. His grandson Alvin Lombardi tells the story of their life and gives exact directions to the art of cheese making.

As a youngster the family raised all of their own food. Alvin had tasted Ketchup and just loved it. His father thought it was foolish to have such a luxury and would not buy it for the young boy. Alvin saved his money and bought a bottle of ketchup for himself, which he hid in his closet so no one else could use it.

From the late1860's until 1927 that portion of the country was the top ice producers in the state. Ice production is detailed in this story. Four sawmills were in the town of Loyalton and the economy was booming. The dairy business was very important to the economy, but with the invention of margarine the butter fat price dropped so drastically that a lot of the dairymen went broke.

The early times in Sierra Valley were marvelous, with the deep snow and cold temperatures, ice skating and sleighing parties. The singing in horse drawn sleighs was heard throughout the valley, stops were only when someone invited them in for cake and coffee.

There were also bad times, such as the train robbery near Reno in 1870. The robbers got away with $60,000 in gold, but all the bandits were found and punished. One tracked through the fresh snow in his high-heeled boots to a boarding house in Loyalton. All but $3,000 of the money was recovered. There is speculation that it is buried somewhere along the Truckee River. If found, the 150 gold coins would be worth over $500,000 today.

Memories Of A Pioneer Lady, tells the story of a brave woman from a long line of hearty pioneers. Laura Miller was born in 1879 in Stone Coal Valley. The lure of gold brought her father, Phillip from Iowa to California. The cumbersome wagons were too slow, so they cut up their harness to make cinches for packsaddles that they made out of the spokes of their wagon wheels. They packed some of the mules and rode the rest to the gold fields. They nearly starved while on the trail only living on what they could shoot which was an occasional jackrabbit. They finally reached Sutter's Mill where six thousand men already crowded the banks of the American River. Shoving, fighting and surviving was all that one could expect.

Moving on to Siskiyou County, Phillip struck gold at Deadwood Creek. Always wanting a cattle ranch he sold his claim in 1869 and moved to Modoc County. Here he and his wife Emily had eleven children and made their home in a log cabin. The first year they moved to the valley they killed twenty-five rattlesnakes.

The winter of 1889-90 caught the Millers off guard. Only enough hay was put up for the milk cows, work teams and saddle horses. The stock cows were expected to graze on the valley floor. The three to five feet of snow covered all of the feed. The men would snowshoe to the mountain to gather brush that they thought the cattle would eat. The straw out of the family's mattresses was fed to the starving animals along with the candles they had made for the winter. The paunches of the dead animals were cut open to let the surviving ones feed on that nourishment. By the dozens cattle perished. They saved only thirty head out of three hundred cows. The horses survived by eating the wool off of the dead sheep.

The Pit River Indians helped the whites, but the Modoc Indian War was on and the Modoc Indians would rob the Pit River tribe of their horses and possessions. Times were tough, but man and beast had to be tougher to survive.

A Fall River Valley History tells the story of the famous Island House, which was built in 1870 by William Winter. This home was a place of grandeur and magnificent parties and entertainment. Winter built the first sawmill and flourmill in the Fall River Valley.

He had promised his sons that he would give the Island House to the son who first brought home a bride. Harry was the first to marry and he and his wife entertained lavishly. Exquisite silver, maids, nursemaids, elaborate parties and fancy food became legends in the valley. The fortune of Harry Winter soon disappeared.

The bank took over the stately mansion and in 1899 Constable and Sheriff Edgar Lansing and his wife Margaret (Straub) rented the house.

Margaret's father William had come to the valley in 1888. He had moved on to Adin where he ran hotels.

Gertrude St John tells the story of her ancestors, the Straub and St John families. Her mother Lottie Straub and father Carl St John raised their family in the Fall River Valley. He was always good at finding a job for Lottie either cooking at a ranch or hotel, but he himself was just a peddler of trinkets.

Cooking at the Malone ranch was one job that Lottie had for quite some time. She also cooked for the crew that built Pit 1 for PG&E. When the water was damned up to build Lake Britton, the water completely covered the Malone ranch.

Lottie ran the McIntosh Hotel in Fall River Mills for her brother who owned it. It was believed that the old wiring was what started the fire that burned the town down in 1934. Almont St John relives the complete account of the fire in this story.

The fate of the beautiful Island House had been foreseen. It was known as the Hoover Hotel and was a home for visiting Hobo's. The sixty-five year home was sold for $100.00 and torn down for the lumber to be reused.

A Bucket Of Blackberries For A Gingham Dress is the story of one hundred year old Eloise Pursley. She has seen the 1800's, 1900's and the 2000's. She has also lived to see eighteen presidents of the United States. Born in Truckee, California the family moved to Red Bluff when she was very young. She and her sister would go to Manton to spend the summers with their grandparents. The thirty miles was an all day trip with their horse and buggy.

Eloise was expected to help with the chores like picking blackberries. She would have to fill a milk bucket for which she would be paid nine cents. At that time gingham material was only five cents a yard and she could buy enough to make a new dress.

Eloise and her sister each married Army Pilots who also flew as stunt pilots. Her husband, Floyd had a specialty of flying under the Sacramento River Bridge at Red Bluff during the Red Bluff Roundup in 1922. He also flew for the Forest Service fire patrol in 1918. His job was to fly over the forests to report fires. They did not have radios at that time, so if they saw a smoke they would drop a message or land and telephone. The practices started of taking homing pigeons along and tie a note on them and set them free to report the fires. This was not completely successful, and the radios were a welcome invention.

They moved to Alturas to work with the Forest Service there. Eloise wanted to drive back to Red Bluff with her baby. It was snowing hard on Hatchet Mountain and she did not have any side windows, only curtains in her Model T Ford. She did have a windshield, but no wiper or heater. She drove with one hand while she constantly wiped the snow from the window with the other. Knowing that she could not stop or she and the baby would freeze she just by-passed all the stalled cars. She met a big truck, but she kept up her speed of fifteen miles and hour and just made him move over.

Eloise is proud to have seen the San Francisco earthquake, sinking of the Titanic, eruption of Mt. Lassen the Jet and computer age.

Lem And The Shining 'E' tells the story of the Earnest family on the move again. They were somewhere in Texas and moving to somewhere in New Mexico with their team and wagon. Lem was born in 1919 somewhere in Texas. His mother died when he was only two years old. The nine children grew up the best they could. Picking was pretty slim and at times all they had to eat were biscuits and stolen watermelon.

When Lem was sixteen he and his younger brother Claude came to Cassel to work for Mrs. Baum. She treated the boys as her own. After graduating from the Fall River high school he went to work on a ranch in Wyoming. He later took a job near Reno, Nevada showing Hereford cattle for $25.00 a month. Traveling in boxcars the young herdsman traveled the west from show to show with the cattle. He worked on many different ranches sometimes showing at as many as twenty fairs a year. His most steady job was with Chandler Herefords from Baker, Oregon for $50.00 a year.

After his tour of duty in the Navy he married Marjorie Bidwell and returned to California. They soon bought some registered Herefords of their own and went into the cattle business.

In 1958 Lem was instrumental with other cattlemen to start a local Feeder Sale to market their cattle.

Lem loved the cattle business and showed and sold Hereford bulls at numerous local sales for many years.

In his younger days Lem could have been called the "King of the Road", riding the rail in those boxcars showing cattle all over the Western United States.

Cattlemen…The Salt Of The Earth, tells the story of the three Hemsted brothers pushing their handcart filled with their possessions from Illinois to California. By the time they reached the gold fields in the west they were so angry with each other that they went their separate ways and never spoke again. One of the brothers, twenty-one year old Timothy settled in Redding, California. Redding consisted of just a few buildings and a river that dried up in the summer time leaving a few stagnant potholes, causing Typhoid Fever and Malaria to run rampant.

In 1890 Timothy took up a homestead of 160 acres on the East Side of the river, this is now where the Costco shopping center is. The Central Pacific Railroad started from Redding in 1869 and had built the first railroad across the Plains. After three years of homesteading Timothy went back home and brought his wife and two daughters out west.

The story goes on to tell the birth of their son Karl and that how later in life he grazed 3000 head of sheep on the free open space that is the Redding airport today. There were three farmers in the area at that time, the Hemsted's, Harrison's and the Pearson's.

Karl was the last freight-line driver for the California-Oregon Stageline Company from Redding to Weaverville. The year of 1936 was a disastrous time for the livestock industry. The Sacramento River nearly dried up and there were only a few potholes to water cattle and sheep. The cattle had to be driven to Red Bluff to find water. In 1940 the building of Shasta Dam began. By 1945 worked stopped on the dam, as the work force and cement and materials were needed for the war effort.

Great Grandma Hemsted told Karl in 1927 to never sell the ranch, because someday the city of Redding might reach that far and their property would be very valuable. She had an incredible forsight.

Hippy, He Never Missed A Lick, tells the story of a Champion Bronc rider and a movie stunt man. Hippy Burmister called Modoc County home later in life, but he had stories that would keep you spell bound for hours. Born in 1894 in Illinois he became part of the famous C.B. Irwin Wild West Show. It was his job as a youngster to ride the Buffalo in the parades before the show. At one of these shows Hippy walked right up to President Theodore Roosevelt and said I want to shake you hand. And as he said, "he just pumped the heck out of my hand."

In 1917 when Hippy was drafted into the Army he was stationed with the Calvary Remount Division. He had to break hundreds of spoiled horses for the soldiers to ride. This is what started him in the rodeo, riding bucking horses. Most of these horses were no worse than the ones he broke for the Army.

After winning the championship at the Reno Rodeo he went on to Pendleton, Ore. As a winner there he was awarded a pair of Chaps from a bronc rider that was retiring. Hippy went right down to the Hamley Saddle Company and had HIPPY put on each side with white leather.

These chaps and much of his memorabilia is on display in the Modoc County Museum in Alturas.

Hippy's movie days were during the silent movies where he worked with Tom Mix, William S. Hart and Will Rogers. One time Tom Mix drove him from the movie set to a rodeo in his new Cadillac. Hippy could not believe a car could go as fast as 60 MPH.

One of his most memorable stunts was when he had to cross a forty-foot wide ninety-foot deep canyon hand over hand on a rope. He had to dress as a woman and act as if he were one. The studio only had one camera so the stunt had to be done twice. By the time he crossed it the second time he was totally exhausted, but he was happy to receive his pay of $15.00. After that stunt, the riding of run-a-way horses, bulldogging steers or jumping on a run-a-way stage coach team was a breeze.

Hippy was credited with the beginning of the Rodeo Historical Society and Cowboy Hall of Fame in Oklahoma City. He was not inducted himself until ten years after his death when he would have been 100 years old.

Left In The Middle Of Nowhere, is the story of Cliff Bailey who when he was nineteen years old was on a train headed through Nebraska at fifteen degrees below zero. Cliff was riding in the stock car with cattle and horses that he was tending on the way to Oregon. After the train started to move, he snuggled down in his bed. In the middle of the night he woke to nothing but the noise of the animals. When he looked out, there was not a train in sight. They had unhooked his car and left him in the middle of nowhere.

He was happy to finally reach his destination in Oregon. It was a long ways from the Sod House in Colorado where he was born in 1919. In his homeland they had severe storms and in 1927 it snowed for five months. All the family of eight children had to eat was a big sack of Pinto Beans.

Moving on to Modoc County Cliff found a job of milking thirty cows for $30.00 a month. He worked on several different ranches and at the Modoc Auction Yard when it first opened in 1948. Now a retired rancher he has stories to tell of the way it was in days gone by.

The Ingram Clan From Scotland, Nell Ingram thought April 1, 1892 was the worst April Fools day of her life. With her husband Jack they arrived in the Fall River Valley after a terrible trip from San Francisco with their team and wagon. They had encountered roads with nothing but ruts and mud and were snowbound for several days. The first winter they lived with and worked for Shird and Emma Eldridge. They soon were able to buy a homestead. They moved a house fifteen miles across the valley from the Craig ranch in 1899. Skidding it with several teams of horses they even had to cross the river two times.

Nell took to her duties as a farm wife and was always willing to feed as many people whose feet could fit under the table. She always kept up her old country custom of inviting the neighbor ladies in for afternoon tea.

Raising hogs and grain were their main lively-hood and the hogs were driven to the railhead at Bartle. In 1907 Jack bought a grain thresher to harvest his own grain and that of his neighbors. Many horses and men were needed to operate this machine.

Jack was the Supervisor of District #3 of Shasta County and was the only Supervisor ever to serve from the Fall River Valley.

ICU, The Brand of Generations, tells the story of the pioneers of Parker Creek east of Alturas. In 1873 the brand was registered and has been passed down through several generations. The Porters, Parkers and other families settled this long narrow valley. Porters built several reservoirs with teams of horses and Fresno Scrapers.

Many years after Leland Porter died, his wife Charlotte, married Joe Covington. They introduced the Romagnola cattle to the area. Joe and Charlotte were the first people ever to import the semen from these massive cattle of Northern Ireland to the United States. Joe first introduced the embryo transplanting in the cattle industry in 1977. 1989 was the first Romagnola show in the United States. This breed of cattle has been shown in Europe since 1850.

The Judge With A Heart. In 1852 the Oregon Trail began to be a steady stream of pioneers such as the Callison's. At the same time the Achumawi Indians in the Fall River valley were restless. There had been raids on the ranches and farms. A military camp was set up near the forks of the Pit River at Lockhart Ferry.

The caravan had started at St. Joseph, Missouri and John Callison kept a daily diary of their journey. He told of the conditions, Indians, illness, price of feed and who died. Cholera ran rampant within the members of the wagon train. Soon John's diary stopped as he became ill himself and died.

The family settled in Oregon, but soon decided to move on to Fall River Valley. Even though the Indians were causing trouble they were not worried as they found shelter at Fort Crook where the Soldiers would give them security. The story tells of what the fort was like in 1866 and life there.

After the family left the safety of the fort and moved to their own home they slept in the fields at night in fear of being burned out by the Indians.

Merton Callison was born in a log cabin near Burgetville in 1890 and one of his fondest childhood memories was when he saw Buffalo Bill at the Wild West Show in Redding.

In 1920 Merton was appointed Justice of the Peace, but found it hard to reprimand a man for killing a deer to feed his starving family. He served the valley as teacher, historian and Justice of the peace for many years.

Not all the Indians were hostile, and some even took Indian Squaws as their wives. When John Taylor took sick and would not eat, his Indian wife said, " I cook up cricket and grasshopper and big green worm, cook it all up for him good and he still no eat."

The Smell Of Sagebrush, is what Boyd Moffitt missed when he left Big Valley to go back to Marysville where he was born in 1917. Boyd started working on the Kramer Ranch when he was twelve years old. Working on most of the ranches at one time or another in Big Valley he called this home for many years. He started to write poetry of his life there, which tells of life on the Will Kramer Ranch and the Cox and Clarke Ranch where there was a lot of buckarooing. There were cowboys mounted on their horses all the time during haying season so they could catch the run-a-way teams that had dumped their drivers and were running wildly across the land with mowing machines and buck rakes bouncing behind them. Pay was $25.00 a month with room and board and the cowboy was satisfied with his life.

In 1937 Boyd hired on as buckaroo at the Bognuda ranch in Little Valley where he, Lil and Clover became very good friends. His poem of the Little Valley Ranch is full of his thoughts of life on that ranch. After serving his time in the Army he moved about quite a bit, finally landing in Yerington, Nevada where he was Foreman at the Anaconda Copper

Mine. This salty character still likes to reminisce with his cronies at the local donut shop every morning and enjoys sharing his book of poetry, "Some Good, Some Bad and Some Indifferent".

A Family Affair, is the story of the Roberti Family in Sierra Valley. How the family came from Switzerland in 1865 and the hard life they led. Working as milkers on dairies and later owning their own dairy which later evolved into one of the larger ranches in the Sierra Valley. Elmer and Elia Roberti learned to milk by hand when they were very young. They were not allowed to go to high school, as they were needed at home to work. By 1944 they bought their first milking machine to milk the large string of cows.

Their parents Josie and Alfred were very strong people in the community. You had to be strong to survive the early times. The winter of 1951-52 was known as the big winter. It snowed for days with five foot on the level and drifts larger than that. Just getting the cattle fed was a major job. They did not get out of the valley for six weeks.

During the depression all of the farmers were getting kicked off of their ranches. They could not pay the 8% to 10% interest the government was charging. Josie wrote a letter to President Franklin, D. Roosevelt and told him that she couldn't make it on the ranch and explained how the government was foreclosing on all the ranchers. She had a registered letter from the Federal Land Bank at the post office in Loyalton but she refused to accept it. Two days later the Federal Land Bank in Susanville received notice that the President had put a moratorium on the foreclosing of the ranches. Josie always thought that her letter was responsible for this action.

Today the Roberti family raises Hay and Cattle on their ranch in the Sierra Valley. The entire family lives and works on the same ranch, which is a feat in itself. Everyone has their own job and each does it well.

The Rancher And The School Marm, is the story of Ray and Dorothy Anklin of Canby, Ca. As a young man Ray came to Modoc County where he worked for Miller and Lux on the Blacks Canyon Ranch. A nineteen-year old school teacher from Sacramento came to the Wild West, but soon the rancher courted her and won. Tales of ranching and teaching intertwine in this story. When Ray told her she rode a horse like a sack of potatoes, he should have bitten his tongue. She told him, "he could do his work and she would take care of the house and children and that was that." Teaching for over thirty years was a big job without doing a mans work on the ranch.

A Time To Remember, is the story told by 100 year old Bessie Bosworth. She tells how her father came to Redding, Ca. when there was only a cookhouse and warehouse out in a Manzanita flat. Her father worked to help build the road up the Pit River Canyon with a pick, shovel and wheelbarrow. She was one of twelve children raised at Goose Creek where her father had the first sawmill in Shasta County. Later moving to the base of Hatchet Mountain she tells of seventeen foot of snow in 1916 and how they dug a trench over the mountain to march the cattle single file to feed at Oak Run. Times were hard and she still remembers them vividly.

Many wonderful pictures help tell the story of this remarkable lady.

Wagons West

Contents

Chapter 1	Fort Sage; The Land Of Sheep, Cattle and Rustling... *Pike Garnier*	1
Chapter 2	The Swiss Families Of Sierra Valley .... *Alvin and Adella Lombardi*	9
Chapter 3	Memories Of A Pioneer Lady.......... *Laura Miller Kresge*	27
Chapter 4	A Fall River Valley History............ *Gertrude St John*	35
Chapter 5	A Bucket of Blackberries For A Gingham Dress........ *Eloise Pursley*	47
Chapter 6	Lem And The Shining 'E'.............. *Lem Earnest*	59
Chapter 7	Cattlemen…The Salt Of The Earth............. *Jerry and Joan Hemsted*	73
Chapter 8	Hippy, He Never Missed A Lick .... *Hippy Burmister*	85
Chapter 9	Left In The Middle Of Nowhere .... *Cliff and Lois Bailey*	103
Chapter 10	ICU, The Brand Of Generations.................. *Joe and Charlotte Covington*	115

Chapter 11	The Ingram Clan From Scotland .... 125 *George and Phyllis Ingram*	
Chapter 12	The Judge With A Heart .... *Merton and Wanda Callison*	
Chapter 13	The Smell Of Sagebrush .... 157 *Boyd Moffitt*	
Chapter 14	A Family Affair .... 173 *The Roberti Family*	
Chapter 15	The Rancher And The School Marm .... 185 *Dorothy Anklin*	
Chapter 16	A Time To Remember .... 197 *Bessie Bosworth*	

Fort Sage: The Land Of Sheep, Cattle & Rustling

The range war between the cattlemen and the sheepmen in Oregon was a troublesome time. The age-old fight and belief that the two kinds of stockmen did not get along and hated each other was true. The cattlemen believed that the sheep ate the grass into the ground and that it was ruined for the cattle. They were sure the cattle would not graze after the wooly animals and they had no love for them or the Shepherds that cared for them. Such was the case with Emmanuel Garnier; who had two bands of sheep; which totaled 5000 head of animals.

Determined he tried to hold his ground and keep his flock together, but it was a losing battle. The cattlemen tried to scare Emmanuel off of the land in several different ways, but the most effective was the shooting of the sheep to scatter or kill them and also shooting at Emmanuel and his herders. The cattlemen won out and scared the sheepman enough that he gave in.

Emmanuel had come from France in the late 1800's and settled in Prineville, Oregon. Buying sheep and keeping the young ewes he finally expanded his flock to the present numbers.

Emmanuel and his bride, Laura who had also come from France feared for their lives. They had a small son, named Emmanuel after his father and they did not want anything to happen to him. They knew they were not wanted in the Prineville community because of the sheep, so rather than get rid of the animals they decided to find a new home.

In 1903 with their teams and wagons and two of Emmanual's cousins, the Graviers, they headed to California. The men herded the grazing sheep along the way. It was a long hard, slow trip, which took several months. They really were in no hurry and not sure of their destination.

After traveling over 300 miles they came into Grasshopper Valley north of Susanville. Here, they camped for quite some time letting the sheep graze and rest from the trip. It was Fall, and they needed to find a permanent home before winter. Emmanuel decided he wanted to move farther south. He had heard of the wide-open spaces at Fort Sage near Doyle, California.

Fort Sage really had not materialized as a Fort. It had been in the process of being built and stories tell of an Indian uprising. The U.S. Calvary had gone on an assignment to take care of this situation. When they returned the Indians had burned the Fort down. The Army never rebuilt it, but the area is still called Fort Sage.

The country was wild with miles and miles of sagebrush desert. Emmanuel let his sheep graze on the vast open spaces. He did not realize that the land had been claimed. This did not meet with the approval of the Bureau of Land Management who had control of the range and they soon forced Emmanuel to sell his two bands of sheep.

With the money from the sale of the sheep Laura and Emmanuel were able to buy a place of their own and some dairy cows. They bought a

A Cattlemen's meeting at the Herlong NCO Club in the 1950's.
Left to right: Dorothy and Pike Garnier talking to Murray Doyle.
In back Laveana, Claude and Leda Harwood, Gene MCallister and Frank Flux

homestead with a small cabin on it. Laura called it "Lanham" after the people that they bought it from. Soon Emmanuel built a two-story home for the family.

After settling in California a second son, John was born then a daughter Mary. Their third son, Felix (Pike) was born September 1917. Two year old Mary could not say Felix and it sounded like "Pike," so that became his nickname for his entire life.

Emmanuel had forty head of milk cows and the boys milked them. Pike was only six years old when he started milking his share of the cows. The milk was separated and the cream was stored in ten-gallon cans in the cellar to keep cool. Once a week two cans of cream was delivered to the railroad at Doyle to be shipped to Sacramento. The skimmed milk was fed to the calves. It only took one time to teach the calves to drink out of a bucket. The kids would let the calves suck their fingers and dipping their hand down into the bucket of milk; the calves just kept sucking the milk up. The rest of the milk was fed to hogs to fatten them for market.

Emmanuel started to increase his cowherd and breeding them to good Hereford bulls he started a beef herd. One year it was so dry that he was not able to put up any hay to winter his cattle. The cattle had to be driven 100 miles north to Adin, California where hay was purchased. The hay could not be moved to the cows, so the cows had to be driven to the hay. Hay was bought from Marcel Kresge on his ranch north of Adin in Round Valley and John Dish went with the cattle to spend the winter there to feed and care for the herd.

Pike and his brothers and sister went to the school at Bird flat. It was a one-room schoolhouse with living quarters for the teacher attached. Pike went for nine years at this country school. Eight years of elementary school then one year of high school. At that time a school bus was purchased and the high school students rode 40 miles in to Susanville.

Pike graduated from high school in 1937. He helped his dad on his ranch some, but soon went to work at the Sierra Army Depot at Herlong, California driving heavy equipment. Shortly after the declaration of war in December 1941, the site for Sierra was selected in the south central part of Lassen County. 36,000 acres are within the confines of the military reservation.

There were mixed feelings in the county at the thought of having any Army activity in it; however; the quick and overwhelming response to the new demand of the war showed the challenge and the facility was

Dorothy and Pike Garnier of the NCO Club at Herlong where the Cattlemen burned their brands into a board. (1950s) Brands on the left side, top to bottom: Frank Rowland, Perry Main, unknown. Second row, top to bottom: Gene McCallister, Claude Harwood, Sam Robbins, Jack Humphrey. Third row, top to bottom: Marcus Gaston, Emmanuel Garnier, Pike Garnier, Dr. A. H. Amesbury. Fourth row, top to bottom: Jack Humphrey, C.C. Rowland, Murray Doyle

accepted. The Army Depot was completed by February 1943 and turned over to the Ordnance Department for accomplishment of the primary mission; receipt, storage and shipment of ammunition.

Located in the wide-open spaces, the site for the Depot contained no shopping or other community facilities. As a result, a typical small town developed. Originally, the community was known as Hackstaff after the Western Pacific Railroad station of that name. Later, at the request of the War Department, it was changed to Herlong in honor of the first ordnance officer to lose his life in World War II.

Pike went to work at the Depot as soon as the groundbreaking took place. He drove heavy equipment, building roads, buildings, ammunitions storage shelters called Igloos and any job that needed done. He worked there through the complete building of the military facility.

To provide the needs of the residents, the Post Restaurant council operated a shopping center, cafeteria, service station, barber and beauty shop and the NCO Officers Club. Schools and churches were built to accommodate the 2,500 residents of Herlong.

There was approximately one thousand Federal Service employees to cover a range of some one hundred different skills. Herlong boosted the economy of Lassen County and local people like Pike Garnier were able to obtain jobs to care for their families, or like Pike, was able to buy a ranch of his own.

In 1938 Pike married Dorothy McCarty. Her family had come from Texas and her Father was the foreman of the lines for the Power Company in Doyle. Two weeks after the young couple met they were married. At that time they were living with Pike's folks. Soon after that Emmanuel became ill and he and Laura moved to Susanville. Pike was renting the place from his father, but Emmanuel raised the rent so high that Pike decided to buy his own place.

In 1944 Pike and Dorothy bought a place from his cousin, Mr. Gravier along highway 395. The property was on both sides of the highway. The ranch was 520 acres and forty head of cows came with it for the price of $10,000. The owner had been milking the cows and selling the cream. The herd was a mixture of every breed of cow there was. Pike bought a good Hereford bull to breed them to and left the calves on the cows. Dorothy said, "but these are milk cows." Pike's response was, "they use to be, they ain't milk cows no more." He had all the cow milking he wanted when he was a kid.

Three generations of Garniers – Pike, Jeff and JJ

Pike Garnier, 1987

Pike and Dorothy had two children. In 1947 a daughter Loretta was born and in 1952 a son Jeff was born.

The Garnier home was about the only place along this lonely stretch of highway between Susanville and Reno. The Highway Patrolmen along this route stopped in for a cup of coffee and check up on the local news. Not able to give the officers the cup of coffee as it was against the law, the officers left a quarter on the table. Pike saved the quarters for many years, which helped him remember the good visits from the officers.

Pike and Dorothy loved the social life and he enjoyed visiting with everyone. He never forgot a name and never met a stranger. Dances at the NCO Club at Herlong were attended every Saturday night. In 1975 the Garnier's were divorced and Dorothy moved to Susanville. She passed away about fifteen years ago.

Pike built his cowherd up to 335 head and ran his cattle on the Bureau of Land Management. He never kept his cows on the West Side of the highway because if they headed to the mountains they could end up in Quincy. When they pastured on the East side of the highway they were next to their range permit and could just be headed up the mountain when the grazing season started.

Grazing in the mountains and on the desert had its drawbacks. Rustling of cattle was very prevalent in this part of the country. Time and time again Pike would find a carcass of a cow or calf that had been butchered out and only the hind quarters was taken. He spent a lot of time camping on the desert with his cattle to keep an eye on them. He would find tracks and following the tracks he usually found the carcass of a dead animal. It kept getting worse and worse and more cattle were lost all the time.

Not many years ago forty head of Pike's cattle were stolen. The local brand inspector told of the time he had been out on the job and watched men working and loading cattle into a trailer in broad daylight. He just figured Pike was working his cattle and moving them to another pasture. Little did he suspect that those cattle were ones that some thief was rustling. The cattle were never recovered.

Pike usually sold his calves to the Shasta Livestock Yard. Norm Elston who worked for the yard was a good friend of Pike's and they had done a lot of business together. At one time Pike sold some cattle through the yard and a neighbor who Pike didn't trust bought them. Pike went to the owner of the yard, Ellington Peek and told him he did not want this man to have his cattle. He would have a brand inspection slip for Pike's cattle and who was to say that he might not slip a few more through the fence. Ellington stopped the ruckus before it started and bought the cattle back from the neighbor. Pike went home much happier.

Pike Garnier, 1999

Pike was quite a buckaroo. He rode a lot of rough broncs and broke a lot of horses. He had done quite a bit of mustanging in his day and caught several wild horses. He would watch the wild horses at Fort Sage and when he saw a nice colt or two year old he would catch it and break it for his ranch horse. He only caught one every three or four years, when he needed it and only for his own use.

Ranch life is hard and tough, but Pike says the hardest job he ever had was as a kid when he stacked loose hay all day. Maybe that is one of the reasons that he never put up hay for his own cattle, but always bought all of his hay.

Up until a few years ago he was feeding his cattle by himself. He would tie the steering wheel of the tractor tight so it wouldn't turn. He would jump on the feed wagon and put off the hay to the cattle. Pike sold his calves off of the cows in the Fall when they weighed 475-500 pounds so he didn't have to winter them.

When the grazing season was over the cows knew their way home. At times Pike would go out with his pickup and a few cowboys and the cows would follow the pickup home.

When Pike was nearing his 80th birthday he was still running his ranch by himself. He had cut his cowherd in half, but still they had to be fed and cared for. It was only ill health and several strokes that slowed this rancher down.

Pike has only been out of the Doyle area for two weeks in his lifetime. He went to Washington D.C. to visit his friend Ann Terral. She had been his steady companion for fifteen years and he helped her raise her two daughters.

Pike enjoyed having coffee at the local coffee shop and eating out with friends instead of doing his own cooking. Now the strokes have taken their toll and he is unable to drive and visit with friends and neighbors like he did. Only last year he sold his ranch, but still remains in his home he built in 1944 by himself for $2,500.

This admirable cowman, that raised good cattle from those forty head of milk cows fifty-five years ago has a lot of thoughts and dreams of the past to share. Happy times and sad times were remembered. Even though it is hard for Pike to convey them because of the speech inability that the strokes have left him with, he wanted his story told. His good friend Barbara Lee was able to help me communicate with him. Ranching until he was eighty years old has been quite an accomplishment for this cowboy. He has made his mark on the livestock industry.

May 13, 1999

The Swiss Families Of Sierra Valley

The year was 1884 when 23 year old Ponpeo John (P.J.) Lombardi decided to leave Airilo, Canton Ticino, Switzerland and make his move to the United States. In the land where he was born in 1861, he worked in a tunnel to pay his way to the United States.

In his native land P.J. attended school and learned the secrets of successful dairying under the instructions of his father, who conducted a dairy during the summer months. He was not satisfied with the prospects for individual advancement in his own country and having knowledge of the splendid opportunities offered in America, he immigrated to the New World. His ship docked at New York City on March 1, 1884. No job was too small or low paying for him, as he was a hardworking man that was contented just to be in this new land. He crossed the continent directly to San Francisco, California where he found menial jobs of washing dishes and selling newspapers. He then found employment on a dairy for two years, and for the same length of time he drove a milk delivery wagon. He also worked on various dairies teaching the art of making cheese in that area.

In P.J.'s homeland his parents Joseph and Clemetina Lombardi were mountaineers. Their home was a public place after the order of St. Bernard, where unfortunate travelers could be taken care of. Many tired and stormbound wanderers though the deep snows of an Alpine winter were rescued and cared for in their home. The family was granted an annual stipend by the Swiss government for their services.

Their home was on Mt. Gotthard, and there P.J. and his three brothers and two sisters were reared. The oldest brother, Caesar moved to Dallas, Texas where he was president of the Dallas News, other brothers Ferdinand and Pacifico and one sister lived near San Francisco. One sister

Angelina and P.J. Lombardi, January 12, 1886

remained in Switzerland. If any young men had any thought of migrating to the U.S. they left before they reached the age of 18 for at that age they were required to serve two years in the Swiss army. P.J. had already served his time in the military for his country.

January 12, 1886, P.J. married Angelina Ramelli in Sierra Valley who was also a native of Airilo, Canton Ticino, Switzerland. She was a sister of Emilio Ramelli and one of eleven children. Emilio had settled in Sierra Valley in Northeastern California and this lured his sister and her new husband to this beautiful valley. Angelina had been brought to this country by the efforts of her brother Amillo several years before.

P.J. and Angelina had a son Caesar who was born in San Francisco and he was two years old when the family moved to Loyalton in Sierra Valley.

Besides their son Caesar, they had Attilio, Louis and Marie. P.J. had bought the Smith Raines Ranch of 360 acres, which was two miles west of Loyalton, California. He saved his money and soon owned 3000 acres, which was one of the larger ranches of the valley.

Angelina's uncle, Angelo D'Agostini was in partnership with Vic Dotta but he wanted to go back to the old country. They settled on how to divide the property and then tossed a coin to see who got what share. He gave his share of the ranch to his nephew Emilio. All that he asked was for Emilio to send for the rest of the half-starved children in the family. Two at a time as he could afford it, he sent the money for their tickets and all ten siblings eventually came to this country. One of which was Angelina.

P. J. worked on ranches near Loyalton where they settled, and in 1890 he started milking cows for Mr. Frank Rowland. Every day he went six miles to the Rowland ranch to milk the cows. Rowland wanted out of the dairy business and wanted to move to Standish. He told P.J., "you take the cows to your house to milk them, there is no sense in you coming all this way every day to milk these cows." Then Rowland made P.J. an offer he could not refuse. He said, "you keep the cows, take the buckets, milk cans and all the equipment that you need to take care of the cows, and pay me when you can." What an opportunity for a young Swiss man who was trying to get a start in life.

Every Fall P.J. took Mr. Rowland a wheel of cheese and what money he could spare to pay off his debt. He wanted to let him know how he was doing and how faithful he was to make his yearly payments.

P.J. Lombardi and his milk delivery wagon in 1902. The Loyalton school house in the background

Starting out with a herd of ten cows that he acquired from Rowland, P.J. built his herd up to 60 head of Dairy cattle. During the 1890's and early 1900's P.J. operated a milk route, delivering to the town of Loyalton with his team and cart. He sold cheese, butter, milk and eggs from his "Excelsior Dairy". The milk was carried in a ten-gallon can and the housewives would come out with their containers and he would ladle out the milk to fill them. He would come to town twice a day to deliver the milk. No one had refrigeration at that time, and the milk would not keep.

In the summer the butter would melt on his route. He would have to wait for a cool moonlight night to deliver the butter to Truckee. In the summer time is when he made cheese as the butter could not be kept or transported.

P.J. went into the beef cattle business in 1935; a few years later he discontinued his dairy business. He became one of the most successful ranchers and best known residents of the Sierra Valley. The home ranch was located three miles west of Loyalton; in addition, he was the owner of other valuable lands, combining about four thousand acres. He was also the owner of the only hardware store in Loyalton and a creamery. He was recognized as a businessman of marked ability.

One of the Swiss traits, which P.J. excelled in, was the making of Swiss Cheese. A complicated task for some, but he was so skillful at it that it seemed rather simple.

To make the cheese, the whole milk was put in a large cast iron pot over an open fire. It had to be heated slowly stirring constantly to a temperature of 94 degrees. When it was all the same temperature, rennant (a product derived from a calf's stomach) was added to curdle the milk. When it was curdled to a Jell-O consistency it was ready to be cut. A rake with long wire teeth was used to cut one way then the other to cut the mixture into small squares the size of a large pea. Keeping the temperature up to at least 90 degrees you started to stir and stir with a large paddle, now you let the temperature drop by sprinkling water on the fire. At this point you had to stir very hard, stirring the dickens out of it until curds gathered. Next, you would scoop under the curds with a large piece of cheesecloth and tie it in a knot to hang from a rope and tackle attached to a pulley on the rafters. It took quite some time for all the whey to drain from the curds. The whey was then fed to the pigs. Nothing was wasted.

Cheese molds were made out of very thin wood into rounds. The second day the curds were put into the molds with another board on top and weighted down with a large rock. The third day the mold was taken off and the salting process began. Every third day the cheese was salted on all sides completely. The salt flavors it and kills the bacteria. If it is done just right the bacteria is not all killed at first and that is what causes the holes in Swiss Cheese. The salting process takes 30 days. On the 40th day paraffin is melted and the 20 pound cheese rounds are coated with this. Good Swiss cheese can be kept two or three years in the cellar and the flavor improves with age.

P.J. also made Jack cheese but this did not keep as well so he did not enjoy all the work it took to make the cheese then let it spoil.

The eldest son, Caesar married Emma Ramelli whose family lived in Long Valley near Bordertown, Nevada. There they had a dairy, raised cattle, hay and grain and had summer range for their livestock.

In 1918 a son, Alvin was born to the young couple. He was their only child. Being raised next door to his grandparents, he spent as much time with them as at his own home. P.J. and Angelina doted on the youngster, but were not the kind to spoil a child. Alvin idolized his grandparents. He helped his grandfather make cheese and with the curing of hams, bacons, sausage and the rendering of the lard when the hogs were butchered in the Fall of the year.

P.J.'s and Angelina's children went into business with them. Attilio ran the creamery and hardware store in Loyalton. Louis ran the home ranch; Caesar operated the ranch next door where his son Alvin was born. And Mary was on another one of the ranches. All of them inherited their respective ranches and businesses when P.J. died.

The Swiss people were very frugal and saved their money to buy their land, never wasting a dime. Angelina had hand knitted all of the curtains for their home. They were beautiful and she was justly proud of them. She never learned to speak English so the Swiss language is what Alvin was raised to learn to speak. He never spoke much English until he started Grammer school at the Long Point School. This was a one-room school with seven to fourteen students, and outstanding teachers. Alvin loved every minute of school and enjoyed the company of the other children. Otherwise he lived a serene life with his Parents and Grandparents as his only companions.

Soup was one of the main meals that Grandma made. Most of the time it was parsley soup and Alvin just did not like that parsley soup. On those days he went home to eat with his parents, and grandma didn't care, as she was not going to fix anything different just to please him.

Alvin's parents were like the other Swiss people and there was never any extra money to spend. The house was not the best, and he did not have enough clothes to wear, but his father thought it was important to always have a good car. So many times they drove a new car when they had nothing else.

The family had lots to eat as they raised most of their own food, but when Alvin was a boy he loved Ketchup on his food. His father thought it was not necessary to have such a luxury and would not let him buy it. When Alvin saved a little money he would buy himself a bottle of Ketchup and hide it in his closet so no one else could use it.

A family by the name of Lewis had a sawmill at Loyalton; they helped to build the school and the church. An influential and religious family in the Sierra Valley, they helped to establish the City Limits, which took in forty-eight square miles. The law was that there was to be no liquor sold in the city limits. To keep the liquor out they made these lines to incorporate quite a large area. There were pool halls in the town, but they could not serve liquor.

Alvin went the four miles to Loyalton to attend High School. This is where he met Adella Dotta whose family had a ranch in the middle of the

Caesar Lombardi's hay wagon on the Loyalton Bridge

1910 steam tractor at White Pine Lumber Co., Loyalton, California

valley. The Dotta children went to Grammer school at the Island School as their ranch was in Plumas County.

Adella's grandfather Caesare Dotta was also born in Canton Ticino, Switzerland in 1861. He came to the U.S. and directly to Sierra valley in 1883. He went to work for Lodovico Dotta, an uncle, who had come to the Valley in 1879. With his brother-in-law, Antone Laffranchini, Caesare established a ranch about six miles west of Vinton, California.

Vic Dotta had sponsored many boys from Switzerland. Caesare Dotta was one of these sponsored young men. The men in America would send a ticket to a young man in the Old Country and they were obligated to that man to work for him when they reached America. The sponsor was responsible for the young men and they would work for him until the price of the ticket was paid off with 18% interest. The Swiss helped the Swiss and there was nothing but honesty and hard work.

Caesare sold out to his brother-in-law in 1896 and rented 320 acres. Here he operated a dairy and sold butter and cheese. He was among the first to make butter in Sierra Valley. In 1889, Caesare purchased the Gould ranch in Sierra County, which later became known as the Dotta Home Ranch. It consisted of 840 acres of some of the finest meadow and hay land in the Valley. Dotta's continued to enlarge their holdings so that in 1903, they owned 5200 acres with a herd of about 1000 cattle and 60 milk cows. Caesare incorporated his holdings with his sons under the name of Caesare Dotta and Sons Co. Inc.

Five sons and a daughter were born to Caesare and Caterina Vella Dotta, Antone, Daniel, Albert, Leon, Caesare Jr. and Edna.

Antone and his siblings received their early education in the Island District School in their home neighborhood. He went on to a business career with commercial courses in the Polytechnic Business College in Oakland, California.

In Oakland, Antone met Edna Hamilton and in 1910 they were married. Her father was a prominent and successful mining man in Nevada. The young couple moved back to Sierra Valley where they had eleven children in fifteen years. From 1911 to 1926, Emil, Agnes, Thelma, Antone Jr., Aileen, Elmer, Alice, Adella, Anna Marie, Annetta and Donald Theodore (Buddy) were born to this devout Catholic family.

In 1920 Antone Dotta bought the McNear place and moved his family into the large home on this beautiful ranch of 550 acres.

Caesare Dotta was the president of the company until the time of his death, on July 1, 1929. At this time Antone succeeded to the presidency. Besides Antone Dotta's individual land holdings, he was the owner of two meat markets in Portola, Plumas County, which carried the names of Portola Meat Company and the Quality Meat Market. Mr. Dotta raised beef cattle and operated a dairy farm with sixty milk cows. Thoughout the Sierra Valley, the Sacramento Valley and the Honey Lake Valley, Antone bought beef cattle, hogs, poultry and eggs for his own markets. He also was an extensive buyer of cattle, hogs and sheep, which he shipped in carload lots to the San Francisco market.

Antone Dotta, became one of the leading ranchers, dairymen and livestock dealers and influential citizens of the Sierra Valley. The Dotta family was poor when they came to this country, but they were hard and persistent workers, exercised sound judgement in the management of their affairs, particularly in dairy farming and the handling of livestock, through which they became wealthy. They eventually owned fourteen thousand acres.

Edna Dotta died when she was 46 years of age. The eleven children in fifteen years had taken the toll on her health. Antone remarried Ottilia Gudecii who helped him raise his younger children. Of the eleven children there is only Emil, Adella, Agnes, Aileen and Alice living.

When Alvin Lombardi was young his father had a small sawmill. Caesar was an industrious man and was wise in the ways of the business

Alvin Lombardi on his donkey in 1925

world even though he quit school after the third grade. He and a friend had loaned money to a man to build a small sawmill. When the man could no longer make his payments, Caesar repossessed the sawmill and his friend took what lumber was there to satisfy his debt. Caesar cut lumber for his own use and cut lumber for other ranchers. The logs were all skidded with teams of horses. Alvin was old enough to help with the skidding of the logs. The milking always had to be done first thing in the morning then they ran the sawmill until time for the evening milking. No time was wasted, as time was money to the hardworking Swiss people.

Caesar always liked horses to work with and even though he did have a tractor he felt the horses were more dependable. At the sawmill they had a solid iron wheel wagon to deliver the lumber with. The mill was run by a water wheel and the rest of the work was done with teams of horses. Caesar would drive eight horses, (four teams) with one jerk line. The wheel horses, pullers, slack team and the leaders were stout horses, but more agile than the heavy draft type.

Alvin's job was to run the Johnson bar to slow the wagon down when it was going down hill with a load. The Johnson bar was a ratchet type brake handle on the back of the wagon and he would pull down on it with all his might. He was only thirteen years old and not very big. His father put a long rope on it with a snap. There was a ring attached to the wagon and Alvin would snap the rope into the ring to hold the Johnson bar down. He then would run along side of the wagon and throw dirt onto the Cottonwood brake block to give it more friction and be more effective. Everything was done by hand, sawing the trees into logs, loading them, unloading them, piling the lumber, running the mill; it was all hard work.

After Alvin got out of high school he skidded a lot of seven foot Cedar logs. These were used to make split cedar posts and rails, which he sold for twelve to fifteen cents a piece to the ranchers.

A lot of small sawmills dotted the hillsides of the Sierra Valley. The lumber that was cut was hauled sixteen miles to Truckee, California and sixty-five miles to Virginia City, Nevada with teams and wagons for the building of these towns. Oxen and wagons hauled the lumber when the gold mining town of Bodie, California was built in the late 1800's. Only two trips a year was made as it was so far. Spring and fall the teamsters would hook up their oxen and load their wagons for the long 170-mile journey one way.

From the late 1860's until 1927 the eastern Sierra Nevada was an ideal region for the production of natural ice. Pure Mountain streams and some of the coldest temperatures in the state and an average snow depth less extreme than at the summit resulted in quality ice that was easy to harvest, transport and store.

There was an ice plant at Grizzly in the Sierra Valley and one at Boca, 25 miles south of Loyalton. Caesar Lombardi would shoe the horses that were used there with ice shoes. The shoes had knobs called corks made of sharpened metal and attached to the shoes. This kept the horses from slipping as they pulled the ice cutters on the ice. The teams of horses would pull the cutter with a huge sharp cutting disc on it along the ice, making strips about 16 to 20 inches wide. The next team would crosscut the ice strips cutting it into blocks. Then a man would use a flattened fork called a "Spud" to break the blocks apart and they would float on down to the outlet to the icehouse. The ice was made on a flat area that could be flooded and the water controlled. The water was let in, to a depth of six inches then it was left to freeze. Again the floodgates of the dam were opened and six more inches of water was let in to freeze on top of that, making a depth of twelve inches of ice. In the dead of winter when the thermometer registered below zero for days on end was the prime time for making ice. Boca had an ice storage house forty feet by sixty feet by seventeen feet high with a capacity of 8000 tons. The blocks of ice were covered in sawdust and they kept through the summer.

Ice from the Sierra first supplied the luxury hotels in San Francisco and the residents of California's gold country. But it was the Comstock mines of Nevada and California's developing agriculture during the 1870's that proved the greatest importance for ice production. With the completion of the Virginia-Truckee Railroad, the Virginia City mines became an important new market for ice. As the mines reached deeper into the earth the temperatures inside rose as high as 140 degrees. Miners working at the deepest levels would work for fifteen minutes and then rest in nearby cooling chambers filled with natural ice from the Sierra. At the same time experiments were being conducted to show how ice could be used to keep California produce fresh as it was shipped in boxcars to markets in the east. This resulted in the Pacific Fruit Express Company who soon became one of the largest users of Sierra ice. By 1881, the ice industry was at its peak employing over 500 men. By 1927 this industry was a thing of the past.

Caesar Lombardi had the only livestock scales in the area on his ranch. All of the cattle that were near by were weighed there. They then had to be driven thirteen miles to the railroad at Beckworth to be shipped to the packinghouses in Reno. Alvin let it be known to the buyers of the cattle that he was available to drive the cattle for them. The cattle buyers were generous with their money, and the days work paid him a couple of dollars. Any other job on a ranch only paid a dollar a day, so this was a welcome opportunity.

When Alvin was eighteen years old his mother told him he was on his own and he was now responsible for himself. His parents gave him freedom, love and responsibility and it was up to him from now on to make the best of his life. Alvin said he was a pretty wild kid when he was young, but the good upbringing with his parents and grandparents never failed him.

His Grandmother was very strict with him, but he loved this woman so very much. She expected everything to be done perfect, even to the stacking of the wood. Same size pieces from twigs to larger pieces had to be stacked neatly, according to their size. When new straw was put in the chicken nests for the hens to lay their eggs he had better smooth it all out and not leave a straw sticking out of the nest or his Grandmother would reprimand him. He learned so much to help him through life from these wonderful Swiss people that never spoke English in their home. Grandma was so strict that you couldn't believe it. If you did not live by her rules, you just better not come around, no matter who you were. Everyone took

The Antone Dotta family in 1931. Standing L-R: Emil, Agnes, Aileen.
Front: Adella, Alice Anetta, Antone, Edna, Anna, Donald (Buddy), Antone Jr. (Toots)

their shoes off when they entered her immaculate home so as not to track any dirt in. No matter if it was the Priest of the Church or anyone else, off came the shoes.

When P.J. finally gained his citizenship to the United States he gave his full support to the Republican Party and showed an active interest in public affairs. P.J. stood among the leading and influential men in that section of the valley and was respected by everyone who knew him.

It took him many years to pay Mr. Rowland off for the cows that he sold him, but the debt was finally paid. In turn, P.J. loaned money to many of the Swiss people that needed a start in life or were suffering from hard times. When he passed away in 1938 at the age of 77 all of the unpaid debts were written off as paid. Angelina had passed away in 1936.

Before 1900 Loyalton had four sawmills and maybe 100 people lived in town. When the railroad came in the lumber business boomed and Loyalton really grew. Nearly 200 people worked at the mill when it was running. Now with all the mechanization only about 80 people work there and they cut three times as much lumber, cutting as many as 3000 logs a shift. The Sierra Valley boasts of the largest lumber mill in the world at Quincy, shipping lumber all over the world.

February 20, 1939 Alvin Lombardi married his high school sweetheart Adella Dotta. The young couple went to Reno to be married where Alvin spent $20.00 for a ring and $10.00 for the Priest. He said it was the best deal he ever made. Two sons were born to the couple, Randy in 1940 and Mark in 1943.

After their marriage, Alvin and Adella worked on the ranch with his father and also worked for Caesare Dotta as well as working for other ranchers. The dairy was doing fine with butter being their best cash commodity. When Oleomargarine was introduced on the market the price of butterfat dropped from .25 cents to .18 cents a pound. The dairy business was really hurt by this artificial butter that was flooding the market. You couldn't even sell your cream and the creamery at Loyalton closed down. This was during the depression and things were tough enough for the farmers and ranchers without this obstacle. It was time to close the dairy.

Caesar Lombardi lived to be 96 years old and died in 1983, he had never been sick a day of his life and was an exceptional hard working man. His wife Emma died in 1978 at the age of 83.

After three years on the ranch, Alvin left and he and Adella and their sons moved into Loyalton where he went to work at the lumber mill in 1941. In 1944 Alvin went into the Navy and was stationed on an amphibious ship. He saw battles at Iwo Jima, and Okinawa where he was stationed on a supply ship. After eighteen months he was discharged in January of 1946. He was happy to come home to his wife and sons. The service is still an unpleasant memory for Alvin and he still has bad dreams of all the death and destruction that he witnessed.

When Alvin returned from the service he went back to work at the lumber mill where he worked for thirty years except for his tour of duty in the service. He worked under four different owners, Clover Valley Lumber Co., Feather River Lumber Co. De Giorgio Corp., and Sierra Pacific. He retired in 1971. Arthritis took its toll on Alvin and by 1975 he was forced to spend the rest of his life in a wheelchair.

The early times in Sierra Valley were marvelous times with wonderful memories. The pace of living was serene and peaceful. Horses and buggies were the main mode of travel until Dr. Crow; a dentist in Sierraville bought the first automobile in the valley. It was quite small and a shiny red thing that made a terrible lot of noise. You could hear it several miles away; causing the children to run and climb up on the front gates to see this wonderful machine that ran and got places minus a horse. Dr. Crow wore a cap, goggles and a tan duster, which were all needed to protect him from the dust flying up from the road. He was quite a spectacle in the community and everyone was in wonderment of his amazing machine.

Freight teams traveled between the railroad terminal at Truckee and Sierraville, Sattley and Sierra City. Mr. Sol Rousseau owned one of the teams and Mr. Copren owned two teams. Eight horses or mules pulled each wagon with teaming bells strapped to their collars. The bells could be heard for quite some distance and their purpose was important. The noise of the bells let the other driver know there was a team and wagon approaching around a steep narrow turn and it gave one of the driver's time to pull to one side to let the others pass. Each team had a different sounding set of bells and you knew who was coming up the road by the sound of them. Mr. Owen Williams of Sierra City also owned one of the teams. He was the victim of a murder when he was robbed for his cargo. Mr. Copren was killed when his team ran away and he was thrown from the wagon.

Winter time was the time for the men to head to the hills to cut logs that could be skidded in near to the homes to be cut into stove wood and give it time to cure for later use. It took lots of wood to keep the heating stoves and cook stoves going 24 hours a day during the cold winter months. Even during the hot weather the wood cook stoves kept a fire most of the time to cook the three large meals a day for the big families and ranch hands.

Mrs. Nonie Dearwater and Mrs. Grace Wilson got together a plan to get electricity into the valley. Neither P.G.& E. nor the Sierra Electric, which came from Reno, would bring the electricity in, as it was too expensive. Finally the two ladies with the help of Alden Johnson got together a plan to get the Rural Electrification Association to bring the power to the area. These people worked hard and unselfishly to get the electricity to the community but were never recognized for their accomplishment. How wonderful it was in 1937 to have electric lights and all the wonderful things that electricity brought to the homes.

Wintertime was cold and the snow was deep, but this did not stop the fun of the young people or the socializing of the neighbors. Sleighing parties were held on moonlight cold nights with a horse drawn sleigh filled with hay. Rocks, irons and bricks were heated in the oven of the wood stove then wrapped in blankets to keep their feet warm. Stopping at someone's home for cake and coffee ended hours of riding through the valley with the sleigh bells jingling and singing. Lots of ice skating parties, candy-pulling parties, popcorn popping; playing games and visiting filled many long winter evenings.

With the coming of Spring, Easter was always a special event to look forward to. The eggs were saved to have enough to make Easter eggs. A few days before Easter the eggs were covered by sewing bright pieces of calico cloth snuggly around the egg making a little cover for each egg. The eggs were then put in a big iron pot with water and wood ashes to cover them and boiled for about an hour, then left to cool. On Easter morning the covers were removed to reveal the loveliest assortment of eggs that a child's eyes ever beheld. On Easter Monday the children took their eggs to school to share the beauty with their friends. The dye from the bright calico cloth had been transferred to the eggs.

Soon the 4th of July Parade would be held in Loyalton, and this was a big event. There was usually a medicine show in town. This was a man that traveled about the countryside with his team and wagon and had all sorts of things to sell. A sideshow was usually a part of his entertainment to get people interested in his wares. Everyone participated in the parade and events, what a celebration. Now with all the festivities over it was time to start the months of haying on the ranches and back to the lumber business for others.

P.J. Lombardi Ranch

The Lomardi family. Back: Randy, Jeanette, Domi, Mark. Front: Adella, Alvin

In the early days hay was put up loose in huge stacks throughout the valley. But then came the invention of the hay press and thousands of bales of hay were put through this machine. In the central and northern part of the valley bunch grass hay was baled. This was some of the best beef hay in the world. The southern end of the valley baled a large tonnage of red top and timothy and wild clover. The market was for the logging camps, which used hundreds of horses and cattle, and they also used tons and tons of barley and oats. It took many tons of feed to supply the freight teams that were used at the mines at Sierra City and Downieville. Nearly every family in that country had one to three cows and a few horses that needed hay. The livery stables which supplied teams and saddle horses to rent out to the drummers and the 8,10 and 12 horse teams in the Marysville country took a lot of feed. The Brewery at Downieville and Boca used hundreds of tons of brewing barley for their beer. This was a good market for the farmer's merchandise.

The ranchers started baling their hay in the field with a hay press. They believed it was a cheaper way to get it to their barns and to the markets. Antone Dotta owned one of the hay presses. One of the earliest presses was called the Petaluma Hay Press. There were four men needed to run it, with one man doing the weighing of the hay and stacking the hay in a pile. The hay was pitched into a trough on the hay press. Men would take turns tromping the hay down. A block of wood was put in at the place the end of the bale was to be. The lid was shut down and locked. The wires were poked in and a heavy team of horses was used to drive the plunger in to compress the bale. The other three men took turns in tramping the hay in the press, completing one bale at a time. Each man tramped what was called a "run", which were five bales, and then change off with someone else. A crew could bale about fifteen tons a day with the bales weighing around 120 pounds according to the type of hay. Another press was called a beater press or Shotgun baler, and it was run with a sweep power. One or two men pitched hay into the press and a pair of horses went on a sweep power in a circle, to press the hay into the bales. This caused the plunger to compress the hay so the men could tie it with wires.

Good horses were in demand and you could sell good horses from $350 to $500 for a team. Horses were used for everything from transportation, farming, ranching, logging, ice cutting and pleasure.

Times were good in those days, and people worked hard. There were the bad times, such as the train robbery near Reno in 1870. The train was carrying nearly $60,000 in gold pieces and silver bars. Five men were holed up in an abandoned mine tunnel overlooking the Central Pacific right-of-way. The train was robbed, but no one was killed. The men split up the money and went their separate ways. All of the bandits were found and one was in a boarding house in Loyalton, another was on his brother's ranch in Sierraville. The thief that was found in Loyalton was wearing high-heeled boots and his footprints were not hard to track in the snow leading the posse directly to him. All but $3,000 of the money was recovered. There is speculation that it is buried somewhere along the Truckee River. If found, the 150 gold coins would be worth over $500,000 today.

Few people are left to tell the remarkable tales and stories of the pioneers of the Sierra Valley. Alvin Lombardi is the last ancestor of P.J. Lombardi left in Loyalton to tell the story of his amazing Grandparents and parents. Adella Dotta Lombardi and her brother Emil are the only descendents of Caesare Dotta who was one of the major ranchers in that area that still calls the Sierra Valley home.

June 15, 1999

Memoirs Of A Pioneer Lady

A brave woman from a long line of hearty pioneers was proud to call Modoc County her home. Laura Miller was born to John Phillip and Emily Miller on August 18, 1879 in Stone Coal Valley along the Pit River in Modoc County, California. The valley was also known as "Lost Frying Pan Valley," or "Pleasant Valley" as the girls of the valley liked to call it. Eleven children made up the family of the Millers, and they were a busy, lively bunch.

John Phillip Miller was born in Germany in 1830. With his parents, a sister and a brother he came to the United States in 1846. The reason so many left their homeland of Germany was to escape the compulsory draft for their sons.

The family first settled in Iowa, but the riches of the land in California soon inspire some of the young men to move west. Phillip and

Laura Miller Kresge

Seward and Laura Kresge wedding photo

several bachelors joined a wagon train and headed west with their teams, wagons and farm equipment to settle farms in California and Oregon.

In 1848 while on their travels they heard of the gold strike in California and they became anxious to get there. Their cumbersome wagons were too slow for these adventuresome young men so they made some adjustments. They cut up their harness to make cinches and straps for the packsaddles that they made out of the spokes of their wagon wheels, so they could load their gear on to the mules. Packing some of the animals and riding the others, they headed to the gold fields at a faster pace.

Not quite prepared for the trip the young men ran out of food. They lived only on the game they could shoot, which was just an occasional jackrabbit. Broke and only one mule left between them they finally reached Sutter's Mill at Sacramento. Phillip was so near starved that he fainted. A kind gentleman bought them some flour and bacon. Phillip was so weak he ate only one half of a hot cake. His friend gorged himself and after not eating for three days he became so sick that he nearly died.

The mining was not that successful at Sutter's Mill. Six thousand men crowded the banks of the American River hoping to find that little piece of gold they all dreamed of. Conditions were crowded and hectic.

Laura Kresge

Shoving, fighting and surviving was all that one could expect. Phillip did not enjoy these kinds of conditions.

In 1851 Phillip left for the Shasta Valley in Siskiyou County where he struck gold in a small creek he named Deadwood Creek. He then homesteaded a small place on the Klamath River. In 1859 the young German man married a German lady, Amelia Syble at Hawkinsville, California. Three daughters, Philopena, Amelia II and Frances were born to the couple. The young mother passed away suddenly, leaving her husband with three small daughters to raise. Amelia's mother helped Phillip with his daughters until he married Emily Sharp in 1869.

The little girls could not speak a word of English, but their loving stepmother was patient and taught them the English language and made a good home for them. Phillip and Emily had another daughter, Augusta within the year.

Phillip always wanted a cattle ranch and in 1869 he sold his place on the Klamath River and traveled due East to Stone Coal Valley in Modoc County. The Pit River meandered through the ranch that he found. It was what he dreamed of and he brought his family and drove his cattle from Siskiyou to this new homestead.

The young couple made their home in a log cabin and began to have more children. Eight more were born to the pioneer couple. Will was born in 1872; Kitty, in 1874; Roy in 1876; Laura in 1879; Phillip Jr. in 1881; Emmet in 1884; Ernest in 1885 and Elsie in 1887. This totaled twelve children for the Miller family.

With the growing family it was time to build a new two-story house as the cabin was getting quite cramped.

Phillip worked as a teamster part of the time. He hauled freight from Redding to Adin and Canby for the mercantile stores. The closest flourmill was the Morton Milling Company at Ashland, Oregon and it took two weeks to make a round trip to bring a load of flour into this area. Phillip would hitch four to six horses to pull the freight wagons, depending on how heavy his load would be.

There were many Indians in the valley and this worried Emily some. While her husband was gone on his freight trips, Emily would sleep with a gun in her bed, as she was afraid of the Indians.

Another of her concerns was that the first year that they moved to the valley, they killed twenty-five rattlesnakes near the house where the children would be playing.

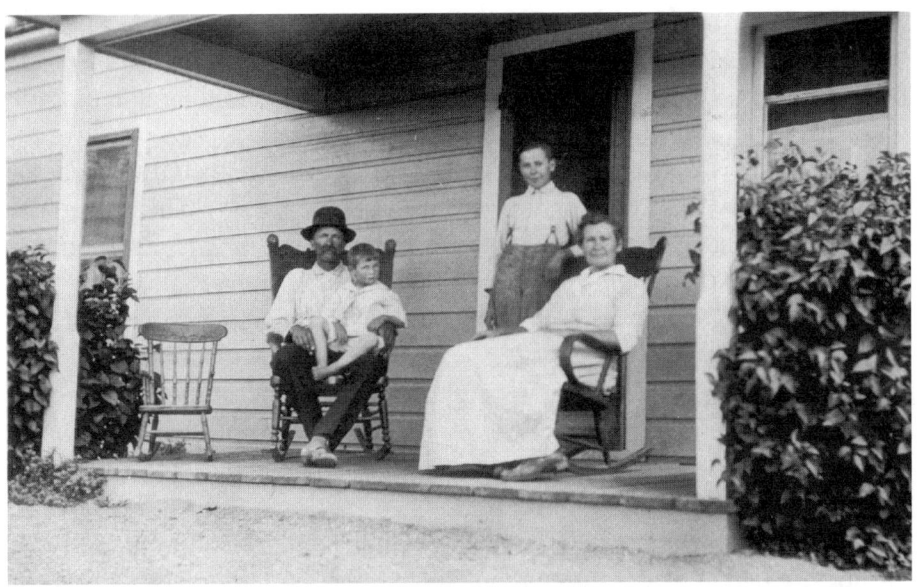

Seward with Marcel on his lap, Owen and Laura Kresge

Like many of the ranchers, the Millers were caught off guard when the winter of 1889-90 hit. Enough hay had only been put up for the milk cows, work teams and saddle horses. The stock cows were expected to graze on the valley floor in the wintertime and the surrounding hills in the summer time. The heavy, unexpected three to five feet of snow of this harsh winter covered all the feed for the livestock.

Gathering the tender willow limbs and mahogany branches to feed the cattle was a daily chore. The men would snowshoe to the higher mountains to gather what feed they could.

Cutting the brush that they thought the animals could consume, they bound it together like a sled and towed the bundles back to the valley. The straw out of the family mattresses was fed to the starving animals. The candles the family had made to keep them from the long winter evening darkness were also fed to the cattle, hoping the tallow had some nourishment to it. The men would cut the paunches open on the dead cattle to let the surviving ones share in that little bit of sustenance, but all was in vain. By the dozens the cattle perished. The family saved only about thirty cows from their original herd of three hundred cows.

Emily's brother Will Sharp who lived close by lost nearly all of his sheep. His horses survived by eating the wool off of the dead sheep.

Will and Phillip would snowshoe over the mountains to Adin, pulling hand sleds to get 200 pounds of flour and some provisions. Barley was browned to make coffee. Times were tough, but man and beast had to be tougher to survive.

The Miller family had to do the best they could to keep things going. Emily learned cheese making and started a cheese factory. She milked the cows, made the cheese and driving her team and buggy she peddled cheese all over the country

As the families grew in the valley a school district was formed and Mrs. Pope taught the first school. The Miller children walked two and one half miles to school. They had to get to the other side of the Pit River by crossing on a footbridge which rested on upright logs in natural holes in the rocks. In 1889 they went to the Stone Coal Valley School with the Sherer, Johnson and Renner children.

When the Indians were restless the Miller, Griffith, Johnson and Pope families would gather at night at one location in case of an attack. The Pit

The children of John Phillip and Emily Miller. L-R back row: Phillip Jr., Will and Roy
2nd row: Francis, Amelia, Philopena. Front: Laura and Elsie at their home in Stone Coal Valley

River Indians helped the whites, but the Modoc Indian War was on and the Modoc Indians would rob the Pit River Indians of their horses and possessions.

In 1890 during haying season the family home caught fire and burned to the ground before the men could get from the field to stop it. A new two-story home had to be built before the cold winter set in.

The family of Phillip Miller Sr. were growing up, marrying and going on with their own lives. The mates they chose and marriages were Philopena to James Essex, Amelia to Alfred Hulbert, Frances to Frank Caldwell, Will to Minnie Fellencer, Kitty to Oscar Tabor, Roy to Lilly, Laura to Seward Kresge, Phillip to Clara Weigand and Elsie to Edwin Clauson and later George Fellencer.

When Laura was young she was a great help to her mother in the home and especially with the cheese making. When Laura was in the eighth grade the family rented a house in Lookout where she and a sister and brother stayed so they could go to school. Their teacher was Nora Kresge Nichols. After high school in Adin, Laura continued her schooling in Chico, California at the Chico Normal School for teachers. Later she returned home to teach in the old school house in Stone Coal Valley, where she had started the first grade. She later taught at another school West of Lookout, the Widow Valley school.

On November 26, 1903 Laura married Seward Kresge at her parents home. After their marriage they moved up the Stone Coal Valley about three miles where she and her husband managed the old Johnson place. They were there only a short time when they moved to Canby to manage the Canby Trading Post.

While living in Canby, twin boys were born to the young couple on March 12, 1905. Owen was small, but quite healthy. Orin was tiny and weaker and lived only a few days. Owen lived a long fulfilling life in the agriculture business in Modoc County.

The family later moved to Adin where Seward built a beautiful home. After moving to Adin, two more children were born. Marcel in 1912 and nine years later, a daughter Leola was born.

From 1906 to 1911 Seward began to build up a ranch in Round Valley, just north of Adin. He acquired 350 acres from several different landholders, namely Gutzman, Rice and Smith. Laura and Seward felt this ranch was the right spot to settle and raise their family.

Here in the middle of the big Round Valley the children grew up. Laura watched a changing world. Gone were the horse and buggy days of her youth, the long cattle drives to market, and the muddy roads. Here the future was bright for her children.

Marcel had married Edna Gould from Gougerneck in 1937. In 1943 Seward decided he was ready to retire and offered for Marcel and Edna to buy the home ranch. They added to the ranch through the next thirty-two years until they had a spread of 3000 acres.

Owen had gone to business school for a time and was working for the Soil Conservation office in Alturas. While there, he met the new Home Demonstration Agent for Modoc County. In 1946 he and Betty Walters were married. Owen soon decided the office work was not for him and he moved back to Round Valley to ranch next to his brother on the Conklin place.

In 1943 Laura and Seward moved near their daughter Leola at Chico and six years later Laura was left a widow.

A courageous lady that lived the pioneer life, as did so many women from Modoc, passed away in 1967. Loved by her family and friends she left a legacy that they are proud of.

July 9, 1999

A Fall River Valley History

The Island House was the most aristocratic mansion in the Fall River Valley. Built in the early 1870's by William Henry Winter, this was a place of grandeur and magnificent parties and entertainment. The house was famous and the pride of Eastern Shasta County. It was the social center of the valley and the home of William Henry Winter, his wife, Sarah, and their three sons, Harry, Frank and Dee who arrived in the valley in the late 1860's.

William and Margaret Straub

William purchased the land along the Pit River and also land in the town of Fall River Mills. That was when the Fall River was a rushing stream, foaming over rapids to join the Pit River. In those rapids lay an island, about 200 yards long and half as wide, with the swift current bubbling by on both sides and connected to the mainland by a rustic bridge. It was on this island Winter built his home, a stately, two-story frame structure, built of the finest native

John St John

Frances St. John

pine lumber, with twelve rooms and open fireplaces in eight of them. Winter added an artificial lake, which he stocked with native trout. The island was alive with lush willows, lawns and shrubs.

This was the first building in Fall River to have running water. A huge water wheel pumped water to the top of the building in a storage tank, then by gravity flow the water was used in the house.

Winter built the first sawmill in the Fall River valley, operated by waterpower produced by Fall River, in which the lumber that was used to build most of the Fall River Mills structures was produced. A fire later destroyed the mill.

This pioneer also built the first flourmill in the valley, located opposite the Island House on the high bank above Pit River.

Fall River Mills derived its name from the mills erected by Winter, who also started to build the first toll road into the Fall River valley. He had started a toll road near Carbon and half way through he contracted to Knoch and Murken to finish it. They were to finish it for $3,000. The construction of the road and a bridge had to be done. Winter was unable to pay for the construction job, so Knoch and Murken had to take over the toll road. The charge was twenty-five cents for horse and rider and seventy-five cents for a wagon with two to four horses to use the road.

They had hoped to recover some of their expenses, but it would take a long time.

Winter had promised his sons that when he was ready to retire, he would give the Island House to the son who first brought home a bride. His son, Harry, was the first to marry and the house became his.

Harry Winter practiced law with an office in a wing of the flourmill, handling the legal work for the entire countryside. But the apple of his eye was the beautiful home where he and his lovely wife entertained lavishly. The stories of their exquisite silver, cut glass and linens, of the nursemaids who cared for their four children and their elaborate parties with fancy food that was shipped in had become legends in the valley.

The fortune of Harry Winter disappeared, as he was not the business manager his father had been. The elder Winter and his wife both died in 1879 just six months apart. A decade or so later the Winter fortune had been exhausted and the estate fell into the hands of a Redding bank. Fred Knoch and his brother-in-law Richard Murken purchased the Pit River Ranch.

After the bank took over the stately mansion in 1899 Edgar Lansing and his wife Margaret (Straub) rented the home for several years. Edgar was the Constable and Sheriff and later owned a service station and the Ford agency in Fall River Mills. They had a son Harold (who died when

Lottie Straub St. John

Carl St. John, Sr.

he was seventeen years old) and a daughter Bertha that was ill. Margaret (Maggie) repeatedly took Bertha back and forth to San Francisco to doctors. All Bertha wanted to do was stay at the Island House that she loved.

William Straub was born in Baden, Germany in October 1840 and came to America in 1859. He landed in San Francisco. His wife Margaret (Gehr) Straub was born in Bavaria, Germany in May 24, 1849 and came to Philadelphia, Penn. in 1850. At thirteen years of age Margaret was married to Albert Kramer in 1862 and divorced him in 1866; they had a son Al, who stayed with his father. When she married Straub in 1868, the couple then had eleven more children, one every two years with the first one being born in 1870. First William and the others to follow were Amelia, Charles, Kate, George, Margaret, Celia, Joseph, Charlotte, Gussie and Gertie.

In 1874 William Straub owned a Saloon on "A Street" in Dixon, California. The advertisement told of the best wines and liquors for Medical and Family use. Also they served the best brands of English Ale and Port. The establishment had a Number 1 Billiard Table for the accommodations of customers and Fresh Eastern Oysters and Clam Chowder on Saturday and Sunday. The I.O.O.F. Installations and Banquets of that lodge were held at the Straub Saloon where Mrs. Straub served a "sumptuous repast."

William had come to the Fall River Valley to homestead 160 acres near McArthur in 1888. His second son Charlie added on to the homeplace by homesteading another 160 acres in 1891. The original patent was signed October 8, 1892. In 1903 he deeded the land to his sister Mary Kate (Straub) and her husband George Rose. After George died and his wife remarried and became Mary Kate Keeler, she deeded the land to her daughter, Lois Edna Ingram, as a gift on February 21, 1923. George Ingram, son of Lois is now the owner of the ranch his ancestors homesteaded.

In 1898 William and Margaret moved to Adin where they ran hotels. For quite some time they operated the Exchange Hotel and later ran the City Hotel. The family lived in this community for several years where the younger children went to school.

While running the City Hotel on February 5, 1903 several men were gathered around the stove in the barroom swapping stories. All of a sudden William took a couple of deep breaths and his head fell back, the 63-year-old man was dead.

At this time many of his children were in the Fall River area and one son George had gone to Petaluma to start the first chicken hatchery there. They named the town Straubville, where he started his hatchery.

John St. John and his brothers Billie and Ed had came to Chico, California in 1870 from Michigan. John had married Frances Decker in Sacramento in 1880. Her family had come to Butte County in 1868. While at Chico, John was the foreman of the Gwynn ranch.

John and Frances's family came into the Fall River area and settled at Bald Mountain on a dry land wheat farm in 1899. The ranch was bought with money that Frances had inherited from her family. To this union were born Carl in 1881, Harry in 1883, Jessie in 1885, Ray in 1887, Lola in 1888 and Effie in 1890, while they lived in Chico. After moving to Bald Mountain and ten years after the birth of her last child, Bruce was born in 1900. When he was six days old his thirty-nine year old mother died. Not being able to care for the tiny infant John gave him to the Creighton family who had a new baby and the mother was able to feed baby Bruce and raise him.

A gathering of friends at Adin about 1903. Standing Back L-R: Buffer Chase, Minnie Chase, unknown, Ira Harris Geis, Alice Bath Walker, Arthur Traugh, Millie Ford Traugh, unknown. Seated L-R: Edwin Pickard, Edna Niles, Gertrude Straub, unknown, Ray Shepherd, Charlotte Straub, and Celia Straub

John and his children lived at Bald Mountain until 1904 when he sold the ranch. In 1906 he had to foreclose on the ranch and the family moved back to their old home.

In 1906, six years after the death of his first wife, John married Ada Zumwalt Noble who had three sons. They lived on the ranch until the time of John's death.

John St. John passed away May 1932 from Pneumonia at the age of 75. His death launched a large court battle between his three sons, Carl, Harry and Bruce and their Step Mother and her three sons.

The newspapers reported a three-cornered struggle to appoint an Administrator of the estate of John L. St. John. Harry filed application for letters of administration in the estate of his mother, Mrs. Frances St. John, who died in 1900, six years prior to his father's marriage to Mrs. Ada St. John.

The petitioner alleged that his mother's estate, valued at "not more that $20,000," was never administered. He sets forth that she left 960 acres, known as the Kesselring ranch, six miles south of Fall River Mills and 152 head of cattle, besides the Bald Mountain ranch.

The petition states that subsequent to her death her widower sold the property and converted it into a note for $11,000, $10,000 of which still is due. $2,293.30 in cash, now in the bank and 200 acres of land near McArthur. This was also the estate of John St. John. Carl St. John also

The Island House with the Edgar Lansing family on the porch, Fall River Mills, Calif., 1914

asked to be name administrator. Mrs. Ada St. John, the second wife, followed later with a contest and a petition asking that she be named. The administration is somewhat complicated because the estate of the first Mrs. St. John was never administered. So there is a problem to determine what is community property and what portions belong to the three sons of the first wife.

A bitter legal battle was encountered and the St. John boys lost the lawsuit in favor of their stepmother and her three sons. They were able to hold on to the Bald Mountain ranch which they later sold to Floyd Bidwell. The stepmother got the Kesselring ranch near McArthur. It cost quite a bit for the St.John children to keep the ranch, but it was something they had to do.

Carl St.John had a sweetheart that had lived in the Fall River Valley, but she had moved to Petaluma and was living with her brother George on his chicken ranch. Charlotte (Lottie) Straub and Carl St. John were married at Santa Rosa on February 26, 1906.

When Carl and Lottie returned to Fall River they lived with his father on the ranch at Bald Mountain. Carl worked as a carpenter for a time, but really didn't like to work at all. He was sure he always found a job for his wife. Her main jobs were cooking on ranches or running hotels.

Their son Almont was born at Fall River in 1910. Gus was born at Shelly Creek in 1916, Gertrude in Pittville in 1918, and Carl Jr. at the Malone ranch in 1922. Working on ranches or managing hotels always gave the family a place to stay. It was a struggle for Lottie to keep the family going and Carl didn't help much. The family was always on the move. When Gertrude was ten they lived in Bieber where Lottie worked at the Valley Hotel for Mrs. Brownell and the children went to school.

He found her a job at the Malone Ranch cooking for the Railroad crew that built Pit 1 for PG&E. The family moved down the dusty road with their meager belongings in their little old car. One of Gertrude's fondest memories is when they would travel that road and stop. Papa would go out and stand on a big rock in the river and catch Salmon for them to eat. Mama would pack a picnic lunch and they would have a wonderful family outing.

The family moved to the Malone ranch when Gertrude was small. Her mother was pregnant and about to give birth when the little girl was four. When Lottie went into labor they sent Gertrude outside to look for the stork. She went round and round the house, looking and looking towards the sky. Suddenly she heard a baby cry and when she ran into the

4th of July Parade in Fall River Mills, 1930

house, the baby was there. She couldn't understand how that could happen as she had watched so carefully for the stork and never saw him.

After the powerhouse was built and they damned the water to build Lake Britton, the water completely covered the Malone ranch. When that job was over and the crew moved on Carl found Lottie another job. The family had to move on also. All Carl wanted to do was peddle things such as salt and peppershakers, shoes, nylons, nick knacks and gadgets going from door to door.

Lottie and Carl divorced in 1928 when Gertrude was ten. They stayed friends, but Lottie couldn't support him and the children also. He just did not want to work and support his family and she was tired of his lazy ways. She later married Al Lorenzen a longtime friend whose wife had died.

Gertrude went to school at McArthur where her Mom ran a restaurant. Her teacher there was Irma Thatcher. Later at Fall River she went to school to Frances Gassaway.

After the divorce the family moved to Glenburn and lived with an Uncle, Phi Reynolds and helped him after his wife died.

When Gertrude was 15 she married Noel Bassett, they had two sons; Harold and deWelden.

At 18 she was divorced and went to San Leandro to go to nurses training at the Fairmont Hospital. She graduated from nurses training in

1940 and worked at the county hospital at Redding for several years. After coming back to Redding to work, she met an attractive man by the name of Bob Barcus who played in a dance band called the "Arizona Wranglers." A daughter Toni was born to this couple. Living the traveling musician's life he did not want to settle down and kept traveling on with the band. Later Gertrude married Richard Hurd.

Gertrude then moved back to Fall River where she worked for doctors and nursed for 46 years before retiring at age 73.

When Almont was old enough he helped Lottie support the family. He worked for Ivan and Arthur Dunlap in their store. He was a very good musician and played with many dance bands in the area. Almont married Hilma Bassett, sister of Noel Bassett.

Uncle George Straub owned the McIntosh Hotel in Fall River Mills. Lottie had inherited $2400 from her parents and he wanted her to put her money in the hotel with him. She was wise and thrifty and finally bought a house for herself. Lottie ran the hotel for her brother George. Gertrude has fond memories of living in the hotel when she was ten years old. The big lobby was like a ballroom to her. They would all set around the radio and listen to their favorite program of "Amos and Andy."

Uncle George dismantled the hotel and built several little motel like cabins using the old lumber and wiring. It was believed that the old wiring caused the fire that burned the town down in 1934. Almont remembered this account of the fire.

"I was sleeping peacefully at my mother's home back of the Odd Fellows Hall when my brother-in-law Noel Bassett, came rushing through the front door (which was never locked in those days) shouting, "Almont your store is on fire!" It was 5 A.M. August 13, 1934. I slipped on a pair of Levi's, ran up the hill to Main Street, and then down main street to the store in my bare feet. The store was called Dunlap's Cash Store, (the first cash store, in the Intermountain area) and was owned by Ivan and Arthur Dunlap, who lived in Glenburn where they operated a grocery store and Post Office. I was the only employee (store manager). The store was located on the West Side of Main Street between Pop Mill's Barbershop and Dr. Pratt's Drug Store. As I opened the front door I could see and hear the fire burning in the warehouse portion in the back so knew I had to work fast.

My main concern was that I had cashed a large number of payroll checks the Saturday before and they were in an old safe. I ran to the safe, turned the combination and to my amazement the door opened on the first try! I grabbed all the money and checks which were in a cash box and took them down to my mother's house for safekeeping. I then ran up the hill and down the street again and back to the store to see what else I could save. I knew we had a large supply of ammunition, so I grabbed a large wooden box of apples, dumped them on the floor and filled the box with shells and put it on the front porch. About that time Ivan arrived and we decided to save as many cartons of cigarettes as possible. We each took a box, filled it with cigarettes and placed it on the front porch. The store had an antique cash register, very large and very heavy, so we took it across the street where we thought it would be safe until later. By this time the fire was too hot, so we loaded the ammunition and cigarettes onto Ivan's pickup and drove it across the street to get the register. Believe it or not, we were unable to lift the register then. Even trying as hard as we could, so it just sat there and burned up when the fire jumped across the street. How we had the strength to carry it across the street has always been a mystery to me.

Gus, Almont and Carl St. John

After Ivan moved his pickup up the street, we watched the fire jump across the street and work its way up both sides consuming every building. It was a helpless feeling.

Bosworth's jewelry was the last building to burn on the west side. Dr. Pratt's large dwelling was the next in line; it's said that it was saved because people were able to hose it down with garden hoses, but I think the main reason it survived was the number of trees between it and Bosworths'.

On the East side, Ready Eddy had built his new clothing store and luckily it was covered with galvanized iron. Using a gasoline-powered pump, the fire fighters were able to spray the building with water, keeping

Gertrude St. John, 1947

it from catching fire, so the fire was stopped on that side.

How did the fire start? I guess we will never know. My uncle, George Straub of Petaluma, had purchased the old McIintosh hotel, located about a block from the old steel bridge. He had torn it down and built several small motel type buildings on the west side of Mechanic Street. They were directly behind Pop Mill's barbershop, Dunlap's Cash Store and Dr. Pratt's Drug Store. The fire started in one of these buildings and worked its way up the hill to the back of the buildings on Main Street, thus practically burning the whole town."

Lottie had mortgaged her home to help Almont start a store on his own and he owned the Modern Market in Fall River for years. He sold the market and put his full efforts toward the insurance business. He owned the St.John Insurance agency in Fall River from 1948-1975. Almont passed away in 1995.

Gus had worked for Almont in the store before he went into the service serving in New Guinea. He later moved to Sacramento where he was a warehouse foreman and died in 1986.

Lottie was born in 1885 and died when she was 63 years old on September 27, 1953.

Carl Sr. died in November 1963; he had been born in December 1881 and was 82 years old.

Dedication of the Lookout Grange Hall in 1951.
The Fall River Dance Band - Floyd Summers, Almont St. John, Lonnie Cleland, Luella Rodman, Bubbles Brewster and young Kenny Eastman in front

Carl Jr. and his wife Mollie owned the Town Hall Theater in Fall River Mills for twenty years. He was the sales manager for the Hiway Garage for twenty-six years. He passed away in 1989

Gertrude is the only one of that generation left to carry on the St.John name. She is a proud ancestor of the Straub's and St. John's who were prominent pioneer families in the Fall River Valley.

The fate of the beautiful Island House had been foreseen. The Red River Lumber Company purchased it and their representatives lived in it for a time. It was then rented to Mr. and Mrs. Edgar Lansing, descendents of the Straub family. Then sold to P.G.& E. when they built the dam to divert the water through the tunnel to the Pit 1 Power House, the flowing water dried up around the beautiful mansion and it became dry and bare. This home that was built of the very finest lumber to satisfy the taste of a wealthy man was now known as the "Hoover Hotel" and was a home for visiting Hobo's. The sixty-five year old home was sold to Raymond Ayers for $100.00 and he tore it down and used the lumber to build his home in Fall River Mills.

The grand parties and lavish dinners in the mansion on the island are history and only memories and clippings in scrapbooks.

August 9, 1999

A Bucket Of Blackberries For A Gingham Dress

"A hundred years you say, it certainly doesn't seem that long." These were the exact words of a fantastic lady that has seen the 1800's, the 1900's and will soon see the year 2000. Yes, it will be one hundred years on November 23, 1999 that Eloise Stockton Pursley can claim she has lived. Born on that date in 1899 in Truckee. California to Mary (Crooker) and (Ira) Louis Stockton she has lived a long and healthy life. Maybe she can't remember if something happened in 1918 or 1919, but that is about the only thing she has forgotten.

Her father Louis Stockton who was born in Decatur, Illinois in 1869 was a frail child. The Doctor told his parents they needed to move to a drier climate for his health, so the family migrated to Red Bluff, California where they homesteaded at Stockton Gulch. Their close

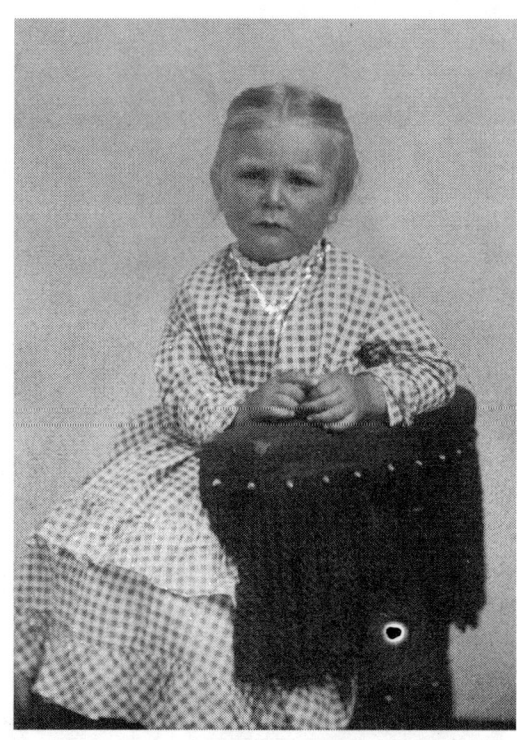
Mary Crooker, mother of Eloise Pursley, 1880

Louis Stockton and Mary Crooker in their wedding photograph, 1894

The Crooker homestead, Manton, California, photo taken around 1910

neighbors were the Owens family and young Louis and Roy Owens were great friends who played together constantly.

George and Etta Crooker traveled by train from New York to California and settled at Henleyville, which was west of Red Bluff. George had a brother Levi that lived there and this is why they chose that area. They had two small daughters Mary and Cora that were born in New York and after moving to California three sons, Bert, Ernest and Claude were born. Even though George was a good farmer, all he could raise at Henleyville were grasshoppers. Trying as hard as they could, they could not drive the grasshoppers from their land and the pests destroyed everything in sight. The family could not even raise enough vegetables and fruits to feed the family, and the hoards of insects ate all the feed for the family milk cow and horses. Giving in to the pests rather than trying to fight them, the family decided to move to Manton, a town thirty miles to the northeast, and closer to Mt. Lassen. There at Manton, George and Etta claimed a homestead of 160 acres where they raised their four children. They were able to raise a wonderful vegetable garden, all kinds of fruit and especially wonderful strawberries. They tried to peddle their strawberries by taking them to Red Bluff. The all day trip of thirty miles of rocky, dirt road and the heat with a team and wagon was useless. The berries were bruised and spoiled by time they got them to the market.

There were many Indians in the Manton area, known as the Digger Tribe. They were helpful in picking the fruit and working on the farms. George needed water for his farming operation, so he and his brother Levi dug an irrigation ditch by hand to bring the water from Digger Creek to their property, the ditch is still known at Crooker Ditch. A flume was built to bring the water on down to the house.

The Crooker children went to grade school at Manton, but had to go to Red Bluff for a higher education. Mary Crooker met Louis Stockton while going to school there, they were married in 1894 when she was 18 and he was 25. The young couple moved to Truckee, California where Louis worked in the mill.

Mary and Louis moved back to Red Bluff in 1900 when their daughter Eloise was seven months old. The other children in the family were, a brother Leo, and sisters Doris and Melba. Their home was near the Lincoln Street school which was out in the country. There were only about 3000 people living in Red Bluff at that time. The other school was the Oak Street school and some of the businesses in town were Cone & Kimball, Bones Dry Goods Store, State Theater, Tremont Hotel and the Red Bluff Daily News. Red Bluff had dirt streets and board sidewalks, but in this small town you knew everyone. Many Chinese lived down on Rio Street and they had tunnels under the town where some of them lived and stored things. Beneath the town was a catacomb of their workings.

Mary and Louis Stockton in their first Model T in 1918

When Eloise was a young girl she would go to Manton to spend the summers with her grandparents. It was an all day trip with the horse and buggy. Dale's station, a stage stop was half way and there they would stop to water and rest the horses. Again they would start on their trip reaching Manton by sundown. The children loved to spend time with their grandparents in the mountains. All the cool wonderful streams were full of fish for fishing and swimming. Eloise learned to fish at an early age and

Eloise Pursley

was an avid fisherman her entire life. She could never stand to put a wiggle worm on a hook so she only used salmon eggs and always caught her limit.

Eloise was expected to help with the chores during the summer at her grandparents. One of the chores was picking berries. Her grandmother would give her a milk bucket to fill with blackberries. And for this task she was paid nine cents. At this time gingham material was only five cents a yard and she could buy enough yardage to make a new dress for a bucket of blackberries. A girl did not have many dresses in those days and the long hot heavy frocks were worn all week to school without washing. The washing had to be done by hand and ironed with a heavy sad iron that was heated on the wood cook stove. Laundry was not an easy chore and you tried hard not to get your clothes dirty before the week was up. Two dresses were all that most young girls had, one to wear and one to wash.

When the summer was over Eloise and her siblings were then taken back to Red Bluff to go to school. Life was simple and content in those days. The family was poor, but happy and had all of the necessities. They had food to eat, a house to live in and clothes to wear, they felt that was all they needed.

Eloise only went to high school one year, then when she was fifteen years old she went to work at the Red Bluff Steam Laundry doing bookkeeping. The owner was very good to her and was like a second father teaching her to be a good bookkeeper. She also went to night school. She worked at the laundry for seven years making a $1.00 a day before she met the man she would marry.

Left, Floyd Keadle, Pilot, and Regional Forester Paul G. Rodington, 1920 at Mather Field

Every Saturday night Louis would give each of his children a dime to go to the movies at the State Theater.

Before Prohibition Eloise and her sister went to Redding with some friends to a "Speak Easy", now know as a tavern or bar. They were dunking pretzels in a glass of beer just fooling around when a young man came up to ask them to dance. When they both refused him, he ask them their name. They said we're the Dunking Sisters. He believed them and went on his way.

Another time Eloise and her sister Doris went to a movie at the State Theater in Red Bluff. Two young Army pilots came and jumped over the back of the seats next to each one of the girls and introduced themselves. Before too long, Eloise married one of the pilots, Floyd Keadle and Doris married the other, Eddie Neher.

Both of the young men were Army Pilots stationed at Mather Field in Sacramento. They had just graduated from flying school and liked to fly as stunt pilots. One of the events that they performed at was the new special event at Red Bluff, the Red Bluff Roundup in 1922. One of Floyd's specialties was flying under the Sacramento River Bridge at Red Bluff.

While Floyd and Eddie were still in the Army they went to work for the U. S. Forest Service on the fire patrol. This was considered a training practice. The fire patrol was established in 1918 when pilots needed jobs and the fire situation for the forest service needed help. An agreement was reached and a trial patrol was flown on May 6, 1919 from Mather Field in California to fly patrols over the Tahoe, Plumas, Eldorado and Stanislaus forests in the central Sierra Nevada. The patrol was encouraging and the actual flights got under way by June 1.

Initially, the airmen flew in DeHavland training aircraft, known as Jennies in airman jargon. These were flimsy and unreliable airplanes with short range and low ceiling. A 100-horsepower engine powered them and their cruising speed was only 70 miles per hour. Some of the more sophisticated aircraft had radiotelegraph, but the pilots like Floyd Keadle only could report fires by dropping messages, or landing and telephoning. The practice started of taking homing pigeons along and when a fire was spotted a note was tied to the pigeon and he was set free to return with the message. This became too costly and unreliable for detecting and reporting fires. The forest service was happy when all the planes were equipped with radios.

Originally, the sole purpose of the air patrol experiment was to discover and report forest fires. The forest Service had an existing network

1920 pilots for Forest Service: Eddie Neker, right and Floyd Keadle, third from right in dark jacket

of buildings on prominent peaks called Lookout Stations. These stations were manned only during the fire season and located fires using a sighting and mapping device. Dispatchers of the fire fighters located fires by plotting lookout sightings as reported by Lookout Station personnel. The measure of lookout success was the number of "first reports" made to the dispatcher by telephone.

The opening of the August 1919 deer season and a summer heat wave caused the Forest Service to request expansion of the aerial fire patrol. This includes all of California west of the Sierra Nevada crest, which included the Trinity, Shasta, Lassen, Modoc and Klamath National Forests. This is the route that Floyd and Eddie flew.

The Air patrol was a hazardous duty. Flying over deep canyons and steep peaks was new to most fliers and it was unnerving. Both Floyd and Eddie delighted in the excitement and danger of it all. After flying under the bridge in Red Bluff for exhibition this was a breeze.

In many ways the 1919 Army Air Patrol was a great success. The sight of regular flights did more to prevent fires than anything the Forest Service had ever done in California. Forest supervisors were convinced that arsonists were afraid to light a fire for fear the observer would see them, and the statistics seemed to prove them right. In one case, on the other hand, the patrol caused a fire to spread. An immigrant sheepherder was patrolling a controlled fire when a patrol plane made a low pass over the fire. The poor scared sheepherder took off for parts unknown, and the fire escaped control.

The sight of airplanes flying overhead every day excited everyone in the mountains and valley towns across the state.

Eddie was killed in a plane accident in 1927 while flying a mail plane at Gustine, California. This was only five years after he and Doris were married.

Floyd had a place rented in Alturas where he was going to run a flying school. On June 14, 1922 Floyd and Eloise headed to Modoc County. They bought their wedding rings and got their license in Redding then went on to Fall River Mills where they were married in the parsonage by the local minister. Traveling on to Alturas that same day in their Model T Ford they made their home. Floyd tried to pursue a career as a flight instructor, but this venture did not prove profitable. He had a very good friend, John Davis, who was the Ranger at the Crowder Flat Forest Service Ranger Station. Floyd went to work there for the Forest Service and Eloise cooked for all the big shots that came up from San Francisco. She cooked for five men, three meals a day for a month and was paid $30.00.

While at the ranger station it was a treat for Eloise to be able to ride her horse off and go fishing. One time while on the way back to camp she had gotten off of her horse to go through a gate. When she went to get back on the saddle slipped and she fell to the ground. The horse went bucking off through the meadow with the saddle under his belly. He finally lost it and when Floyd saw the horse coming back without his wife he was afraid something had happened to her. At a distance he saw Eloise walking home and was really relieved. He had quite a search looking for the lost saddle. John Davis fired the young man that could not even saddle a horse right.

Floyd's mother lived in Arkansas so the young couple went back there where Floyd flew for a charter service in Little Rock for a while. By 1927 Floyd and Eloise moved to Red Bluff where their daughter Arlie was born.

When Arlie was just a baby they were again in Alturas for a time. It was wintertime and Eloise wanted to get back to Red Bluff before the weather got too bad. John Davis told her she had better not chance the trip and snow was predicted on Hatchet Mountain between Burney and Redding. The road was winding and treacherous in good weather without the threat of snow. Eloise had her mind made up, so she bundled the baby up and in her Model T Ford she headed south. By the time she made it to the Hatchet Mountain the snow was falling hard. The Ford had no windows on the sides, only curtains. A windshield did keep the snow out of her face, but windshield wipers and a heater were unheard of. Eloise drove with one hand while she reached out and wiped the snow from the windshield with the other. Cars were off the road stuck along side in the snow banks. She knew she could not stop or she and the baby might freeze to death. She just kept on going and bypassed all the stalled cars not even being able to tell where the road was. She met a big truck, but kept up her speed of 15 miles an hour and just made him move over. What a happy young mother when she reached Redding and it was raining. You can bet she never tried that trip again in the wintertime.

Floyd spent quite some time as a bush pilot in Alaska flying state officials and fishermen to their destination. Another exciting time was when he flew for the Americans during the Mexican revolution in the 1920's. He was flying for the rebels and flew his plane across the boarder to El Paso, Texas. He was promised a big salary but never got a thing. The FBI investigated him thinking he was the enemy. The FBI also came knocking on Eloise's door to check her out. Finally Floyd was cleared and that was enough of that excitement.

Floyd went to Portland, Oregon to fly for United and the Alaska-Washington airlines after the World War. Eloise and Arlie went to New Mexico to visit her mother-in-law. The depression hit hard and it was no time to be moving about. Mrs. Keadle owned a restaurant and service station, so Eloise just stayed there and worked in the restaurant. She stayed several years and they made out fine.

In 1934 after Floyd had been in Portland for six years he contacted pneumonia. Suddenly the 38-year-old aviator was dead. After surviving several airplane crashes and other injuries it was a shock to all that he was gone.

After thirteen years of marriage, Eloise had to go back to work to support her seven-year-old daughter and herself. She could not take care of Arlie and work also, so she sent her daughter to live with an uncle in New Mexico.

Eloise moved to Oakland where she went to work for the Vogue Cleaning establishment. During WWII the gas and sugar rationing was in its height and people were issued stamps to buy these commodities. Shoes were hard to buy and nylons for the ladies were a premium. Eloise loved pretty dresses and you certainly had to have nylons to wear with them. A cosmetic company came out with a lotion that you rubbed on your legs and it was suppose to color them and make it look like you were wearing stockings. This worked fine in the cooler weather, but when it got hot or rained the paint started to run and was a terrible mess.

After being a widow for thirteen years she met a baker, Ted Pursley and they were married in 1951. They were married for eight years when he died of a heart attack. Again Eloise was on her own. Moving back to Red Bluff was like going home to her and this is where Arlie was after she married John Stephenson. Arlie had a son named John after his father and it was certainly Eloise's duty to teach him how to fish. It was great times they spent with the sport she loved, building a lifelong bond between a boy and his grandmother.

Henriette (Burt) and George A. Crooker

So many things in the past 100 years that Eloise can recall, the San Francisco earthquake, the sinking of the Titanic, the wars, depression the eruption of Mt. Lassen, the jet age and now the computer age. There have been so many things that she can't possibly remember them all.

How many people have lived to see eighteen presidents of the United States in office? McKinley was president when she was born, then

Eloise Pursley's 100th Birthday, November 23, 1999

Theodore Roosevelt, Taft, Wilson, Harding, Coolidge, Hoover, Franklin Roosevelt, Truman, Eisenhower, Kennedy, Johnson, Nixon, Ford, Carter, Reagan, Bush and now Clinton. She can remember them all and could tell a little anecdote on each one. Truman was her favorite, she said maybe because she is a Democrat, but she really did like him. She hopes to see another great president in her time.

Living alone for the last thirty-nine years in Red Bluff she did extremely well with help coming in twice a week the past few years to help her with the heavy cleaning. But in March of this year at the age of 99 she fell and hurt her back and had to go to the hospital. She is a long-term patient at the Mayers Memorial Hospital in Fall River Mills, the town where she and her first husband were married. Her daughter Arlie passed away in 1998 at the age of 71 and now the only family that Eloise has are her Grandson and his wife, John and Lori Stephenson and their three sons, Tyler, Jonathan and Ryan.

An avid soap opera fan, she watches four of her favorite shows daily. She has watched them so many years that she feels like they are part of her family.

Contented and happy with a giggle like a schoolgirl and sharp as a tack, this lovely lady is looking forward to her 100th birthday party on November 23, 1999 and seeing the New Year of 2000 being celebrated. Her comment is, "changing to 1900 was no problem, I don't know why everyone is so worried about changing to 2000."

September 15, 1999

Lem And The Shining "E"

The wagon was loaded and the horses were harnessed and hitched to it. The Earnest family was on the move again. They were somewhere in Texas and moving to somewhere in New Mexico. Wherever the work was and wherever the need for a preacher was is what determined their travels. Charles Earnest worked with cattle, horses and did a lot of carpenter work as well as a part time preacher. Later on he went into the ministry full time.

The Earnest family originally migrated from Switzerland and crossed the Atlantic by ship to Hanover, Virginia in the 1640's. The family later relocated to Georgia then traveled through the south to Oklahoma, Texas and New Mexico.

August 23, 1919 Lemuel Walker Earnest was born somewhere between Twitty and Shamrock, Texas. His mother, Abigail Leona Morris Earnest died when he was only two years old so he was never quite sure of his birthplace. His Papa, Charles Henry Earnest never kept records of his nine children. Lem was the eighth child then his little brother Claude was born not long before their mother Abbie died. Abbie's father was named Lemuel and he offered a side of beef to any of his children naming a grandson after him. With five older sisters it took awhile before the honored name could be used.

Lem's Papa was a preacher man and this caused the family to move often. Abbie died after they moved to Elida, New Mexico and she was buried there. Sadness had hit the family earlier. One Sunday after church, their small son who was not more than two years old was out side playing. He was wearing a cowboy hat with a string to hold it on. Somehow while he was near a barbwire fence the string got hung up and the child was choked to death. Abbie never recovered from this terrible loss.

The Earnest family and their home in Georgia

The Earnest family homestead during the flood in Elida, New Mexico.
Abbie, Bill, Cyprus and Minnie Earnest

When Lem was five years old in 1924, his Papa loaded his family into a black touring car, and they headed to California, the land of promise. Leaving the sadness of the death of his wife and son behind. The trip was exciting for the children, crossing the big Colorado River and driving all the way to San Bernideno, California where their old jalopy got hit by another car. They had to stay there for awhile and it was Christmas time. The children were happy to go to a Christmas program at the nearby church where each of them received a peppermint stick and an orange. This was the first orange that Lem ever tasted.

After getting their car fixed they traveled on, following the work to the Delano/McFarland area in the San Joaquin Valley. Here they settled for awhile, then moved on to Watsonville and finally settled at Live Oak where the children went to school. Papa depended greatly on the three girls, Gertie, Inez and Loma, that were still at home to help care for Lem and his little brother Claude. When Lem was twelve and Claude was ten years old, the last sister, Inez, married and left home. The two little boys were pretty much on their own. Pickings were pretty slim at home for the boys anyhow and all they had to eat were biscuits and stolen watermelons.

Lem was ready to get out on his own and see the world. He was old enough to hold down a job. A friend, Bill Spratling was in partners with Mr. Baum on a ranch near Cassel, California. Lem who was sixteen and

Grandma Earnest and her chickens

Claude who was fourteen went up to work on that ranch in the summer time. There they worked cattle and Percheron horses and helped to build Baum Lake on the ranch. Mr. Baum had been an inventor for the Pacific Gas and Electric Company and did a lot of experiments. Mr. Baum was thought to have committed suicide when he fell off of the Golden Eagle Hotel in Redding, California in 1935 and was killed. Later it was claimed to have been an accident.

This left Mrs. Baum to run the ranch. Since Lem and Claude had been at Cassel one summer she ask them to come up to work for her. In 1936 the two brothers moved to Cassel and made that their new home. Mrs. Baum treated the boys as her own. When you had been raised without anybody bossing you around you became pretty independent early in life.

Many of the families took a special liking to the brothers and provided them with a place to live and work. The Doty family especially took them under their wing and provided the home they needed. The Great Depression was in full swing and you were lucky to have a place to eat and sleep.

Lem and Claude went to the Fall River High School at McArthur. Lem was active in all the school activities, FFA, football, track, and baseball and was Student Body President. He also was in the school play,

The Antics of Andrew. Lem graduated in 1938, but had his eye on a lower classmate, a girl from Hat Creek. Marjorie Bidwell made quite an impression on this young man. In the school yearbook it was prophesied that he would become a successful radio comedian.

The high schools FFA program had quite an impact on Lem and he had an outstanding Advisor, Mr. Bequette. He instilled ideas into all of his students that led many of them to doing prosperous things in the livestock industry.

After graduation Lem went to Sheridan, Wyoming where he worked for the Bar 13 Ranch. Lem started showing cattle and came back to California to go to the Lassen Junior College at Susanville. Bethel Brown, Floyd Bidwell and some of Lem's friends from Hat Creek had come over to the Lassen Fair to show cattle. He took his sleeping bag and spent the night at the fair with them. The next morning he was to start work at Kelly's dairy. But he had been offered a job at Reno for $25.00 a month working for Mr. Stead showing Hereford cattle. The Stead ranch was where Stead Air Base now is and it was named for Mr. Stead's son, Cross, who was killed in the service. This was a big operation with lots of money behind it. Lem worked there for six to eight months.

Next the young Hereford herdsman found himself in Sulfur, Oklahoma showing cattle on the Harper and Turner ranch. This is when Lem started traveling the show circuit in boxcars with twelve to fourteen head of cattle in the show string. While working on this outfit he showed the Champion Hereford Bull at Treasure Island for them.

Traveling in boxcars with the cattle from show to show was a thrill for the young herdsman from California. He had a couple of helpers that traveled with him. They took boards and made a little loft above the cattle where they slept. They had a stove and did a little cooking or just carried a big grub box. There were no trucks in those days, everything was moved by rail. Lem was on the road all the time and sometimes he never saw the ranch he worked for. He was making quite a name for himself showing Hereford cattle.

He was offered a job at Chandler Herefords at Baker, Oregon and got a raise to $50.00 a month. For Chandlers Lem started the show circuit early in the year and showed the cattle at as many as twenty fairs a year. From Portland, Oregon; Spokane, Washington; Glacier Park; Great Falls, Montana clear down to the Texas State fair. He saw country he never expected to see. The view from the train was beautiful and spectacular. You had plenty of time to think and enjoy God's handiwork.

Marjorie Bidwell and Lem Earnest before they were married, 1945

While Lem was working for Chandler he was showing cattle at the Cow Palace at San Francisco. His brother Claude who was eighteen years old was an equipment operator for PG&E in Fall River Mills, California. Claude and a friend drove down to visit with Lem. Claude had to get back to work the next day and they got a late start heading back home. A large truck sideswiped them on the highway and Claude was killed.

Lem left Chandler Herefords and went back to the Bar 13 Ranch. Mr. Chandler wrote to him and asked him to come back. Lem felt obligated to stay at least a year with the Bar 13 in Wyoming, then he returned to Oregon.

After the bombing of Pear Harbor on December 7, 1941 the world was at war. In 1942 Lem joined the Navy from Sheridan, Wyoming. He was sent to Farragut, Idaho where he was in Company 58. From there he went to Aviation Machinist school in Norman, Oklahoma and off to the South Pacific Island of New Hebrides. He became part of ACORN 10 at Guadalcanal as a casualty replacement. His tour of duty included Russell Island, Vella Lavella and Green Island. He finally spent fourteen months in CASU 12 as a seasoned trooper of Guam. After four years of active duty he was discharged December 26, 1945 in Bremerton, Washington.

After his discharge he decided to drive back to Hat Creek and see Marjorie Bidwell who had faithfully written to him the whole time he was

Lem Earnest doing his daily milking chore

in the service. He just automatically thought they were going to get married. He arrived at the Bidwell Ranch, after driving from Oregon on January 4, 1946. The next morning Lem and Marjorie drove to Reno, Nevada to get married. They then went back to Chandler's in Oregon for Lem to work with the cattle.

Lem continued to show cattle for Chandler and had entered a string of their show Herefords at every state fair west of the Mississippi River. This created a well-known name for the Chandler Herefords and their herdsman in the entire western United States. Traveling the show circuit was no life for a married man, so that responsibility was soon left to someone else.

That fall Marjorie gave birth to a premature son on September 25, 1946 at the Catholic Hospital in Baker, Oregon. The seven-month infant was believed to weigh somewhere around three pounds. The scales they weighed him on would not weigh less than four pounds and it didn't move a hair. Jim was so tiny that Marjorie had to feed him with an eyedropper, a drop at a time in fear of choking him. Every two hours around the clock the tiny baby boy had to be fed. He was small, but he had lungs that let you know when he was hungry. Lem was always aware of his large hands and when the doctor held him out to the young father to hold, Lem was afraid to touch him in fear he would break. He ask the doctor, "will he live?" The doctor assured him that babies smaller than he had made it. This was certainly time for Lem to stay home and not be on the road with the cattle.

Lem and Marjorie had bought some cattle from Chandler with the money he had saved while in the Navy. They decided it was time to move on and start a little herd of their own. They moved back to California where Lem went to work for John Crowe at Millville, California. They also worked for a time with Marjorie's brother Floyd Bidwell at Hat Creek. Lem added more good Hereford cattle to his herd when he bought some from Floyd.

While living at Hat Creek, a second son Robert was born June 11, 1948 in Fall River Mills, Ca.

John Crowe wanted Lem to come back and work for him. This ranch was originally known as the Wickson & Crowe Ranch. Frank Crowe, John's uncle was one of the main engineers on Shasta Dam. Wickson did the clearing for the trees at Shasta Lake and they had the extra money to put into their 7000-acre ranch. The Crowe Hereford Ranch ran 250 head of registered cattle. Lem and Marjorie spent four years there caring and showing their cattle.

It was time for Jim to start school and he went to the one room schoolhouse with all eight grades in Millville. There were only about fourteen kids in the whole school. This is where Jim received his first spanking from the teacher. When he was in the first grade he called the teacher some names he had heard the men say down at the barnyard. Needless to say she was shocked and less than pleased. Young Jim also helped to tip the outhouse over when one of her pet students was in it. This could have added to her anger.

The Earnest Herefords with the Shining E brand were increasing and Lem and Marjorie had around fifty registered cows. It was too much to take care of their own cattle and also show the Crowe Herefords. They moved back to Hat Creek and worked for Floyd for awhile again. In 1955 they heard that the Herb Totten place near the Day bench in Fall River Valley was for sale. Lem and Marjorie bought the 500 acres and moved into the large two story home where they started out on their own. One of their first herd bulls was Donald Dhu 24th and from him much of the herd is descended. Lem now for the first time was showing his own cattle and selling his own at Bull Sales in the area. He mainly sold at Red Bluff, Klamath Falls, Madera and Cottonwood. He also sold at the Nugget Range Bull Sale in Reno for ten years. Madera was their primary sale and Lem held the record of showing more champion bulls at the California State Hereford sale there than anyone else. His main customer for his good Hereford Bulls was the ZX Ranch at Paisley, Oregon. For many years they had a standing order for 100 bulls a year and left it up to Lem to pick them out and send the bulls to the ZX Ranch. The Hart Cattle

Company of Montague, California also has been a top buyer of the Earnest bulls. One time Lem and Floyd Bidwell held a large production sale in Sacramento.

Lem leased several places to run his cattle. One of the places was the Hardy Vestal ranch near Pittville, which he leased from 1962 to 1965. When Hardy had some heart problems he sold his cattle and Lem leased the ranch. Hardy passed away in 1964 and June Vestal was thankful that Lem was there and was such an excellent tenant. While on the Vestal place Lem ran cattle on the Bureau of Land Management permit.

Jim Earnest riding a Crowe Hereford bull at Millville

The Earnest's later leased the Whipple place near Glenburn for eleven years. While there they had an eighty head Forest Service permit for four months at Indian Springs then moved the cattle closer to White Horse for the remainder of the grazing season.

Lem also leased a ranch in Big Valley between Bieber and Nubieber that was known as the Kenneth Holl ranch. A man named Johnson had bought it and Lem was leasing from him. Lem came over to the ranch to tend to the cattle and decided to take a load of hay back over to Fall River Valley on his pickup. He was loading the hay when a bale from the top of the stack became dislodged and fell, hitting Lem and knocked him off of the pickup. He fell with his leg hitting on a big rock and breaking it just below the hip joint. He tried to get up but couldn't move. The county road department was working on the road just a short ways away so he hollered and hollered. Finally a girl that was flagging the traffic heard him and came to investigate. Lem told her he could not get up, but if she would help him into his pickup he was sure he could drive home. In the meantime a neighboring rancher, Charles Kramer saw Lem's pickup and wanted to talk to him. He also stopped in. Before long the County road crew had called an ambulance and the flashing red lights were coming down the road. Lem felt he had quite an audience and didn't see why all the fuss. Lem was taken to the Mayers Hospital in Fall River Mills where he was cared for. It took awhile for the rugged seventy-year-old rancher to get back to his daily chores.

Another time Lem and Jim were working cattle and Lem got hit in the eye by the cattle chute. It was a serious injury that nearly knocked his eye out, but calmly he took his red bandana handkerchief out of his pocket and covered his eye. The blood was streaming down his face and he quietly said, "maybe you better take me to the hospital". A few years later having a five-way heart bypass also slowed this powerful man down for a while, but he got back in the saddle again.

Lem loved his milk cows and for years and years he milked two or three cows twice a day, and raised some calves on them. It was all part of the cow business.

Lem loved his cows as much as Marjorie loved her flowers. Her Iris and Roses were her pride and joy. Bob was a landscape architect and designed many beautiful gardens in the Sonoma, Ca. area. Through his travels he brought roses from all over to his mother to beautify her garden.

In 1969 things were pretty tough for the Earnest ranch and they had 1000 head of cattle. The note was due on the ranch and they needed to have a dispersal sale to meet the demands of the note. The County Farm Advisor at the time was Walt Johnson and he did a study that proved it cost $40.00 a head to keep a cow through the year. If you had a 1000 head that took a lot of money to keep them.

Jim came home from college and he and his Dad drove the cattle to the Inter-Mountain Fairgrounds in September from the Ivy Horr ranch where they had them on pasture. They were to have their dispersal sale there the next day and wanted to sell all but about 200 head of the best cows. They sold as many as they could, but no one had any money, so there were not many interested buyers. Only a portion of the cattle were sold. Lem said he should have just loaded them up and taken them to the auction yard at Cottonwood and got the misery over with. They only got about half of what those good Hereford cows were worth, but could do nothing about it. The banker stepped in and talked Lem into refinancing and keeping the rest of the cattle. He never was sure that he did the right thing.

In 1970 Jim married Arleen Hayden from Etna who was from a ranching family. Both Jim and Arleen had attended Chico State College, where Arleen received her teaching credentials. In 1974 a son Keith was born, a daughter Jennifer was born in 1975 and in 1977 Jeff was born.

Jim and Lem were showing cattle and selling at bull sales as a father and son team. In 1976 the Earnest duo exhibited the champion and reserve champion Hereford bulls at the Klamath Falls, Oregon Bull Sale. For years they held the record for the highest selling bull of $3,100 at the Cottonwood Sale. At one time Lem was offered $10,000 for a bull from an outfit from Texas. He turned them down thinking it was good judgement at the time.

Lem and Marjorie Earnest did their share of community services. They were 4-H Leaders and were active in the Fall River Chamber of Commerce, he was President of the Cattlemen's Association and she was instrumental in helping to start the Cow Belles where she held several offices. They were members of the California Hereford Association as well as other farm and ranch organizations and church.

In 1958 the local Cattlemen banned together to have a feeder sale to market their animals. On October 10, 1958 the first feeder sale was held to market local cattle. A meeting was held in the living room of Lem and Marjorie and with her as secretary and Lem a committee member were John McArthur, Albert Albaugh, Hardy Vestal, Andy Lakey, George Brown Jr. and Walter Callison trying to set up the new enterprise. Margie did all of the books for the feeder sale for years.

In the beginning they tried to have a Spring and Fall sale, but found there was not enough cattle ready in the Spring to warrant that one, so they dropped it. The Fall sale has proved successful and around 1500 head were marketed annually. The feeder sale brought top dollar and with a good buyer attendance it was a popular place to sell your cattle.

The forerunner of the feeder sale was in 1957 when the Fall River Ag teacher, Ron Hutchins asked Lem and some of the other cattlemen to help sponsor a FFA fancy feeder sale. The sale was held for two years but was not successful. The fancy feeder calf sale where the Earnests, Bidwell's, McArthur's and Doty's just to mention a few, sold some 4-H and FFA fancy calves resulting in ninety-seven calves being sold at an average of .38 cents a pound.

The highest price registered at that special sale was .52 cents per pound paid by Howard Hayward of Overton, Nevada to Morris Doty of Cassel, for a 455 pound Angus steer. McArthur Brothers of McArthur sold the calf which brought the second highest price, a 485 pound shorthorn which Hayward also bought for .51 cent a pound. A 420 pound

Bidwell calf sold for .47 cents and a 520 pound calf from the McArthur Brothers sold for .48 cents.

A Bull sale was tried for three or four years, but this did not prove successful so it went into history. Lem credits Harvey McDougal for helping the cattlemen start their sales. He came up and helped sort the cattle and he had the contacts with the buyers to come to the sale. Harvey owned a large feedlot in California and he had judged cattle all over the country, especially judging at the Cow Palace in San Francisco for many years. After Harvey gave up this position, Ellington Peek and his crew from the Shasta Livestock Yard in Cottonwood have been the backbone of the sale.

After the low cattle prices in the 1950's it forced cattlemen into action. That is what led the local cattlemen into creating their own feeder sale in 1958. The fairgrounds were available and a perfect place to hold the feeder sales. The farm advisor, Walt Johnson was extremely helpful and later on the new farm advisor Sam Thurber was there to help in any way he could.

There were quite a few fifty head outfits in the Inter-Mountain area and they had a problem marketing their cattle. They were at the mercy of any buyer that came along. Most local sales for the small outfits had primarily been to the order buyer traveling throughout the country who bought their cattle for his price, take it or leave it. The rancher ended up taking it.

In 1958 when the cattlemen's association feeder sale committee launched the group's first home spun feeder sale which expanded into a top notch buyer drawing, triple auction success the ranchers had a local market. This helped them one hundred per cent. Some times up to thirty buyers attended the sale. In 1964 the steer calves were bringing .18 and .19 cents a pound. Twenty-three cents was the highest at the sale and the average was 21.50 per hundred, the rancher's felt that was pretty good. Lem was the chairman of the feeder sale for eight years and all the help was volunteered by the cattlemen.

That year the special calf sale followed the sale of the Fall River Cattlemen's Association in which 1,622 head of feeder cattle sold for an average of $162.09 per head which was slightly less than the sale of the year before

The first scales at the fairgrounds would only weigh six or eight cattle at a time. Fair board member Asa Doty told them if they proved it to be a success then he would see to it that a new scale would be put in. The Cattlemen proved themselves and Doty kept his word.

In the mid 1980's, 3200 head of cattle went through the ring and was one of the top sales. In 1995, 1,487 head of cattle marched over the scales and the gross sales was around $580,000. From 300-pound heifers to 1100-pound steers there was quite a variety of cattle. In declining cattle markets and so many ranches in the Inter-Mountain area not raising cattle anymore the 1998 sale only had around 700 head.

With the birth of the video auctions, the fifth wheel livestock trailers and fewer cattle in the Inter-Mountain area, the Cattlemen had to cancel their sale for 1999. After forty years of productive sales there were not enough cattle consigned to warrant an auction. Will it ever come back? Lem thinks not, times have changed, and you have to change with it.

Earnests use to send their cattle south to pasture near Balls Ferry along the Sacramento River. The owner of the property was to keep the fences up and he did not. A bull got out on the highway and a boy hit it with his motorcycle and there was an insurance problem. The subdivisions were pushing the cattle out of that country, then someone came along and offered twice what the Earnest's had been asked for pasture payment and they lost their lease.

Around 1990 the lease was up on the Whipple place and the Earnests bought the Hartley place; 150 acres with a house that joined the home ranch. Jim and Arleen and their three children moved there.

Lem and Marjorie's son Bob died in 1991 and four years later Marjorie died in 1994. Life was just not the same without her infectious smile and wonderful nature. Her caring, loving ways and bubbly personality made her an angel in the outfield. Marjorie had been the Business Manager of the Fall River school district for over twenty years.

In 1995 Lem married a widow lady from church that had been a friend for years. He and Marilyn Ketman went to Sparks, Nevada for the wedding ceremony.

It was time for Jim to take over the reins of the ranch anyhow and this was as good as time as any. Lem moved to Fall River Mills where Marilyn had a home. They spend the summer months there, but by Fall they are packing their car and moving to Yuma, Arizona where they spend the winter.

The steers from the Shining E herd are now sent to a feedlot at North Platte, Nebraska and fed out there. The cattle herd has been cut down to around 125 head. Only 25 to 30 bulls a year are raised to sell. The only

Lem, Keith and Jim Earnest at Keith's graduation from
University of the Pacific in Stockton, CA 1997

bull sales that Jim now consigns to are the Klamath Falls sale and the Cattlemen's Livestock Market Sale at Galt, California.

The wonderful sandy soil of the Earnest ranch is more productive in raising wild rice than pasturing cattle. When you can make $1,000 an acre on rice it is not economically feasible to pasture cows on that ground with the depressed cattle markets that have been seen the past few years.

Lem is proud of his grandchildren. Keith is the pharmacist at the local hospital; Jennifer is showing cattle following in the footsteps of her grandfather and works for a ranch in Illinois that raises Club calves. Jeff is a senior at Chico State College.

Lem has seen a lot of changes in the cattle industry and not all of them have been for the best. This is the only life he has ever known and it has been a good life and he has enjoyed most of it. In 1951 your beef dollar bought five times more than it does today, but hopefully the beef market is getting more positive.

Lem could have been called the "King of the Road", riding the rail in those boxcars showing cattle all over the Western United States for so many years. He was a top herdsman for several big Hereford cattle operations and raising good Herefords of his own. He is a well-respected citizen of the Fall River Valley. But to many he is thought of as a hard working cattleman with a heart as big as the land that he loves.

November 7, 1999

Cattlemen...
The Salt Of The Earth

Before the war of 1812, Soldiers of Fortune were hired by the English to do their fighting. The term, Soldiers of Fortune was used for men who would serve as a soldier in any army for personal gain or the love of adventure. This was what brought the Hempstead brothers from Prussia to the United States. The Great Great Grandfather of Jerry Hemsted of Cottonwood, California was a Prussian General in the Army in his homeland. Settling in New York the town of Hempstead, N.Y. was named after him. As the family scattered west a town in Texas was also named Heampstead. The brothers became dissatisfied with the English and decided they did not want to fight their battles any longer.

Timothy Hempstead (great grandfather of Jerry) and his two brothers decided to travel west. At that time they had been settled in Illinois. Not having the money for a wagon and oxen the three brothers made a handcart with wheels as high as their heads. They started to California pushing their cart loaded with their possessions. It is unknown how long it took them to make the trip, but it must not have been and easy adventure. By the time they reached Redding, California they were so angry with each other that they decided to go their separate ways. They were so furious that they no longer wanted to share the same last name. One brother dropped the "P" in his name and spelled it Hemstead. The other kept the "P" and dropped the "A", spelling his Hempsted. One went to Trinity County and the other went to Happy Camp and was never heard of again. Timothy changed his name to Hemsted and settled in Redding.

Timothy was twenty-one years old in 1890 when he reached California. He had left his wife and two small daughters' back in Illinois. He wanted to establish a homestead and build a cabin before he brought his family to California. Most of the settlers had settled in the foothills away from the Sacramento River. In the summertime the river dried up to just a few stagnant potholes, causing Typhoid fever and Malaria to run rampant in the valley. This caused people to be afraid to settle in this area. In the summer time settlers would move their families to Mountain Gate or Oak Run to escape the dreaded diseases. Timothy had his choice of homesteading wherever he chose. Timothy claimed 160 acres some distance from the river. Here he built his cabin and began his homestead. (Today this is the location of the Costco Shopping Center in Redding.)

In 1893, the third year after his arrival in California Timothy decided to return to Illinois and bring his family west. He walked back to Sacramento where he was able to board the Trans Continental Rail Road and traveled east. He returned to Sacramento, California on the train with his wife Alice and two daughters Tolie and Edith. From there they rode the steamer ship up the river from Sacramento to Red Bluff. They then traveled by stagecoach to Redding where they settled into their home. Grandma Hemsted was able to take up a 160-acre homestead also. She chose a homesteaded close to the East Side of the river. (The location of her homestead was what is now near the Cypress Street Bridge and several automobile dealerships at Hemsted Drive.)

Most of the small communities were settled in the foothills. Oak Run was a popular place and was so named because that was where the Oak trees ran down into the valley through the canyons. At this time Shasta was the county seat and a steady stream of homesteaders were moving into that area. The gold mining and dredging in the Sacramento River brought people in by the hundreds looking for their fortune.

Homes and businesses started to spring up in the Redding area. Shasta's glory days was from 1849 when it was first settled to 1855 when there were 2400 people in the small community. By that time they had a post office, Masonic Lodge, newspaper, a Protestant and Catholic Church, school house, courthouse, a county hospital and two hotels and various stores.

This was considered a typical boomtown. From the placer gold first discovered on Clear Creek in 1848 and the quartz mining in the French Gulch area, some five million dollars worth of newly mined gold passed through the express office of Shasta. The first road from the Sacramento River reached Shasta in April 1851. Freight had to be shipped by riverboat to Red Bluff, where it was loaded onto wagons and shipped to Shasta. The town first was a tent town then structures of board and later brick buildings began to spring up.

In 1860 a road was begun along the Sacramento River. After times of heavy rains washing it out and disasters, it was finally reopened in 1868. The Central Pacific Railroad in 1869 started from Redding and built the first railroad across the Plaines. In 1872 this became a branch line northward from Sacramento, Marysville, Chico and across the river at Tehama and into Red Bluff. The Shasta people tried hard to get the railroad to come to Shasta, but the engineers decided to follow the water grade of the Sacramento River. The railroad needed a town at the head of the Sacramento Valley to serve as a temporary railhead. In consequence, the railroad laid out the town of Redding a few miles east of Shasta. The town was named for Benjamin B. Redding of Sacramento, General Land Agent of the Railroad. The town of Redding continued as railhead until superseded by Dunsmuir in 1886. By 1888 Redding won the claim of county seat and the rise in population started. Sadly, Shasta reverted almost to a ghost town.

When the Hemsted family had business in Redding, it was an all day trip in the wintertime to travel by team and wagon. They had to go clear around the river and come in on the north side of town to cross on the Desselhorse Bridge. In the summer time when the water was low they only had to dodge the potholes with their teams and wagons in the nearly dry river to cross it.

In 1894 a son, Karl was born to Timothy and Alice. Timothy was a crafty person and made all of his own tools, hammers, saws, shovels, axes and any tool that he may need. He was also quite handy at cabinet making. He contacted a lung disorder when he was quite young and couldn't do the farming because of the dust. For this he relied on his son Karl and his younger son Phil after they grew up. The family ran about 300 head of sheep and farmed the land.

August 3, 1912 Karl married Lillian Eastep a daughter of a pioneer family who came to Oak Run in 1850. Lillian had gone to Santa Jose Normal school where she studied music and received her teaching credential. She returned to Oak Run where she taught school for eighteen months. It was a twenty-five mile horseback ride for Karl to court her, but he was persistent. In 1914 a set of twins, Don and Mildred were born to the couple, in 1918 Jim was born, then in 1922 another set of twins, Dick and Bob were born.

Karl and Lillian Hemsted's 50th Anniversary. Back L-R: Don, Mildred, Jim, Dick and Don

Karl and Lillian built their band of sheep up to 3000 head. Everyplace was free open space for grazing and the sheep did well. The sheep grazed what now is the Redding Airport and the Redding Golf Course which was the sheep headquarters. In 1931 Karl bought another 160 acres along the river which is now the Raley's Shopping Center.

The sheep grazed the grain stubble fields at Churn Creek. There were only three farmers in the area at that time, Hemsted's, Harrison's and the Pearson's. The farmers paid Karl to graze his sheep over their grain fields in the early spring to stool the grain. The sheep would be herded quickly across a grain field to clip off the new growth, causing it to stool out which would result in a 20% higher production in grain at harvest time.

Karl was an excellent teamster and could drive a six-horse hitch without any problem at all. He just laced the lines through his fingers as if they were tiny strings tied to puppets. Karl and his friend Ern Elwood helped to build the highway to Bella Vista, by using teams of horses and a Fresno Scraper. Karl was also the last freight line driver for the California-Oregon Stageline Company from Redding to Weaverville. At that time trucks with solid rubber tires came into use and took the place of the stagecoaches.

The Hemsted sheep migrated to what is now Shasta College and grazed that entire area. Karl was farming along the Sacramento River, which was all open leased bottom ground. Today this is known as the Miracle Mile and is a well-established business and residential area. At that time all of the teams of the city of Redding were stabled at what is now the Redding Park. Dozens of teams used for fire, police, cabs and city work were cared for there at the city stable. Young Jim's job was to help his father with the horses. The teams were traded off at noon and a fresh team was hitched to the pieces of farm equipment. Jim was to swim the hot tired horses in the Sacramento River to cool them down, a job that was fun for the young boy.

Karl's sister Edith married Henry Woodrum. She became the first county clerk in the city of Redding. She was the first elected county clerk for California. A position she held for thirty-two years. Tolie never did marry and lived her life as an old maid. She owned several cabins in town that she rented out. She started the Baptist Church in Redding, which she was totally devoted to. The Hemsted roots run deep in the town of Redding.

In 1936 it was a disastrous time for the livestock industry. The Sacramento River nearly dried up and there were only a few potholes to water the cattle and sheep. The cattle had to be driven to Rio Street in Red Bluff to water them in the potholes. That was the only source of water during the great drought. There was a big die out in the livestock industry because of no water and feed, the animals could not survive. Cattle could not be driven to the mountains, as it was a long hard trip. It would take months to get the cattle to summer range and by then it was time to drive them back to the valley for the winter. The trail drives were difficult and an all summer job that was hard on the cattle and the cowboys. There were many cattle run between McCloud and Mountain Gate more than any other area, as there was water and feed there. Hardenbrook's, Ern Elwood, and Mentzell's, drove their cattle into the draws of the rivers that drained into the Sacramento River.

The coming of the railroad to Redding made a complete change in the livestock industry and cattle could be transported more easily. Before that Redding was only three blocks long and one block wide, which consisted of California and Market Streets. Later, the coming of the livestock trucks made another change in the livestock industry.

June 21, 1941 Jim married Barbara Kelly who was born in 1921 at Arcata, California. Her father Irvin John Kelly owned the Redwood

Jerry Hemsted, ten years-old, buying his first 4-H heifer at the Crowe Hereford Ranch Sale in 1952. John Trusdale looking on

Ranch in Rio Del; he lost it during the depression for a $5,000 note. From there the family moved around to many different places, where Barbara and her brothers and sisters, Romayne, Jim, Jack, Patsy, Glenna and Margie (who died when she was 12 years old) went to several different schools. The family spent quite some time in Oregon and then back in California they finally settled at Churn Creek near Redding where they bought the Hunt Dairy from A.N. Hunt and sons from Eureka. Eventually Kelly sold the Dairy back to Hunt and moved his family to Vina, California where he went into ranching.

In 1942 Jerry was born to Jim and Barbara Hemsted. At that time there were only about 7,000 people in Redding, a fairly small community. A daughter Judy was born a few years later.

In 1940 the building of Shasta Dam was begun. This started the large development of Redding and all the small communities in the area. Small towns sprung up overnight to accommodate the working force. The city fathers of Redding did not want the labor force to live in their city. But they did want them to spend their hard-earned dollars there. The five year

Curly Hines, truck driver. L-R standing: Bill Verdugo, Bill McDonald and Jim Hemsted. First feeder cattle to be flown from Hawaii to the mainland and hauled by Hemsted trucks

project of building the huge dam which was to be the ninth largest and highest in the United States took hundreds of men to build. By 1945 work stopped on the 600 foot dam as the work force and the cement and materials was needed for the war effort. The original plans were to have built it another 100 feet higher.

After the building of the dam, the Sacramento Valley became a lush valley of production. With plenty of water and the warm weather farmers were sure to raise excellent crops. No longer was there a shortage of water for the livestock. The rapidly moving river was no longer a source for the stagnant pools that carried Typhoid and Malaria. Cattle did not graze the meadows of the rivers that flowed into Shasta Lake as they were now filled with water.

Jim Hemsted and John Crowe started in the trucking business in 1956. His good friend Ellington Peek went into the cattle buying business and Jim did the hauling for him, they had a good working relationship. Jim was the first one to double deck cattle in trucks and he designed the cab over truck boxes. The sixteen Hemsted trucks ran in thirteen states. In the 1960's and 70's lots of cattle were moved to California feed lots and packing houses. Many cattlemen customers moved their cattle in the Spring and Fall to their respective pastures. The days of long trail drives were over. By 1972 the land in the Sacramento Valley became too valuable to run cattle and raise cereal grains. It had been changed to orchards and homes. Through 1965 the Hemsted trucks hauled for sixty-five different feedlots and forty-seven packinghouses from Bakersfield to the North.

Jerry had gone to school in Redding most of his life, but in his senior year the family moved to nine-mile hill south of Cottonwood to run the livestock trucks. Jerry finished his senior year at Red Bluff and went away to college for one year. Jim suffered a heart attack, so Jerry came home to help with the dispatching of the trucks and also took his turn at driving them.

Some of the packinghouses in California at that time were Armour, Cudahy, James Allen & Sons and Swift around the San Francisco bay area. These larger plants had squeezed out seventeen different packinghouses around that area. At one time there were three plants in Dixon besides Elk Grove Meat, Roderick Meats and Valley Meat at Marysville. Farther north there was Minche's at Red Bluff, Crum Meats and Royce in the Fall River Valley, also the Cedarville Meat Company and three different slaughterhouses in Redding. After World War II, automation came along and now the large plants were killing 3000 head a day. Minch, one of the larger packers in Red Bluff only killed eighty head a day. That was a big job without the automation of today. They killed one load of butcher cattle and one load of fat cattle a day. Even this kept their buyers Herb Flournoy and Oakley Kerber busy. They bought for Minch full time traveling the countryside to fill their orders. With the increase in automation, the medium plants of today butcher more cattle than the largest plants of that day.

As the high rollers came along they increased that number of beef butchered even more. There were little feedlots all over the country. In the Klamath Falls, Oregon area there was a feed lot every few miles feeding the cull potatoes. Most of those no longer exist. Now in California we have Orvis Meats, Avala, Los Banos Meats, Beef Packers Incorporated in Fresno, Hanford Meats in Hanford and Hallmark Meats in Vernon, Ranch Meat at Petaluma, Harris at Colinga and Brawley Meats in Los Angeles. Nobody north of Stockton is killing cattle at all. The Air quality control and OSHA (Occupational, Safety & Health Association) has made a big difference. These plants were all started in the 40's during the war when there was such a demand for beef. The strict regulations of the government have shut down so many of these plants. The hard work and minimum pay was not attractive to the younger generation and this phase of the livestock industry was cut back.

Great Grandma Hemsted died in 1927. Before that she told Karl not to sell the ranch. She had an outstanding foresight and she knew that someday that the city of Redding would grow out to their part of the country. Even though at that time it was a long way from town.

Karl Hemsted died in 1979 and after that the ranch was sold. Jim bought some from the estate to run cattle. Don was one of the three people in the nation qualified to teach twin engine aircraft flying at the beginning of World War II, even though he was never in the military. He had Hemsted Van and Storage in Redding and H&H Flying Service. His twin sister Mildred married George Summerfield and moved to San Francisco. Jim went into the livestock transportation and cattle business. Dick was a rodeo cowboy and now produces rodeos. His twin, Bob was a pilot for TWA Airlines. He had joined the Royal Canadian Airforce when he was sixteen and Lillian took a train to Canada to bring him home as he was under age.

Joan Jarrell soon came into the life of the young Jerry Hemsted. Joan was raised in Red Bluff where she was a very protected child. Her father John was a First Lieutenant in the Air Force in which he flew thirty-five missions over England. Joan was busy with school, 4-H, Rainbow Girls, piano and clarinet lessons, church and teaching swimming lessons. After the service her father worked for PG&E for thirty years. He taught Joan and her sister Patricia his love for hunting and fishing.

Although active in high school, Joan was not allowed to go to public dances. One night at a friends slumber party the girls went to a dance at the Red Bank schoolhouse. There she met Jerry and after a persistent courtship they were married June 21, 1965. He courted Joan, but he also won her fathers approval when he brought him a quarter of venison that he had killed. The young couple started their family and in 1966 Jamie was born, Jesse in 1967 and Julie in 1968.

Running the Hemsted Livestock hauling business was a busy time. Before the days of cellular phones and answering services someone had to be at the office at all times. Three phones kept Joan busy at the house. Ranchers that were just getting in at midnight would be calling for trucks, and then the ranchers who started their day at 4 A.M. would call at that time. It was a full time job and someone had to be on duty at all times. Jim sold out part of the trucks from the original sixteen he was now only running seven. One of the memorable trips for the Hemsted Livestock

Joan and Jerry Hemsted engagement photograph, 1965

trucks was when they met a 707 Airplane that was loaded with two and one-half truckloads of cattle that had been flown in from Hawaii. The Hemsted trucks picked them up at the Oakland airport and took the cattle to the Bill McDonald ranch. The plane had flown registered bulls and horses to Hawaii and brought the cattle back. These were the first feeder cattle to ever be transported from Hawaii to the mainland. A half load of Santa Gertrudis heifers went to McDonald and the rest to the Newhall Land and Cattle Company. He and Jerry then went into the livestock and horse trailer business and opened Hemsteds Trailer Corrals. Jim said, "it took him fifteen minutes to get into the trucking business and forty years to get out of it."

In 1981 Barbara died of Leukemia at the age of 61. Jim died in 1985 at the age of 69 of a heart attack. In 1980 Jim had sold the last seven trucks to Cottonwood Livestock Transportation. They closed the Hemsted Trailer Corrals for awhile then it was leased to Halco for five years at which time they were bought out.

Jim and Jerry had gone into the cattle business, which is still carried on by Jerry and Joan. They are running 300 head of mother cows year round and lease summer pasture for 400 yearlings at Hat Creek. Everything is run on leased ground. At Hat Creek the water rotation is on a ten day on, ten day off system and Jerry is there to take care of that job.

Jerry has always been an active cattleman and in 1985-86 he was President of the Tehama Cattleman's Association, before that he was Vice President, Secretary and it seems he has been a director forever. He started being involved in the association when he was sixteen yeas old to take over his dad's place when he was sick. He was State Membership Chairman for 89-90,the second State Vice President for three years, first Vice President two years, and now he is going into his second year as California Cattlemen's President for 1999-2000. A position he is very dedicated to. A member for 43 years he has seen many changes in the beef cattle industry. "Better marketing of our beef product is so very crucial to our existence. It has never been more important for producers to be supportive of our Beef Council and the check off programs than now. Food safety should be everyone's number one concern."

Jerry is a man that will only do a job if he can give it his all. He doesn't want to hire people to take over his job with his cattle. He loves people, but he loves his cattle and wants to do his job himself. Jerry has good neighbors and friends to help work his cattle when he needs them and he in turn helps them.

Jerry spends a lot of time on the road. He had just returned from a meeting with California Governor Davis. The education that he is receiving through this job is invaluable and the people he meets are the salt of the earth.

Because of the livestock transportation business he is not afraid to travel and knows people wherever he goes. He has met so many wonderful people and ancestors of the people he knew years ago.

Jerry feels that all of the cattlemen need to come together in a livestock partnership. The packers, feedlot operators and the cow/calf operator have to join together and market our cattle and become a part of the industry as a whole. We are going to have to take a part of the risk and produce a product that they want. If we have good bulls and a good cowherd we have to stand behind that product all the way to the consumer. Our product is beef, not calves, cows or bulls, but the end product, which is all, packaged and sold as BEEF. We have to be proud of our product and the genetics and choice cattle are our end product. Quality assurance, is our goal and the bottom line in an accredited product. The livestock business is run in a cycle and we have to create these partnerships we are producing for the consumer. Competition is still what our business is all about. All of us aren't as creditable as some of the others, but the public throws us all together and they judge all of us as one.

Jerry Hemsted 1999-2000
California Cattlemen State President

One rotten apple can spoil a barrel full. Jerry said, "we are going to be a world market and let us bring the rest of the world up to our level, lets not go down to their level."

We do not produce enough lean meat for the hamburger market, which consumes 53% of our product. The fat is trimmed off of our grain fed fat beef to mix with the lean meat from foreign countries so it will stay together and be more palatable and be able to be used in the vast hamburger markets of today. The Canadians are using our grade on their cattle. Their beef has an USDA stamp on it and this is one of Jerry's pet peeves. He is working hard on this issue and this has to be negotiated with Canada to get this changed.

Jerry and Joan promote the cattle industry, something that they definitely believe in and work for. Jerry is in his role as 39th CCA President and Chairman of California State P.O.S.S.E.E. (Protecting Our States Stewards of Environmental Economy). Joan has worked hard for Ag In The Classroom and was National Chairman. Their family is important to them and their five grandchildren are the sixth generation of the Hemsted's to claim that their roots go deep in Redding, California.

Jerry's favorite quote is "Change is inevitable, success optional," no truer words have been spoken. He definitely has his job cut out for him as President of the California Cattleman's Association. But if anyone can handle it, he can.

December 9, 1999

Hippy, He Never Missed A Lick

The " hip-shot" colt came trotting up the lane to the ranch at Little Horse Creek dragging his reins, his saddle was empty. The ground was frozen hard on that cold January day in Wyoming in 1915 when the 19-year-old cowboy got bucked off of his horse. Young Arthur Burmister had left early that morning to take the mail twelve miles to the other ranch at the Divide for his boss C.B. Irwin. When he had ridden six miles from the ranch he got off to warm up a little, as it was really cold. When he got back on the colt he blew up and bucked him off. Landing in a snow bank, only his pride was hurt. It was just as close to one ranch as the other, so he walked on to the Divide, and the colt went back to the barn at Little Horse Creek.

The skinny young cowboy was always the brunt of the jokes and laughs at the bunkhouse anyhow and this was not going to help none. The cowboys had waited quite awhile with their noses pressed against the frozen glass of the bunkhouse, taking turns waiting for young Burmister to come limping in. Arthur had walked the six miles to deliver the mail to Mr. Irwin, which impressed the boss quite a bit. He nicknamed the young cowboy Hippy after the colt that had bucked him off. Mounting another horse, Hippy rode back to his outfit, knowing he would be teased.

The cowboys were beginning to think they should go looking for him, when they saw a form in the distance riding up the road. The cowboys made the most of the situation, anything to break the monotony of a long Wyoming winter.

As the young buckaroo approached the bunkhouse he was greeted with jeers and jokes. "Hey Burmister, how's the walking, did that old hip-shot horse get the best of you? They also thought he should be called Hippy after that colt had got the best of him. The name stuck like a cocklebur under a saddle and the rest of his life he was known as Hippy.

Hippy Burmister, 12 years-old

He won the admiration of the cowboys there on that ranch and many ranches in the future. He was a tough little wiry bronc peeler that was known to try anything, at least once.

Who would have ever thought that a tiny baby, fragile and frail born in Evanston, Illinois on May 26, 1894 would ever become a champion bronc rider in the world of Rodeo. It can happen, and it did to Arthur Henry Burmister. Arthur was born to John von Joachim and Mathilde Wassmund Burmister. When Arthur was three years old his father died and later his mother married L. O. Schuettes. His stepfather owned a hardware store and was also a sheet metal worker. For a time the boy went by the name of Schuettes.

In 1905 the family moved to Denver, Colorado. While there the nine-year-old Hippy had a paper route for the Denver Post. A couple years later they moved to Greeley, Colorado for a year then moved on to Fort Collins, Colorado. While living there the young boy saw his first rodeo. He thought it was the most exciting and greatest thing he ever saw. In 1910 the family moved again to Cheyenne, Wyoming. Mr. Schuettes made stovepipes and young Hippy helped him. Their home was a block from the post office and right across the street from the post office an old man by the name of Dan Fallen had a horse corral. Hippy spent his spare time there working with the fifty horses Mr. Fallen had. There were a few at the corral all the time the rest of them were out in a pasture about twelve miles from the city limits. The young boy got the job as horse wrangler and chased horses for the old man.

A memorable experience of young Hippy was when Theodore Roosevelt, President of the United States visited Cheyenne. Hippy just walked up to him and said, "I want to shake your hand." The President just pumped the heck out of the young boy's hand. Even though Hippy never went to school past the fourth grade he gained a lot of knowledge through life's experiences. The family moved around a lot so it was hard for the boy to keep up with school.

In 1912 it was an exciting time for Hippy when it was time for the Cheyenne Frontier days. A man by the name of C.B. Irwin who had a Wild West show, furnished most of the stock for the rodeo. He owned a famous bucking horse by the name of Steamboat.

The young boy was so thrilled with the Wild West Show of Irwin's that he just had to have a job on his show. Hippy could not ride very good, but he told the owner of the show he wanted a job as a bronc rider, just anything to be able to travel and work for the show. It didn't take Irwin long to realize the boy really was not a bronc rider, but he took a real liking to the boy and wanted to give him a chance. He gave him a job for three dollars a month to ride buffaloes. The buffalo would be brought out in the arena with hobbles on, then they would pull him down and saddle him, then Hippy would ride him off the ground which was like trying to ride a bull with a saddle on it. The saddle took about ten jumps while the buffalo made one. The saddle just didn't fit. The skinny kid would get dumped off in the dust, pick himself up, brush himself off and wave and smile to the crowd. Everyone loved him.

Hippy would ride the buffalo in the parades in town to advertise the Irwin Brothers Wild West Show. He would yell and wave at the crowd saying, "come see me in the show tonight." One day the program for the rodeo came out and there in print it said that Hippy Burmister would be riding the famous bucking horse Steamboat. Hippy was surprised and scared. He told Mr. Irwin that he really didn't want to do it, but he didn't have any say in the matter. He was a skinny kid that would be tossed like a feather from the powerful horses back. He had no choice, the boss said he was going to ride and this was no crybaby outfit, if he wanted to keep his job he had to do what Irwin said. He did mount the horse and rode him for ten seconds before being tossed into the dirt where the clowns picked him up. It wasn't so bad after all and he was exuberant when he heard the screams, applause and shouts from the audience. Hippy was hooked on bronc riding.

The show moved on to Winnipeg, Canada and back. By that time Hippy was tired of falling off those Buffalo and was glad to get back. His folks had moved on to Los Angeles, California and he had no place to stay so he went to spend the winter on Irwin's ranch forty five miles north of Cheyenne on Little Horse Creek. He also had another ranch twelve miles away on what they called the Divide. This was when he got bucked off the horse that gave him the nickname.

In the spring of 1913 Hippy left for Los Angeles where his folks had moved. About the first thing he did was buy a horse. His folks lived in Boyle Heights where he could keep a horse. He met a young fellow named Hank Potts, and they rode around together having a good time. They met Fat Jones who had a stable full of horses he furnished to the movies; he needed help so they went to work for him. In those days a lot of cowboy, Indian and soldier pictures were made and there was a lot of work for the young men. Their main job was to double for the stars

1916 silent movie stuntmen and star William S. Hart. Back Row L-R: Bert Rollins, Ben Corbett, Fat Jones, Walt Whitmore. Front Row: Hank Potts, William S. Hart and Hippy Burmister

and get shot off of horses and have running horses fall with them.

A faded and torn newspaper article from the Los Angeles times that was glued hard and fast in Hippy's scrapbook tells of a hair-raising experience. The headline read, "Boy Victor of Animal Seriously Hurt When Mount Falls, Sustaining Fatal Injury." Los Angeles, Cal. 1915. Saturday—Grey Eagle the outlaw, is dead. The notorious mouse colored bucking horse that made it's name historic for ten years in the country killed himself in a mad attempt to dislodge Art Schuettes, the champion nineteen year old rider of Cheyenne, Wyoming. Schuettes lies in the Receiving Hospital with an injured skull and a dozen minor wounds.

The final rage of the old outlaw was spent in a death struggle occurring in the northern part of Los Angeles. Schuettes had for several months heard of Grey Eagle. Bartlett Brothers, on a foothill ranch owned the unmanageable horse. Schuettes decided he could ride the outlaw.

For months Grey Eagle made a route of the various motion picture shows where Wild West scenes were staged. None of the cowboys assembled for the film could handle the treacherous bucking animal. Grey Eagle had become notorious for peculiar character of his buck, a rotation motion of his back when in midair, then dislodge the most skillful equestrian. One after another of the champions of film squad of roughriders had been tumbled over his arched back and Bartlett Brothers accepted him as a freak in the collection of horses.

Last week Schuettes sent word to the Bartlett ranch in the foothills that he would ride Grey Eagle. The horse was taken to the Schuettes home for the boy to mount. Without preliminary he launched upon the back of the beast and the contest started across vacant lots, along clotheslines, against the sides of houses, under bushes that a maddened but cunning horse selected for a conquest. Schuettes clung to his seat. Once Grey Eagle dashed down a seven-foot ditch, scrambled along it for a few yards, then climbed the precipitous bank and continued his wild pitching, with the boy siting in the saddle.

His energy was nearly spent when Schuettes guided him toward the paved streets. At the first touch of the asphalt at Fairmont and Blade streets Grey Eagle's feet slipped. He made a last separate stand in defiance of his title, bucking wildly and viciously, and then he started to run again. He continued slipping across the street and launched into the curb, lying flat, where his head was crushed against the solid block of concrete. Astride him was Schuettes, also knocked unconscious, but still clinging to the bridle reins.

Spectators took the boy to the Receiving Hospital, where his wounds were dressed while Grey Eagle was taken back to the Bartlett ranch for honorable interment, even though his title of Grey Eagle unridden was gone. (This was an account of a ride by Hippy Burmister, but he was still going by the name of Art Schuettes until he was drafted into the Army.)

In October of 1917 Arthur "Hippy" Burmister was drafted into the U.S. Army and sent to Camp Lewis, Washington. At that time he reclaimed his birth name and dropped the extra e in his last name changing it from Burmeister to Burmister. He was assigned to the Remount Division, which had hundreds of horses. This suited Hippy just fine. Horses were used for everything in the Army, the Calvary, pulling the supply wagons and it took six horses to pull every canon in the Artillery Company. Every day was a rodeo, as there were a lot of spoiled horses.

The ranchers that sold horses to the Calvary only sold them their spoiled and hard to break outlaws. Every weekend Hippy and his friends put on rodeos and rode those spoiled bucking horses for the fun of it.

In June of 1918 Hippy was made a Sargeant and was paid $44.00 a month, he had been making $30.00 as a buck private, so this was a big raise for him. He was sent to Camp Johnson in Jacksonville, Florida getting ready to go overseas. Just as his company was to be shipped out they got the word the war was over on November 11, 1918. When he was discharged from the Army in 1919 he went back to North Hollywood and the Fat Jones Stables.

That year he heard of a big rodeo in Reno, Nevada and decided to try his luck there. He had ridden so many bucking horses in the Army that he was pretty confident of his skills. Hippy won the bronc-riding contest. In those days bareback and bull riding was just mount money. They drew a line twenty feet out from the chute, and if you made it to the line, you got paid $3.00. If not, you never got a dime, so he never took to that. From there he went to Pendleton, Oregon. In September Yakima Canutt, a famous bronc rider won first and Hippy won second in the bronc riding on I. B. DAM. Another bronc rider, Ben Oaks was giving up riding at that rodeo. For the second place rider he gave his chaps as a prize, and Hippy won those chaps. He went right over to the Hamley Saddle Co. and had them put a big HIPPY in white leather down both sides of those chaps. He was really proud of them and in all of his bronc riding pictures you can see those famous chaps. (Hippy's chaps and other memorabilia are now on display at the Modoc County Museum in Alturas, Ca.).

Hippy had hit the rodeo trail and was doing real well for himself. He won second in Garfield, Washington, then back to Los Angeles for a big show at Ascot Park. The first money was $500, in Pendleton they paid $300, $200, $100, which still was a lot of money. There was no day money in those days, and you had to ride three horses to win it. Hippy won it.

The cowboys needed to travel to get to the next rodeo, and no one could afford a car, so they traveled by train. If twenty-five cowboys bought tickets to ride the train they were given a boxcar to carry their horses. When the horses were unloaded they rode them to the rodeo grounds. Sometimes riding double on the roping and steer wrestling horses, as the cowboys that rode bulls and broncs didn't have to keep a saddle horse.

Hippy's first real job in the movies was in the movie "Days of the

Hippy Burmister, 1920, when he won 1st at Weiser, Idaho

Hippy Burmister on a rough bronc in 1923

Thundering Herd," as an extra. Another cowboy that was new on the job that day was a fellow that became a mite more famous. His name was Tom Mix.

As a stunt man Hippy saved the stars from having to do the dangerous stunts, as they couldn't afford for them to get hurt. He doubled for the stars in bulldogging steers, riding broncs, and catching runaway horses and all the dangerous things. One time he was shown jumping off of an airplane to catch a team of runaway horses. The airplane wing was mounted on a truck to look like he was jumping from a real plane, but he only jumped from the fake one, the truck.

Hippy had been in several movies with William S. Hart and with Will Rogers. In 1920 Hippy was working on a picture with Will Rogers and riding rodeos on weekends. At the Los Angeles rodeo he made the finals but it got rained out and they were postponed for a week. He went back out to Mojave where they were making the picture he was working on. When Friday came, Will Rogers told him he could get him back to Los Angeles in plenty of time because he had a Cadillac that would go 60 miles an hour. Hippy couldn't believe any car could go that fast, but he proved it on the way by racing a passenger train and beating it. That is how they knew how fast they were going and Hippy was really impressed.

Ray Kane and Norman Cowan and Hippy picked out a few roundups to go to back East. The first one was Mason City, Iowa. They traveled by train and the three cowboys made a pact that they would split their winnings with each other. The first horse Hippy got on fell with him and broke his collarbone. He was laid up for a few weeks, but his fellow cowboys kept their promise and shared their winnings with him. By the time he was able to get back on a horse it was time for the Cheyenne Rodeo and they had doubled their purse. It was now $600 for first and they also put up $100 for the best ride each day. Hippy won first and took home the biggest purse of his career, $700.00. The young cowboy went on to win first at Weiser, Idaho; he was having a fantastic year.

In 1921 the three cowboy buckaroos started out again. There was a show at Deer Creek, California that was half way between Chico and Red Bluff. One account from the newspaper in Red Bluff, California when that rodeo was in it's early heydays, stated. "Hippy Burmister, a little runt of a cowboy who has been capturing prize money in every big rodeo of the Northwest, walked off with the huge percentage in the World Championship bucking horse event yesterday at the roundup. He was hard pressed by some of the other cowboys including up-and-coming Perry

Ivory, a mean hand with a bronc, who copped second honors."

Hippy had been running into this other top-notch cowboy that was eleven years younger than he was. Perry Ivory from Alturas, California was hitting the rodeo business hard, and he was good, real good, and he was only sixteen years old.

There was no accepted point system to determine a world champion, and those top riders were acclaimed according to the amount of money they collected during the rodeo season. Hippy's peak was reached in 1921 when he figured he had earned over $10,000 during his bronc-bustin' career and he had collected $750 in a single day at Minneapolis.

Again in 1922 Hippy won the Reno, Nevada show and one at Susanville at bronc riding. In the winter when the rodeos were all over Hippy went back to Hollywood and worked in the motion picture shows

"Coyote is Some Surprised Horse", Unridden outlaw with record of throwing 25 men is ridden: Coyote was some surprised horse yesterday. He has a little trick of spinning the top, which has proven the defeat of over 25 men. Eddie Martin stayed with him six seconds in Oklahoma, but he had never met his match until Hippy Burmister mounted him yesterday.

Burmister is some rider, even if he did have bad luck here. He won the Championship at Reno, Nevada last Fourth of July.

He knew Coyote's inclination for spinning and took the same tactics that have broken many a team of run-a-ways. When Coyote began to spin Hippy encouraged him in it and when the horse showed signs of slowing up Burmister began to whack him on the side of the head to make him whirl faster. He kept on whirling until he lost his head and tumbled over. Burmister stuck to him until he went down, a total of sixteen seconds.

When Coyote got up he staggered around a few seconds and then started for the corral. He had enough whirling to satisfy him for one day at least. Burmister received a great ovation from the crowd on his work in riding the horse. The horse Coyote was brought here at considerable expense for exhibition purposes. (This is one of the faded newspaper clippings from the scrapbook that Hippy kept. The article had no date, and no place, but it is believed to have been in San Francisco around 1923.)

In 1923 Hippy never left California, one of the reasons could have been that he had met a girl. While at the Salinas Rodeo, Perry Ivory introduced him to Vera Armstrong Hafer, a rancher's daughter from Alturas.

In September he split first and second with Al Biscaro at the rodeo in

Hippy Burmister and Perry Ivory around 1923 at a Bakersfield rodeo

San Francisco. After the show Hippy and Vera were married and went north to her families ranch. Vera had a year old daughter, June. She had been married to Roy Hafer and he died of pneumonia before their daughter was ever born. Hippy lovingly raised June as his own child.

Every time a good job came up in Hollywood the Burmister's would go down and go to work. Vera worked in the movies with her husband doing bit parts. They both had parts in Bill Hart's last picture "Tumbleweeds." About the last picture Hippy worked in was "The Iron Horse", which was made in Wadsworth, Nevada. The picture shows at that time were silent movies, so they only had to act, not remember their script.

They stayed in Pullman Sleepers and ate their meals in the diner cars. Hippy doubled the star George O'Brian. When the Indians were chasing him and shot his horse out from under him just before he got to the train and meets the girl, that was really Hippy. He had to do a running W for him and he was paid and extra $75.00 for that stunt. The running W was when they would string a wire along the ground in the path of a horse to trip him and make horse and rider take a nasty fall. It was dangerous, but Hippy had done it many times. The humane society made them stop that as they said it was too tough on the horses.

One of his most memorable feats and difficult stunts was when he had to cross a forty-foot wide, ninety-foot deep canyon hand over hand. The big problem was that in this scene he had to dress as a woman and act as if he was one. In those days the studios only had one camera and nearly all the stunts had to be done twice. He made $15.00 for each trip across the canyon. By the second time he crossed the canyon he was so exhausted that he wasn't sure he was going to make it. He had no choice; there was no way out but to cross the rope.

By 1923 Hippy felt that he was going down the other side of bronc riding, and he figured when he couldn't always win it was time to quit. In 1924 Hippy won the bronc riding at Salinas and Victorville and that was the end of his riding in rodeos. Hippy hung up his spurs as he had a family now and needed to settle down.

The young couple went back to Alturas to the ranch and changed their way of life. His father in law William Armstrong who had been the Justice of the Peace in Modoc County for twenty-three years decided to retire and give his ranch to Vera and her brother Jack. Hippy and Vera soon bought out Jack and went into the ranching business in full force. They later bought more land to add to their ranch.

His start in the cattle business occurred while working for Charles

Hippy on one of Fat Jones horses in Hollywood in the 1930's

Demick, the manager of the Corporation Ranch, who gave him a leppy calf. Hippy raised the calf to a 1500-pound steer and received enough on the sale of it to buy four more heifer calves, starting his cowherd.

Running the 3200-acre historic Armstrong Ranch became a full time commitment for the couple. Raising cattle, haying, feeding cattle in the winter and calving them out was a big job that he enjoyed for 35 years. Hippy said he had some of the best neighbors in the world in the South Fork Valley and he loved every minute of it. Hippy was active in community affairs and was on the board of directors for the Federal Land Bank and Bureau of Land Management. He was Past Master of Masons and Grange and a member of the Elks Club. He was an avid promoter of the Modoc County Historical Society. He was also honored by the Modoc County Cattlemen as the cattleman of the year.

Hippy kept up with the rodeo life by judging bronc riding at various rodeos including Reno, Klamath Falls and Salinas.

The Modoc County Roundup, was held annually at Alturas, and was quite an attraction. It was started in 1920 with many Modoc ranchers being very instrumental in its beginning. When Hippy moved to Alturas he worked directly with the committee and was responsible for some of the best riders in the country to come to the Alturas show. It was his idea to open the roundup events each afternoon with a parade of the riders and cowboys down Main Street. At the 1925 Roundup Perry Ivory was one of the winners in the bronc-riding contest. The Roundup Association was thrilled that the receipts were over $800. Hippy was manager of this event for several years.

Vera passed away in 1943. In 1945 Hippy married Alice Mary "Tiny" Toreson and gained two more stepchildren, Joan and Jerry.

At the age of 64 Hippy became the manager of the Modoc County Fair. An event that he had been director for sixteen years. This

Hippy Burmister receiving Modoc County Cattleman Award from John Weber

was one of the most enjoyable jobs he ever had. He retired from this position at the age of 70 in 1964 due to their mandatory retirement regulations. The Burmister's sold their ranch and moved to Reno, Nevada for several years. Modoc was home, so they moved back where their real friends were. Tiny passed away in 1980.

Hippy began to realize that much of the Western American History was going to be lost unless someone somewhere could start a collection of all the artifacts, memorabilia and building a perpetual monument to the disappearing West. For people who had joined their lives with his in the ways of the western cowboy. Real range experienced cowboys and cowgirls, who also rode in rodeo because they loved the sheer excitement of testing themselves against all kinds of stock. Whether it is calf roping,

In 1982 the group of Front: Hippy Burmister, 87; Nels Monroe, 87; Gop Sloss, 81; Masten Ramsey, 83. Back: P.B. Harris, 85 and Davey Grove, 87 were featured on the front of a Modoc County magazine playing poker

steer wrestling, or riding the toughest bucking horses in the world. Even riding race horses in relay or pony express or in those exciting Roman standing races. Those riders, men and women in that era preceding and following WWI were the rare breed of riders who could enter into any and all events of the rodeo program and perform in each. No one would ever see or experience this again in the True Old West. Rodeo was changing and the olden days of rodeo needed to be preserved by records and art galleries, photo collections and recorded memories.

With Hippy's cowboy enthusiasm he spoke out and asked his friends and acquaintance in the rodeo world to help him to start building the Cowboy Heritage Center in Oklahoma City, Oklahoma. It took many people many years to get the idea off the ground and into action. Hippy had accomplished so many of his dreams and he knew this one was possible. With all of his acquaintances in the world of motion pictures, rodeo and fairs gave Hippy more leverage than most cowboys to continue to bolster the forces of that freshly budding National Cowboy Hall of Fame. From a member of their Rodeo Historical Society, he graduated to their President, then stepped down to become their roving "Good Will Ambassador," for many years to come.

The Rodeo Historical Society was founded on December 9, 1966 in Oklahoma City, Oklahoma. The founders were: A.H. "Hippy" Burmister, Alturas, Ca.; W.H. Bill" Donovan, Los Angeles, Ca.: George Williams, Oklahoma City, Oklahoma; Tad Lucas, Fort Worth, Texas; Ida Lee "Babe" Knight, Hot Springs, Arkansas; Frances "Flaxie" Fletcher, Fort Worth, Texas and Dean Krakel, Oklahoma City, Oklahoma.

Hippy was proud of the accomplishments of this society and to this day they are going strong. In 1967 Hippy was named 'Man Of The Year' by this society. An honor and achievement he well deserved and was very proud of.

The National Cowboy Hall of Fame along with the Rodeo Historical Society was a dream of Hippy's. He had helped to induct many a cowboy, cowgirl or animal into the great halls of this extravagant building. Proudly he presented the gold medallion to some of his friends, or in their memory, taking part in their induction.

When he was asked one time if he ever thought he would have the honor of being inducted, he said, "no, I never went down south to Texas or some of those places, so I really wasn't known that far away." At that time a person had to have been dead five years to be inducted into the Hall of Fame. That rule no longer applies.

If Hippy had only known that his daughter June Graham did not have the same thought on that subject that he did. She always felt he was due to being honored in such a way. Hippy passed away January 18, 1985 at the age of 90, and ten years later he was inducted into the National Cowboy Hall of Fame in Oklahoma City. June had been at work at this endeavor for quite some time and had hoped to have the induction take place in 1994 the year that Hippy would have been 100 years old. This is no easy feat, many letters were written, and a lot of research and many copies of pictures and articles were made. But finally the honor was bestowed on Arthur "Hippy" Burmister, and was well deserved.

Hippy lived life to the fullest. He never met a stranger and was a friend to all. He and several of his old friends that shared the same stories, dreams and eventful years had weekly poker games at the Niles Hotel in Alturas. In 1982 the group of Hippy Burmister, 87; Nels Monroe, 87; Gop Sloss, 81; Masten Ramsey, 83; P.B. Harris, 85 and Davey Grove, 87 were featured on the front of a Modoc County magazine playing poker.

Hippy never met a horse he couldn't ride, and he never met a person he didn't like. Hippy Burmister will be remembered forever as a legend in the world of rodeo and a legend in the county of Modoc.

January 8, 2000

Left In The Middle Of Nowhere

It was fifteen degrees below zero and the wind was blowing hard drifting the snow. Cliff had been hard at work loading the railroad car all day long. Barrels of water, 50-gallon drums of silage, bales of hay, a bed, bedroll, some grub and finally the livestock. Five horses, one colt, five milk cows and one calf.

Cliff Bailey was only 19 years old and he wanted to go to Oregon from Nebraska to see his brothers that had gone west three years before. He had the chance to ride in the boxcar and take care of all the animals for a man that had bought a ranch near Portland, Oregon. He was to take care of the animals and not get paid, but it would be a "Free Ride." Well, in this world there is no such thing as a free ride, and Cliff found that out.

They didn't get done loading the boxcar on the Burlington Railroad until late that night, and it was really cold. When the train started to move, Cliff snuggled down in his bed, dead tired and fell fast asleep. In the middle of the night he woke up. The train was not moving; the icy night air was dead still. No train sounds were to be heard, only the stirring and snorting of the animals in the car with Cliff. His bed was built right in between the two doors. Stalls for the horses were on one end of the car and a pen for the cows on the other. He got up and opened the door to look out and all he saw was nothing. There was not a train in sight. They had unhooked his car, he was all alone. He was left in the middle of nowhere. Blowing snow and ice in the pre-dawn hours was quite lonesome out there on the Wyoming prairie.

In the far distance down the track he could see a little station house. A half-mile away was the only sign of life. He put on all the clothes he could and decided he had better investigate to see why he had been left. "It was plum nippy", exclaimed Cliff. One guy was at the small depot and he explained to Cliff that the train had left a boxcar of sheep back down the line at Scotts Bluff, Wyoming and they had to go back and get it. They just decided to unhook his boxcar and go back. They didn't bother to let Cliff know the plans.

Finally the train came back and hooked up the boxcar and they moved on. Cliff's job was to take care of the livestock in his charge. He had to milk the cows and feed and water all the stock for the six days and nights the trip took. Every day he had to break the ice on the barrels to water the livestock. It was quite a job packing water in a bucket to that many animals. Cliff had been milking since he was five years old, so that was no problem for him. He was also glad to have the warm milk to drink, as all he had was some cold fried chicken and bread in the grub box the bosses wife had packed for him. He and the calf drank all the milk they wanted then he just threw the rest out the door. At first the calf was sucking the cows, but he was getting too much and going to get sick. Cliff had to milk the cow and teach the calf to drink out of a bucket. The calf was pretty big and just ran loose in the pen. Cliff had to lift him up over the fence to get him out or there, and it was a pretty tough job.

Everytime the train would stop, the two doors would slide open and let the cold air in, so Cliff nailed and wired them shut to keep warmer. When they reached Laurel, Montana they shifted his car over to the Great Northern Railroad. This time they hooked the boxcar with Cliff and the animals in it right next to the coal car. By the time he got done with the trip he was as black as the coal with the dust in his hair and clothes. He was running out of cow feed and he had to buy some bales of hay. The boss had paid for twenty ton on the railroad, but when the car was weighed they were over weight and it cost another $100.00.

The first thing that Cliff did when he got to Portland was find a café and had his first hot meal in six days.

Cliff's grandfather Sherm Bailey had come from Iowa to eastern Colorado. His son Earl Bailey had married Ida Young from Bristol, Oklahoma. Her father Melvin Young had a ranch right next to the Cherokee Indian Reservation. When Ida was two years old her family moved to western Kansas. After Earl and Ida were married they lived in a sod house near Lyman, Colorado. There was not much lumber in that part of the country and many of the homes were made out of sod. Boards were put up, and then tarpaper over that and the thick blocks of sod was stacked up against that to insulate from the cold weather. Then sod covered the roof. It was quite cozy and warm. Cliff was born in that sod house in 1919. There were eight children in the family. Bill, Melvin, Earnest, Don, Durward, Mildred, Tressie and Cliff.

In 1927 it was a terrible winter and the family was snowed in for five months. They had a big bin of Pinto Beans and that is what they ate the most of. When they ran out of flour Earl and another neighbor were able to drive a team and wagon the twelve miles to town to get flour and provisions. The 29th of April they had a blizzard for three days. The kids didn't even get out of the house. Earl only went out long enough to do the major chores. A very large ranch, the Hash Knife outfit was close by. They had thousands of cattle, and many bands of sheep. They just opened the gates and let them go wherever they could find feed or shelter. You could go thirty or forty miles on open range before they would hit a fence. But when the spring thaw came, they found where twenty-five or more head of cattle were huddled in a corner and the snow had drifted over them suffocating them.

Cliff's grandfather Sherm Bailey was quite a horse trader. At one time Earl and his older Brother and Earl's son Melvin drove about thirty head of horses one hundred miles to the Denver stock yards to put them on the train. These horses were called wild horses, but they were not the wild horses that are known in the West. They were all ranch raised horses that had been turned to the range and people just never bothered to gather them, so they were considered wild. When they got to the stockyards Melvin and his uncle sold their horses along with the rest of them, and they took the train back home. Earl did not want to sell his, so he had to ride the 100 miles back home by himself.

After his sophomore year Cliff went to Nebraska where his uncle had bought a ranch. Bill was already there. Bill decided he wanted to go back home, so Cliff stayed to work for his uncle. He helped with the haying, and then he and a neighbor kid built a trailer house to go to Scotts Bluff to pick potatoes and beans. They never went hungry as they could shell all the beans they wanted to eat. They also worked in the sugar beets. Everything was picked in bushels in that country and they got 3-1/2 cents a bushel for picking potatoes. When the corn picking was finished that is when the man they were working for bought a place in Oregon. This is the person that Cliff went with his animals to Oregon. He knew Cliff wanted to go west so he asked him to care for his animals in exchange for the free ride.

Cliff's older brothers Melvin and Bill had gone to Oregon to plant wheat in 1936. Cliff had not seen them for three years. Melvin went by

Durward and Cliff with a 6-horse hitch, 2 row corn planter

the name of Kansas after coming west. They were in Malin, Oregon and that is why Cliff decided to come west to find his brothers.

After Cliff delivered the cows and horses to Portland he caught a bus to Merrill, Oregon. The mail carrier gave him a ride to Malin. He asked in several places for Melvin Bailey, they hadn't heard of him, no one knew him. Cliff was afraid he had made a mistake, maybe Melvin wasn't there after all. He got a room at the hotel and was sitting in the lobby. A man came up to him and ask him if he wanted a job. It was Chet Thompson and he put Cliff to work grading potatoes. The next night Cliff went into the Drug Store and there was his brother Melvin. How happy he was to see him, the older brother explained that everyone there called him Kansas. He was working on the Pitchfork Outfit for Bill Dalton. It was good to finally get to see his brothers again.

Cliff bought an old 1926 Chevrolet with no top and an open box behind. He and Bill took off in search of jobs. They went to Alturas, Fort Bidwell, Surprise Valley and all over. Bill finally found a job and went to work for Sharky Doris at Alturas. Cliff found a job milking thirty cows two times a day for Maggie and Hans Heesch and Felice Leoni on their dairy near Alturas. He was making $30.00 a month with board and room, which he thought was pretty good. He wrote to his younger brother Don and told him to come to California, there was work for him also. Not only Don, but the other brothers Durward (Dode) and Earnest (Buzz) came out and went to work at the dairy where they also had 300 beef cows.

The cook during haying was Grace Dunn from Jess Valley. Grace was the daughter of Walter and Ada Brooks. The other Brooks children were Floyd, Ralph, Dora and Clyde. Their Grandparents, John and Samantha Brooks were the second settlers in Jess Valley, east of Likely. They settled on Soup Creek in 1875, and their son Walter was the first white child born in Jess Valley in their little cabin on December 26, 1876.

John Brooks built the first sawmill in Jess Valley on Mill Creek. It had saws that ran up and down like a crosscut or rip saw blade, rather than the circular saw blades. He was quite constructive and inventive. He also had a small mill on Soup Creek where he ground grain into flour. John Brooks is credited with building the first road out of Jess Valley which is the old road that goes up the hill to Hacker Flat.

John Brooks leased an acre of land for the school to be built on for a $1.00 a year. He had a great interest in a school as he had nine children. The stipulation was that if the school ever closed that the land and buildings would revert back to the Brooks ranch, which eventually it did.

Walter Brooks drove a team of Oxen to deliver the lumber that was cut at the sawmill. He would make trips to Alturas to deliver the lumber, flour or grain whatever needed to be hauled.

In 1886 and '87 James E. Addicott was the schoolteacher in Jess Valley and he boarded at the Brooks family. He wrote an account of the home that he lived in.

"The house had a large fireplace. John Brooks came in, shut the door quick to keep out the cold north wind after being out to feed his livestock. A genial, smiling little man with joy and sunshine radiating from his squinting eyes that spelled fun and humor. He pulled up a three-legged stool and sat next to the warm fire. When supper was ready Walter Brooks stepped out the door and hammered a gong made of a crow bar bent into a triangle that hung on a long rafter extending beyond the kitchen door. The children climbed the ladder up the corner later that evening to go to bed in the loft."

Mr. Addicott described his own bedroom in the John Brook's home; "The door on my private room was two boards hung by old leather shoe tops, and fastened by buckskin strings. The room was 6ft. X 8ft. and the bed was 4ft. X 6ft. made of straw and the straw was covered by old burlap sacking. The only light was an old candle on a box in the corner. Six nails in the wall for to hang my clothes. A piece of glass tucked up against a hole in the wall was the only window. No sheets, no pillow cases, just blankets. There were big cracks in the wall that revealed the beautiful landscape but also allowed the snow to blow in and often covered my bed. One morning it had blown fine powder snow in 4 feet deep in the corner of the room. There were times that winter it was 40 degrees below zero and the bedroom was the same temperature as the all out doors."

The teacher had visited some of the other homes and none of them had quarters as good as John Brooks', so he felt quite fortunate to have such a good place to stay.

Grace Brooks married LeRoy Dunn whose Father Charlie ran a freight line through Modoc County down to the town of Bieber. They settled at the south end of Goose Lake where he cut wood on the Devils Garden and sold it at Davis Creek. The Dunn's came across the plains in a covered wagon. Generations back they came from Ireland in 1753 and settled in Virginia. When that part of the colony was cut off to make Pennsylvania they moved to another part of the Virginia colony, only to be chased from their homes by the British and the Indians. They moved on to Missouri then in 1850 Colonel William Anderson Dunn crossed the prairie in a covered wagon and settled in Vacaville, Ca. where his son Charlie was born. Later Charlie and his wife Elizabeth moved to Modoc County to claim their homestead.

Grace and LeRoy had five children, Lyle, Vivian, Gene, Lois and Warren.

When their youngest child was about four years old LeRoy had a terrible fall. He never recovered from it and soon died. About a year later Grace married Farlan, her husbands younger brother. She never had to change her name and it was good that he was there to help her raise her children.

Grace was the cook on the Heesch Dairy where Cliff was working. Her teenage daughter Lois came to help her and that is where she and Cliff met. After a short courtship Cliff proposed. When Lois was sixteen years old her mother signed the papers for she and Cliff to get married. He was twenty-three and had a good job and was a steady hard worker.

October 26, 1942 the young couple went to Carson City, Nevada. This is where Lois's Mother and stepfather had gotten married so they decided to go there. They found the Preacher who was out digging a ditch and his wife was doing the laundry. They stopped their chores long

Cliff and Lois Bailey wedding photo, October 1942

marriage ceremony.

At that time there were no paved streets in Carson City and only a little clapboard hotel with board sidewalks.

The young couple went back to Alturas where they both went to work at the dairy. Cliff and Lois both milked 15 cows morning and night and Cliff pitched hay all day. Lois kept going to high school, but had to get up pretty early to milk the cows before she could go to class.

Lois and Cliff moved to Surprise Valley in the Fall of 1943 where they leased a ranch from Frank Kerr. Frank owned the mortuary in Cedarville also. After the harvesting was done Frank sold the place then Cliff and Lois moved back over to the Alturas side of the Warner Mountains and leased the Stanton place on Parker Creek in 1944.

Bill Smith had a place up Parker Creek for sale. It was 560 Acres and he only wanted $10,000 for it. It had a two story ten-room house on it that was built in 1900 for the cost of $1,200. How could Cliff and Lois go wrong, this would be the perfect place for them if they could only swing it? Frank Kerr thought a lot of the young couple and he offered to finance them. Bill Smith stayed long enough to help Cliff put up the hay then it was up to him.

They were milking six or eight cows and selling the cream in Alturas to the Mountain Lily Dairy and running beef cows also. They had a thirty-five-head permit on the Forest Service not far from the ranch, and they still have the same permit.

Cliff and Lois had two sons, Roy and Gordon. The school bus came right up the road to the house and picked the boys up to take them to Alturas to school.

When Fritz Nozler built the Modoc Auction Yard in 1948 Cliff went to work for him hauling cattle and working at the yard on sale days.

In 1955 Lois and Cliff went to Marysville where he worked in a feed lot for three years. They had someone stay on the ranch to look after it. After they came back in 1959 Cliff went to work for Fritz at the Auction yard for eleven years full time.

Tom and Blanch Bragg owned the Ranchers Feed and Supply Store next door to the Auction Yard and Lois worked there for many years.

Cliff worked on several ranches and he rode with the Willow Creek bunch when Bidart owned the Willow Creek Ranch on Devils Garden. Ed Ivory was the cow boss out there and his wife Ellen was the cook. Bidart ran around 2500 head of cows and didn't have enough hay to get them through the winter. He bought hay all over Modoc County and drove the cattle to the hay. Around 300 head were wintered on the Bailey Ranch and Cliff fed them hay that had been bought from the Fogerty Ranch.

Cliff and Buryl Mulkey were sorting out some of the cattle and Cliff's four-year-old son Roy was watching gate on his old black mare. They were picking out cows to take back up to Devils Garden. After about a half-hour the four-year-old got tired and rode over to his Dad and said, "I don't like watching gate no more." He wanted to be where the action was.

When the cattle were sorted and ready to be moved there was still two-foot of snow on the Devils Garden. They had Al Ingram doze a road to the ranch. Ed Ivory, his sons, Jim 11 years old and John 10 years old, Red Driscoll and Buryl Mulkey were to drive the cows the two-day drive to the ranch. The first night they got as far as Ingle Swamp and left the cows overnight. Mulkey had a jeep and they went back to the ranch to spend the night. The next day they were getting ready to head the cows out again. All the saddles were in the jeep and they were going to unload them. Young Jim Ivory started to get out of the jeep when Buryl backed into a tree mashing Jim's leg.

Jim couldn't ride that day, so they just let his palomino mare run loose behind the bunch. She got rather frisky and kept running up in front of the cows stopping them and causing a wreck. She came back and forth, back and forth through the herd. Finally Ed Ivory took down his rope and was going to rope her. He got a little deep and caught her around the flanks. She went bucking up through the bunch scattering cattle, but she never

The Bailey Ranch, Alturas, California

came to the back of the bunch again. The snow was so deep the cattle couldn't get out of the trail, so they were strung out for quite some distance.

Another story Cliff likes to tell is when they were going to Weed Valley up on the Devils Garden to work cows. Again there was deep snow on the ground and snowing pretty hard. Oscar Haise was driving the old jeep station wagon and he had a veterinarian from Lakeview with him. There was about two-foot of snow on the road and Oscar let the vehicle lug down and it died. The battery was dead and they couldn't get it started. They did have a scoop shovel in the rig and the cowboys shoveled snow for quite a ways in front of the car and kept pushing it and they finally got it started. They sure liked to tease Oscar about that.

Cliff helped Randall Collis run his packing outfit out of Pepperdine Camp in the Warner Mountains. Lois and Jackie Collis did the cooking for 35-40 hunters. The packhorses belonged to the Likely Roping Club and the pack outfit used them during deer season. There were about 80 camps set up and they were strung all over the Warner Mountains. They were all separate parties with separate camps. Some with just one or two hunters others had several hunters in them. Randall, his son Don and Cliff had to pack in all the camp gear and hay for the horses and then when it was all over, they packed out the deer and the camp gear again.

Cliff was riding his saddle horse that had come from one of Ed Ivory's bucking horses. He was a pretty nice horse, but when he decided he wanted to buck he knew how. One time it was after dark that Cliff was

Cliff and Lois Bailey, Grand Marshalls of the 1997 Modoc County Fair

packing out of the Warner's and the packhorse he was leading got the rope tangled under his horse's tail. His horse would only stand and buck in one spot and not go anywhere. Finally the pack mare came up along side Cliff just as he was about to go off on the right side. She crowded in and Cliff just pushed on her pack and pushed himself back in the saddle. By that time she had jerked the rope out from under his horse's tail and he quick bucking.

Cliff has been a long time member of the Modoc County Sheriff's Posse. They have been out on a few rescue missions and represent Modoc County in many parades. For thirty-one years Cliff has gone on the Modoc Tribe Ride. He has only missed one ride as one year he had his appendix out. He didn't ride, but he didn't miss the play day, although as he said he didn't do much playing.

The Tribe Ride was instigated nearly sixty years ago. The ride was started one day when during a Rotary meeting it was mentioned that the Forest Service was going to cut the range permits in a certain area. This meant a cut in personnel in the Forest Service and a cut in the people that the ranchers helped to support. It would mean a cut at the machinery businesses, the gas plants, grocery stores, feed stores and clothing stores. The town of Alturas couldn't stand the loss in revenue. The businessmen decided it would be a good idea to go out on the range and take a look at the situation and see for themselves just why the Forest Service needed to make these cuts. The Forest Supervisor said if they could get some horses gathered for their people to ride that they would go make a study. The ones that couldn't ride went in a truck. Cooks were brought in from the

Cliff Bailey on Modoc Tribe Ride

Forest Service and the Sheriff brought some from the jail. They went to the Warner Range and rode to Patterson Mill, Pepperdine Camp and Mill Creek. Bleachers were brought out and they would have lectures and speakers, learning about the range conditions. This began to be an annual event and everyone looked forward to it.

The ride has always been held the third week in August and men from a far distance come to take part in the ride and companionship. You have to be invited to participate in the ride, as it is not a public thing. Cliff Bailey has been a director of the Modoc Tribe Ride for over twenty years.

Lois was a member of the Modoc Auction Yard Side Saddlers sponsored by Fritz Nozler. They went as far as Pendleton, Oregon with the group to ride in the parades in their long skirts on their side saddles. They made quite a show and represented Modoc County royally.

Not slowing down much to retire, Cliff and Lois still bowl in a League. They both started in 1971 and are still going strong. Lois won first in 1990 and they have placed first in the mixed doubles. Plaques and trophies are seen throughout their home.

In 1994 Lois and Cliff were the Grand Marshals of the Modoc County Fair in Cedarville, riding in a convertible. But they both would have been more at ease on a horse.

Their son Roy leases the ranch but Cliff still has a free rein and helps him out when he wants. Riding to the range to check the cattle or what else needs to be done. Roy is also a plumber. He has two children, Fred and Mindy.

Gordon works for California Highway Department and he has two children Kenny and Brenda. Between the two boys children they have honored Lois and Cliff with nine great grandchildren.

Milking cows, riding the range, ranching, pack stations and cooking have been a way of life for this ambitious couple. After fifty-eight years of marriage they are still going strong and haven't a complaint in the world. It is doubtful that they would change a day of their life as they have enjoyed it all.

February 13, 2000

ICU, The Brand Of Generations

One hundred and twenty seven years ago in 1873 the Parker family held a branding. You can imagine the cowboys with their rawhide riatas picking a calf or unbranded yearling out of the herd and swinging their loop and catching the animal. Once they had caught the critter by the head another cowboy came in to catch the hind feed. The animal was then taken closer to the fire to be castrated if it were a bull and branded. The ICU brand was heated in the fire and the brand was placed on the right rib of the animal.

Charlotte and Joe Covington

The Parker Ranch was in a long narrow valley a few miles east of Alturas. They were the original homesteaders is that area that is known as Parker Creek. They owned many cattle and the large ranch supported a big family.

Cowboys always liked to have a little fun. One of them caught a coyote and branded it with the ICU brand. Several years later when a Government Trapper trapped the animal he found the brand on it. This particular trapper spoke with quite an accent and could not pronounce his "R's". He came to the ranch and told them, "I have found some of your Popperty."

The Parker's daughter Phear married Howard Porter. The Porters also owned a large ranch a little farther up Parker Creek. At one time about the only acreage around there that some of the Porters did not own was the Fogerty Place and the Smith Place. Howard and Phear's children were Lester, Howard, Johnnie, Jim, Nettie and Mary.

There was a homestead cabin along the road where Porters lived. Lester Porter married Alice Smith who lived about five miles up the creek. In 1914 they built a new home west of the road. They had moved the original cabin to this location, but it was later burned down when a fire in the stove got too hot.

Lester and Alice had three sons, Leland, Floyd and Oakley. Their first born, twin daughters had died at birth. When Leland was eleven years old in 1925 Lester died of cancer. He was only in his 30s. After Lester died, Alice' brother Cleveland Smith came to help her with the ranch work.

The boys rode horse back to the Hopewell School several miles from their home. Leland's first teacher was Norma Studley from Adin. She was boarding at the Ebbe home.

The Porter's were buying some horses from Mr. Steward at Cedarville. The horses were out in Nevada and had to be driven back over the hill to Parker Creek. Young Leland Porter was sent to drive the horses' home. Mr. Steward had a Granddaughter, Charlotte that was quite a sweet young thing and Leland was really taken with her. It seems that he made quite a few trips over the hill to Surprise Valley. In 1938 twenty-four year old Leland Porter and nineteen year old Charlotte Steward were married at Reno, Nevada.

The young couple moved in with his mother and brothers until other arrangements could be made. They built a smaller home for Alice a little way down the road. Floyd went to work for Pete Weber when he got out of school. Oakley quit high school and moved to Sacramento to live with a cousin. He then went to work for United Airlines as a mechanic. His

Charlotte Covington and a Romagnola cow and calf

mother had to receive his high school diploma for him. He then was promoted to a flight engineer, flying on transport planes to Hawaii.

Leland and Charlotte bought the ranch from his mother and that is where they raised their children, Beverly, Lawrence and Carolyn.

In 1946 Alice Porter died from Pneumonia, she also had been treated for Tuberculosis. She was only in her early 50's.

The Porter Ranch ran commercial Hereford cattle. A couple hundred head of cattle was run on the Forest Service and Bureau of Land Management allotments. Leland had also bought a permit from Chris Hansen who had a ranch in Surprise Valley.

ICU Carolee Romagnola female

Four Porter Reservoirs dot the landscape along the Parker Creek countryside. All but the one in the mountains was built on Porter land, which belonged to one member of the family or the other. The reservoirs were all built using teams of horses and Fresno Scrapers. The days and days of labor paid off with the use of the water to irrigate the croplands of the ranches.

The original ranch was 1140 acres on Parker Creek and another 320 on the Mountain.

The ICU brand was passed down to Jim Porter from his parents, when he sold out to Randall Collis he sold him the brand along with the cattle. When Collis was ready to relinquish the brand he handed it down in his family to Diana and Fred Derner. Several years later the brand was again for sale. This time Charlotte (Porter) and Joe Covington found out about it and was able to buy the brand back and it was finally back in the Porter family where it originally belonged.

In 1975 Leland and Charlotte were ready to retire and sell their ranch. Warren Weber bought the ranch from them, all but twenty-three acres that they kept along with their home and barn. In 1978 Leland passed away at 64 years of age.

Many ranches line the banks of Parker Creek and cattle and horses roam the pastures. Only a few of the original families still remain in the area and Charlotte Porter Covington and Cliff and Lois Bailey are the only original members of homestead families that still live in the beautiful little valley.

Charlotte spent several years alone after her husband passed away, spending time with her daughter Beverly. Still very much interested in the cattle business she was pleased to see her Grandson getting started in the Polled Hereford business. While searching for a Polled Hereford heifer for him they visited the Whitmire Ranch at Burney. At that ranch they were doing some embryo transplants on their cattle. This is where Charlotte met Joe Covington who was there doing the procedure of transplanting for the ranch.

Joe was born in Utah in 1927 on the family ranch. His family also had a mercantile store. Joe was ready to go off on his own and he went into partnership with some friends at Boulder, Utah where they ran 600 mother cows. He began doing Artificial Insemination work on his own cattle about 1950. The practice was fairly new at that time. He started in doing the process to improve his own herd and soon started doing the work for other cattle producers. The ranch sold and Joe went out on his own and bought a ranch in Arizona. The Artificial Insemination work soon transpired into embryo transplants for this Reproduction Specialist.

Joe decided to move to California after his son Joe Jr. was hurt in a car wreck so he could be there with him. They bought a ranch at Round Mountain, California.

His studies led him into the field of Embryologist and Geneticist. A pioneer in this field his work was in demand everywhere.

Joe Covington and Charlotte Porter both had the same interests in life. They liked good cattle and enjoyed the cattle industry. They soon decided to combine their likes and their lives and they were married in 1986.

Joe had been raising Simmental cattle but he was looking for unique tougher cattle. He had seen a breed in the 20 degree below zero winters of Montana that were out grazing while all the other cattle were huddled trying to find protection. He had also seen this same breed of cattle in the heat of the Texas deserts.

The big gray Romagnola cows with husky, fat calves at their sides really impressed Joe. The Romagnola cattle are an Italian breed, selectively bred in the rugged Romogna region of Italy. They are the old breed of cattle that people used for oxen. The massive, hardy looking animals are really very docile. They were never sent to the United States until 1974. They are very adaptable to climate changes. When they are in the colder climate they just put on more hair. With good feet and strong legs they survive extremely well in the steep Italian countryside. The Italian breeders refer to them as goats because of their unusual ability to forage for food. Their number one trait is their high quality of lean mean, with little backfat and high quality of marbling.

Joe and Charlotte bought two heifers from Montana to start their new breed of cattle. At that time there were only about eighteen Romagnola breeders in the United States. The Covington's paid top dollar to have the pick of the herd from these Romagnolas. They soon knew they had made the right choice when they were offered $10,000 for one of the heifers.

Charlotte thought if the heifer was worth that much to someone else she was worth that much to them and they kept her. That cow turned out to be one of the top producing Romagnola's in the nation. The beginning of two heifers had turned into a herd of fifty head, which is a good-sized herd for that breed.

The National Romagnola breeders now number around 500 and Joe served as president of this organization for three years.

As a Reproduction Transplant Specialist, specializing in bovine embryo work, Joe has been able to maximize efforts in improving the quality of their herd.

Originally, Joe worked with some of the first veterinarians doing embryo transplanting when the idea took off in 1977. He served on the team doing the first non-surgical transplant in the United States. Because of that he was invited to Italy, where he conducted the first on-farm embryo transplant in that country.

Having the ability to multiply offspring from genetically superior cows is the primary advantage of embryo transplanting. A superior cow is bred artificially to a genetically superior bull, then at day seven the embryos are pulled and either transferred to surrogate mothers or stored. The embryos are flushed from the cows and can be frozen and stored in nitrogen tanks for use at a later date. They are not thawed until they are ready to be implanted non-surgically, which is a lot like the procedure of artificial insemination. The eggs are so microscopic that they can be hidden under the smallest pinpoint. The procedure is complicated to some, but to Joe who has done it so many times it is just another job.

Unno the Champion Romagnola bull from Ireland that the Covington's purchased

A surrogate mother cow receiving the transferred embryo can be of any breed as long as she is healthy. They use a lot of Holstein, Brown Swiss and Hereford crosses as long as they have a lot of milk to produce a healthy calf.

Because of this transplant process, a superior cow can produce more calves in one year than she would normally produce in her lifetime. Joe flushed 28 eggs from one cow at one time and transplanting them there were 21 calves born that were the same age. Another cow had 13 calves that were all her own. A 50% success rate is the usual, but then there are some that are unusual.

Romagnola calves are born a fawn color then start to change color at three months. By five months they are completely gray. The average birth weight is 85 pounds and then they grow like crazy. The Romagnola make outstanding crossbreds with any other breed of cattle.

In 1991 Joe and Charlotte received the first semen ever exported from Northern Ireland to the United States. They had been searching for

Claudina and Flodina, 1996 Grand Champion Cow and Calf, California State Fair

superior cattle to strengthen the existing Romagnola cattle in the United States. The Covington's had traveled to Italy, Northern Ireland and Scotland looking for the bull they knew existed somewhere in those countries. They found him in Italy and their negotiations finally were a reality.

They purchased an outstanding bull "Unno" for $5,000 in Italy and had him imported to Northern Ireland. There the Covington's attended the Province's top cattle show, the "Royal Ulster" in Belfast and were pleased to see their bull win Grand Champion Romagnola when he was shown by Ule Kennedy of the Hazlewood Ranch. Their bull would never come to the United States but his semen was collected to introduce to the Romagnola breed in America.

In Italy there is no crossbreeding of cattle. All of the cattle are gray and white, but different breeds. They have to meet a certain criteria to be kept in a breeding herd. All breeding cattle have to be graded and if they do not meet the specifications they have to go to slaughter and not be used for reproduction. Each section of Italy only has a certain breed of cattle and that is the only kind that can be raised there.

The Romagnola cattle that come from Northern Italy are normally horned. But their horns are so vicious that they are cosmetically removed when the calf is five months old. The skin is cut and the horn removed then the hide is sewn back together producing a smooth polled look.

When Joe was at a convention for cattle breeders in Ireland they had someone from each country present the flag from their country. Joe was very proud when they asked him to present the United States Flag. He also received a certificate recognizing him as an International Expert of Cattle Breeders.

1989 was the first Romagnola show in the United States. This breed of cattle had been shown since 1850 in Europe.

Joe, Bob Blagg and Jerry Hitchings started a Romagnola Invitational Sale in Reno, Nevada, which was held in March. The entry's are limited to 50 Bulls or Females. The Covingtons took seven head this year and their cattle always sell at the top end of the offerings with Bill Lefty at the microphone.

The other interests of Charlotte and Joe is hunting. Charlotte started hunting Modoc Mule deer with her father when she was ten years old. After she and Joe got married they went to Texas hunting and their trophies hang on the dining room wall. Charlotte shot a Black Antelope Buck and a White Tail Deer in Texas and an Elk in Wyoming. Joe is the proud hunter of a large Mountain Sheep. The last time they went to Colorado hunting Charlotte missed an enormous trophy deer that had so many points she couldn't even count them. She has never lived that miss down.

The many trophies, banners and ribbons that fill their home and office from all the livestock shows are only a portion of their winnings. Joe Jr. has as many or more at his home in Round Mountain. Cow Palace in San Francisco, California State Fair and the largest show in the world, the Houston Livestock Show are their favorites. They have had many champions at all shows with their Silver Cattle with the Golden Future. For five years in a row from 1993 to 1998 they had the Champion heifer at Houston, Texas. In 1992 they had the National Champion Bull.

With thousands of straws of semen from some of their top bulls in their Nitrogen tanks frozen for eternity the Covingtons keep up with the business. Although Joe does not do as many embryo transplants as he once did he has not lost his touch.

Still living in the home that the Porters built in 1914 where they have twenty or so Romagnola to feed and care for the Covingtons keep busy. One of their top selling bulls that they sold to a Texas rancher was sold for $40,000. They have sold cattle that have been sent to Tennessee, Kentucky, Louisiana and Mexico.

The largest growth of Romagnola cattle breeders is in Colorado and Wyoming. They are used for a terminal cross because they grade so well and the outstanding cutability of the carcass.

Charlotte and Joe are proud of the contribution they have made to the beef industry with their Romagnola cattle. They traveled far from Modoc County to follow their dream and their dream is reality in the pastures of their Parker Creek ranch. Their dream is the big gray cattle with the ICU branded on their rib.

April 5, 2000

The Ingram Clan From Scotland

This was the worst April Fools day a person could ever have is what Nell Ingram had on her mind when she and her husband John Ingram Sr. (Jack) arrived in the Fall River Valley on April 1, 1892. Nell was not the least bit happy about the move from San Francisco. It had been a terrible trip. They had bought a team and wagon in Redding and headed north. The roads were nothing but ruts of mud and they became snowbound north of Whitmore. Their son Johnnie was only eight months old and it was a hard trip on the baby. Luckily they were not traveling alone as Jack's sister Maggie and her husband William Tocher were also with them.

Jack had traveled a long way to get to this new place he hoped to make his home. He had been born in Keith, Scotland June 12, 1863, the oldest of six children and the only son of John Ingram. The Ingram's were part of the Colquhoun Clan. His father was a farmer, on land that was not owned by them, but leased for ninety-nine years. When Jack was twenty-five years old he left Scotland and traveled into Canada, settling near Ottawa. He was traveling with his future brother-in-law Will Tocher and an uncle of Tochers. The only job that Jack could find in Canada was on a dairy milking cows. He never did like to milk cows, even on his own farm for his own family. The winter was harsh in Canada and Jack's feet were severely frostbitten.

Only staying one year in Canada the men traveled on to San Francisco. Jack secured a job as a streetcar conductor and thoroughly enjoyed his work. His route was from Market Street out McAllister to the Cliff House. Will Tocher also worked on the streetcars and Bill Crombie who had joined them from Scotland worked in the iron works.

Jack's two sisters Margaret (Maggie) and Katherine (Kate) soon emigrated from Scotland. Will Tocher married Maggie Ingram.

Jack and Nell Ingram with baby Helen; clockwise: Elizabeth, William, Johnnie, Robert and Alex

Nell Crombie was the oldest of eight children from Leuchers by Elgin, Scotland. She had gone to school with Jack when they were youngsters. A marriage agreement had been made and she came to America by herself to marry this man. Traveling by herself all of the way she was most happy when Maggie met her at the Ferry Building in San Francisco, just before her wedding day. July 5, 1890 the 27-year-old Jack married 26-year-old Nell and they started their life together. Their first child Johnnie was born July 17, 1891.

A cousin of Will Tocher's, Mary had married Archibald McArthur and they were living in the Fall River Valley. This is what lured the two young couples to this North Country. They were very happy to finally end their journey. They spent the first night in the valley with John and Kate McArthur at their home ranch.

Jack and Nell soon made friends and found a job. The first winter they worked for and lived with Shird and Emma Eldridge at Mountain Home near Jellico. Jack had saved his money and within the year he was able to buy the homesteads of Bill and Jim Coen one and one-quarter miles south of Pittville. Part of the purchase price was compensation from McArthur's for Jack and Nell using their names to purchase timber claims of 160 acres each.

The Ingram family began to grow. The first four were boys, besides Johnnie, there were William (Billie) born in 1893, Robert born in 1895 and Alexander (Alex) born in 1897. Then the three girls came along, Elizabeth in 1899, Helen in 1902 and Margaret in 1906.

The children attended the Rocky Comfort school, which was a couple miles from their home, and they walked to and from school every day.

Jack and Nell lived in the Bill Coen house, which was about halfway between the upper place and the present homestead on the corner of Dee Knoch Road. Nothing remains at the original home site, on the East Side of Beaver Creek. Not even the old locust tree that gave them shade and was a landmark for such a long time.

Billie, Robert and Alex were all born in that house, but the last two were born after the house had been moved to the new farm site. This building later became the shop and storage shed. A larger house was needed, but it was impossible to believe that a house could be moved fifteen miles clear across the valley. A house was bought from the Craig ranch and in 1899 it was put on skids and with several teams of horses it was drug the fifteen miles to the Ingram ranch, even crossing the river two times.

Will and Mary Tocher spent their first winter with the Cathcarts. They then were able to buy the Jimmy Cooper ranch, 160 acres to the East and adjoining Jack's property. The two men built a dam on Beaver Creek, which was on the Tocher property. This dam irrigated the meadows of both of the ranches. Will Tocher built a rail fence between the Ingram ranch and the Cathcart's to the North. Jack and Will were so close that they even shared their livestock brand. The brand "IT" for Ingram-Tocher was used on the left side of the animals and was recorded October 19, 1901. Even though the brand was never listed under Tocher, the brand stood for and was jointly used by both the men with never a bit of squabbling. This was the time they had gone into the cattle business and required the use of a brand. Up until that time they had raised hay, grain and hogs.

Their first major crop was hay, which was sold or exchanged to Eldridges. For several years the Eldridge ranch wintered their cattle on Jack's and fed the hay there. In the late 1930's Jesse Eldridge was still buying the hay crop and wintering his cattle in the Ingram feedlot and hired Alex to feed them.

Jack Ingram always carried a long buckskin leather purse with two $20.00 gold pieces in it. It was to take care of Nell if anything ever happen to him.

Nell was always willing to feed as many people whose feet could fit under the table. Her gingerbread cake was famous and she always kept up the custom of having afternoon tea, inviting the neighbor ladies to stop by. The fresh churned butter and scones were a favorite and the ladies loved to visit. Neighbors had time to stop by for a visit or cup of tea and enjoy each other's company. Box socials at the grange were a regular affair. Mrs. McCoy came by in her buggy every Sunday to take Nell to church in Pittville, then on the way home she would stop in for tea.

Hogs were one of the main cash crops. Grain was raised to fatten them, but in the early days hogs were allowed to roam the sagebrush. The butchering and curing of the pork was winter work. The neighbors would all get together and have a butchering day several times each winter. Eighty to one hundred head would be butchered in one day. The halves of fresh meat would be delivered to Bartle and Sisson (now Mt. Shasta) to the west and to Westwood and Susanville to the east. The first trips were by teams and wagon or sled and later by trucks.

Live hogs were also driven to the railhead in Bartle. All of the neighbors would get together to drive their hogs to market. In the early years Jack supplied the McArthur's with their fresh pork, hams and bacon for their hotel. In the 1930's the scalding tank, hanging racks and smokehouse were still in use with Jack in charge of the salting and smoking.

Jack raised many horses and at one time he had as many as fifty head on the place and grazing the hills. Beef cattle were run on the ranch but only enough dairy stock was kept to supply the family with milk. Sheep men from the valley, Matthews, Callahan and Wing would graze their sheep on the stubble fields in the fall. This provided an extra income and also cleaned and fertilized the fields. The sheepherders would always leave a few sheep behind as a gift.

In 1907 Jack Ingram had a grain thresher he had bought second hand. It required a lot of horses to run this operation. It was a stationary thresher and all the equipment was moved from ranch to ranch. It took six horses to move the separator, six more to move the steam engine, four to move the derrick, two for the water wagon and two more for the cookhouse. If Jack didn't have enough horses some of the men that worked on the crew were hired with their teams.

Almost as many men were needed to run the operation. Two to man the derrick fork to load the grain on the wagons, two drivers, three or four hoe down (to feed the separator) one sack jog to fill the sacks and pass them to the two sack sewers. One engineer for the steam engine, one water buck with a hand pump, and the cook with his kitchen on wheels and a roustabout to move the feed wagon and to tend the extra horses.

Jack was a good rancher and father, but his main interests were beyond the boundaries of his ranch and family. The children, milk cows and garden were Nell's domain. Jack was always a trustee of the Pittville School while any of his children attended. All of them graduated from the Pittville elementary except Billie who lived with "Grandma" Hulbert for several years and attended Rocky Comfort School. He tended to the chores for the elderly widow lady and took her where she needed to go.

Jack also served as trustee of Fall River Joint Union High School. The first trustees besides Jack from Pittville, were Mrs. C.G. Bosworth and L.M. Rose from McArthur, Carrie E. Sylvester from Glenburn and John Snell from Cayton.

Jack was also instrumental in founding the Presbyterian Church in Pittville and served as a trustee all of its existing years.

Even though Jack and Nell came to American at a very young age they intended that this would be a permanent home. They acquired their naturalization as soon as possible. They never lost touch with their homeland of Scotland and kept in contact with family members and other immigrants from the "Old Country." Some of the neighbors that also had traveled the same trail as the Ingrams were Joe Bruce and Jim Parker.

Neighbors and relatives gathered for Christmas dinner and other occasions. In 1909 Nell had gone to Scotland for a visit with her Mother and she took baby Margaret with her. Even though Nell was not there a gathering of the neighbors included Sylvester "Vess" and Mary McCoy, Ira and Dora Campbell, Will and Maggie Tocher, Steve Collett, Mrs. Wendt and Arie, (who later married Joe Bruce) Ollie Cathcart, Howard and Harve Wendt and Mr. and Mrs. Press Fine.

It was a good opportunity for Nell to go to Scotland as Blacksmith Bill Tocher, her cousin was going and she could travel with him. Margaret had her third birthday party at Christmas in Scotland in her Grandmothers thatched cottage. While their mother was away ten-year-old Lizzie stayed with the Wendt's and seven-year-old Helen stayed with her Aunt Maggie Tocher at their Hotel in McArthur.

The Tocher's left the valley in 1913 and moved to Cobb Mountain above Middletown in Lake County. They sold their thirteen-room hotel to Shird and Emma Eldridge who ran it until 1942 when it burned down. The hotel was on the main road through McArthur and was a flourishing business, and was a welcome place for travelers and salesmen.

Jack was very social minded and he joined the Masonic Lodge in Adin in 1916. Roderick and Luther McArthur recommended him. His father had been a Mason and he had memorized much of the work from listening to his father. He demitted the Adin Lodge and affiliated with Fort Crook Lodge in Fall River Mills in 1925.

The Ingram boys enlisted in the Army. Bob and Johnnie both enlisted in 1918. The Armistice was signed before they were shipped to Europe so they were discharged in 1919. They both were stationed at Fort Lewis, Washington.

Billie received his induction notice on his wedding day when he and Mable Hendricks were married June 26, 1918. He also was soon released because he was needed on the ranch at home. In 1939 Billie married Alice Swan and adopted her son Jackie. In 1954 he married

Lucy Manilla and they had a son William in 1955 and a daughter Melissa in 1960. Billie did a lot of custom farming in the valley. He seeded all the McArthur swampland. He inhaled so much alkali dust that it caused lung problems for him and he died in 1967.

When Bob returned from the service, he went to work for the McCloud River Lumber Company at Bartle for a year before he married Lois Edna Rose Smith in June 1920. Lois was married to Grover Smith first and he and Charlie Moore were running a trap line. Charlie crawled through the fence first then Grover crawled through second. The gun went off and shot Grover in the back killing him.

Lois's grandparents had a homestead over the rolling hills from the Ingram's. Their homestead was known as Starvation Gulch. The next gully over was known as Skunk Hollow. As in the Ozark Mountains every little gully, gulch and homestead had a name. Bob and Lois moved to her grandparents Straub's homestead when they were married and this is where their children Eileen and George were raised. They walked across the field to attend the Beaver Creek School

Johnnie had some cows of his own before he went into the service. While he was away his mother cared for them, milked them and churned and sold the butter. She put the money in the bank for her son. When he returned he was able to use these savings toward the purchase of half of the Hendrick's ranch. Billie and Mable bought the other half.

Johnnie moved onto the property when he married Mary Eva Dickey in 1926. They had planned and built a house that was ready by their wedding day. Mary had been a schoolteacher at the Beaver Creek School and had boarded with Bob and Lois.

Johnnie and Mary started their family and in five and one-half years they had five children. Erma Jean was born in 1927, Ruth in 1928, Vera in 1929, Caroline in 1931 and Donald in 1932. In 1938 Mary and three of the children contracted pneumonia. Penicillin had not yet been put on the open market and it was only used for the Armed Forces. Mary was really sick, she was so run down from having so many children in such a short time and all the hard work. Her brother was able to get some penicillin in Redding and he was on his way up to Pittville with some for her. She died before he got there. The children survived the sickness, but with their mother gone this left Johnnie with quite a family to raise. He had to hire a housekeeper and she had a child of her own. He could not stand for her to correct his children so he decided to make other arrangements. Some of the aunts would take one or two of the children, but no one had room for all five of them. He did not want his children to be separated, so he took them to Gilroy, California and placed them in the Odd Fellows Home. Erma Jean was ten and Ruth was nine so they were old enough to help care for their little five year old brother Donald. It was not the most perfect situation, but at least the children were together.

They all went to school at Gilroy and graduated from High School down there. Johnnie never did remarry.

Alexander married Kathryn Hight and they did not have any children. He remained on the home place and worked on various ranches. He worked for the McArthur's, Albaugh's, Byrne's, Cathcart's and Wendt's.

Elizabeth married Arden Reynolds and they had Joy and Marion. After her first husbands death she married Dudley Wymore. Helen married LeRoy Shaffer and they had Theresa Lenore. She later married Bert Orbell. Margaret married Ralph Edwards and they had one son Glenn.

Jack Ingram was supervisor of District #3 of Shasta County. He was the only Shasta County Supervisor ever from the Fall River Valley. In 1925 he began his term of office and one of the first projects he was involved with was a bridge over the slough near Ball's Ferry. Having succeeded C.R. Heryford, Jack attended his first meeting in February 1925. His only absence was in October of that year when weather and road conditions prevented him from making the trip to Redding. At one time it had been too wet and muddy for the car, so Jack had traveled by horseback the two days to Redding and two-days home. He arrived home so wet and cold that he went in to pneumonia. Mrs. Wendt was called in to nurse him. His other major sickness was in earlier years when he suffered sunstroke. It left him so incapacitated for several months that Nell had to wait on him for everything. He could not even light his pipe.

At a very early age he had a fever so severe it caused him to lose his red hair. The new hair growth was black which turned to gray at a very early age.

Jack's first car, which was his transportation to Redding, was a long bodied Studebaker. It was second hand but a good car and it was also used as a hearse for the Pittville community.

The years as Supervisor added to the circle of friendships that Jack already was blessed with. The trips to Redding required at least an overnight stay and always at the Golden Eagle Hotel. He stopped many times enroute to visit with friends along the way. At reelection time George Darrah defeated Jack.

Another of his community offices was as Deputy Assessor for Shasta County. At that time the deputies worked only from the first Monday of March through June and reported to Redding once a week. They were mainly responsible for the listing of personal property and new additions or improvements of property.

Jack and Nell celebrated their Golden Wedding Anniversary July 5, 1940. It was a memorable gathering of the clan. All seven of the children were in attendance and most of the grandchildren except Johnnie's five that did not come home that summer.

In 1939 when Jack was seventy-six years old he injured his foot while chopping wood and it would not heal. He went to the McCloud Hospital and Dr. Dickinson amputated the big toe of his right foot. Two other operations were performed, taking more of the foot. The last surgery was to remove his right leg just below the knee. He was fitted with an artificial limb and he learned to walk with the aid of a cane. The reason the foot could not heal was because of the time when in Canada as a young man he was severely frostbitten.

His grandson George could remember his grandfather walking with his cane out to the field where George was raking hay. He just came out to see if his grandson was doing it right.

Nell passed away in 1943 at the age of eighty. She had become severely stooped and was afflicted with palsy. She became bedridden and remained at home where Alex's wife Kathryn took care of her. She died the same day that her first great grandchild was born.

Jack lived another ten years after his wife passed away. During this time he made his first trip to Ottawa, Canada to visit his sister Kate in 1945. He had not seen her since she moved there in 1891. After that he made the trip two more times before he passed away in 1953 at the age of eighty-nine. He remained ramrod straight, clear minded, witty and always enjoyed his pipe and a "wee nip".

Many of the homesteads in the Pittville area were built in the gullies so they could save the higher ground for the farming. Starvation Gulch was where George Ingram's Grandfather William Straub homesteaded in 1888. The original homestead was 160 acres and in 1891 Charlie, William's second son added another 160 acres. The original patent was signed October 8, 1892. In 1903 Charlie deeded the land to his sister

Eileen (back), L-R; Ruth, Erma Jean and George Ingram

Mary Kate and her husband George Rose. After George Rose died and his wife remarried and became Mary Kate Keeler, she deeded the land to her daughter Lois and her husband Bob Ingram as a gift in 1923. The young couple was living on the property and that is where their daughter Eileen was born in 1923 and their son George in 1926.

The children walked across the field to go to the Beaver Creek School with the nine of the Crum children, five of the Bruce and the Dawson, Knoch and Bean children. There were thirty-seven students in the one room.

George Ingram belonged to the Lasta Paiute 4-H Club where Maple Perkins was his leader. The Lasta Paiute name came from Lassen and Shasta, as there were members from each county. That club later evolved into the Cloverleaf 4-H Club of today. He showed his animals at the InterMountain Fair and who would have ever thought that one day he would be the Fair manager.

Eileen and George then went to McArthur to High School. In high school George was very active in FFA. His instructor was Jesse Bequette and George was one of his favorite students. After graduating from high school he went into the Armed Forces. He was a secretary in the service as typing was one of his best subjects in high school.

After his discharge in July he was ready for some rest and relaxation. He went to San Francisco to visit his best friend David Schneider who was in the hospital. A log had rolled on him and crushed his pelvis.

In 1946 Jesse was leaving the valley for another job and the fair needed a manager. He was sure George was the man for the job.

A telegram was sent to George in care of David. Come home, I have a job for you. Signed; Jesse Bequette. Although George was only nineteen-years old he was offered the job of the manager of the Inter-Mountain Fair. At the time it was up to the FFA Advisor to be the manager of the fair. Before that the McArthur Grange had taken over the fair and it was mainly a rodeo. They even had their own rodeo stock and ran them on the McArthur swamp. Jesse was hired in 1936 and he had done the job for ten years. At that time Willis Albaugh, Asa Doty and Hugh Carpenter were the fair board and when Jesse convinced them he was sure that George could do the job they certainly agreed with him.

When George started his position with the fair in 1946 he was paid $200.00 a month. This was a lot of money and how hard could the job be. His only tools were a shovel and a hammer. Frances Gassaway was the volunteer secretary and Clarence Whipple was the Treasure. The fair ran smoothly, no real problems. People were great to volunteer to help with the projects. Any time a job demanded more than George's hammer and shovel he would just go over and borrow anything from a tractor to a wheelbarrow from the McArthur's.

In 1946 the Inter Mountain Fair was changed to the Labor Day weekend and ran for three days. Jesse Bequette was still the fair manager as George did no take over until after the fair that Fall.

George was lucky to have such capable Committee chairmen as Floyd Bidwell for Livestock; Roy Hoffman, Feed; Elizabeth Albaugh, Domestic Science; Hazel Kaufenberg, Domestic Art; Alice Burton, Flowers; Police Protection, Roy Duggens and Clair Engle, Congressmen.

The 1947 Fair was George's first fair and Frances was doing the job of both Secretary and Treasure by this time. Jim Bruce was taking care of the Livestock responsibilities and Della Wiertzba, Louise Crum and Anna McArthur were seeing to the Domestic fair exhibits.

George was lucky that he had the typing experience that he did, because to get the premium book approved a hand typed book had to be submitted to the state division of fairs and exposition to be approved before you could have it printed. George typed the entire premium book by himself and it was approved.

The fair kept growing, 1947 was the first year for a carnival. 1948 the board approved the purchase of 98 acres from the PG&E for nearly

Phyllis Totten and George Ingram wedding photograph, April 1950

$900.00. 1949 Hugh Carpenter was added to the board of directors along with Willis and Asa. This was the year a new exhibit building was started and a new grandstand was added to the fair grounds.

During the years of 1949 and 1950 the main hall, known as Ingram Hall was constructed. For the grand opening of the hall a dance was held and all of the ladies attending received and orchid corsage. The second racetrack and exhibit building were also ready for use.

The development of trees and shrubs started taking shape in 1950. The trees, shrubs and rose bushes were ordered from Stark Brother's nursery in Missouri and were sent by railroad to Alturas. Albert Kenyon was the first caretaker of the fair grounds and he and George went to Alturas to pick up the order from the nursery. Albert and George planted all the shrubs and trees and then planted the lawn. There was no

George Ingram (left) and Willis Albaugh (right) discussing the days business

sprinkler system, so George and Albert watered everything with the fire hose to get it started.

The fair was going great guns and George was handling things quite well and was also active in all the community activities. While attending a Grange meeting he met a very nice young lady. Phyllis Totten was at the meeting with her aunt and uncle the Arnold's and she certainly took George's eye.

Phyllis lived in Oakland, California when she was young. When she was six years old she and her parents were in an automobile accident. Both of her parents were killed and she was unconscious for several days. She was the only child of Phillip Totten but her mother had three children from a previous marriage. Phyllis was sent up to live with her father's sister Nora Arnold and her family. She had other uncles in the area, Clarence, Peter and Herb Totten.

1971 George Ingram (right) receiving the 25 Years of Service Award from the Western Fairs Association by Robert Finch (left), counselor to President Richard Nixon

It was hard for the little girl to adjust to this new life. The colder weather, wearing heavier clothing and just a whole new atmosphere besides having a new family to live with and a new school. Phyllis was going to high school at McArthur when she and George started dating.

In April of 1950 George Ingram and Phyllis Totten were married in the living room of the old Arnold house with Shirley Neuerburg McArthur and David Schneider standing up with them. Phyllis wanted to get married in the home because two of her cousins had been married

Phyllis and George Ingram's 50th Anniversary, April, 2000

there. She was not going to graduate from high school until June, but the old house was to be torn down. The day after the wedding they started to destroy the old home so they would be able to build a new one in its spot before winter came that year.

George had a good job and the newlyweds rented a place in Fall River for a year. His father had been quite sickly so George and Phyllis decided they had better move out to the ranch to help him out. They remodeled a shop building into a house and they lived in that for ten years before building a new home. All of their children Anita, Alexis, Lynn, Robert and Jennifer grew up on the ranch.

In 1983 George was President of the Western Fairs Association. He really enjoyed that position and during that time traveled to some very interesting places, always being an impressive representative for the Inter-Mountain Fair.

George retired from the manager position of the Fair in 1988 after forty-two years of dedicated service. He enjoyed every minute of his job and did it first rate. He was proud of his achievements as fair manager and the fair board was proud of him.

The Ingram roots run deep in the Fall River Valley with many ancestors still living there. They are proud of their Scottish heritage and the contribution that their Grandparents Jack and Nell made to the community. Nell was happy there, but she never forgot the worst April Fools Day of her life.

March 9, 2000

The Judge With A Heart

By the mid 1800's the Oregon Trail began to be a steady stream of horse and ox drawn Conastoga Wagons. Pioneers by the hundreds were moving westward to find their fortune and start a new life. They carried all their worldly possessions in the wagons.

Among those pioneers was the family of Gilmore and Elizabeth Callison. His father Joseph had farmed in Kentucky and served in the war of 1812. Joseph and his wife Susannah had ten children and their fifth son Gilmore was born in Kentucky in 1808.

At the age of 22, Gilmore was married to Elizabeth McClure and three years later the family moved from Kentucky to Carthage, Illinois. The family settled into farming there for many years and raised their eight children. One of their sons William Thomas Callison who was the second born into a family of eight children in 1832 would later be a witness to the murdering of the great Mormon leader Joseph Smith in 1844.

In the spring of 1852, Gilmore Callison had received several letters from his brother Robert, who had immigrated to the Oregon territory four years earlier. Gilmore was intrigued by the stories related to him by his brother and decided that making the move west was a good idea. The family consisted of six healthy robust sons and two daughters. It would take several wagons and teams and a large amount of supplies to get them to Oregon. The arrangements were made for the trip and they packed their most treasured possessions. As so many of the settlers did they held a sale and sold the rest of their belongings.

The starting point for their westward caravan was St. Joseph, Missouri. John at 22 was the oldest of the sons and he drove one of the wagons. He kept a daily diary of their journey. He kept an account of the miles they traveled, weather, road conditions, the Indians they met and a

William T. and Rebecca Callison. The first Callisons in Fall River Valley.
Photograph taken before 1867

record of their expenses. The journal also included daily events, and the descriptions of the Platte River, Fort Kearney, Chimney Rock and the people they met along the way were all entered in his journal.

Following are some excerpts of John Callison's daily diary.

April 6, 1852- Started to Oregon, traveled fourteen miles. Paid 30 cents for a bushel of corn and 50 cents for 100 pounds of hay.

Averaging 15 miles per day through rain and muddy roads they crossed the Mississippi River by the 16th.

April 17- passed through Unionville, took the right hand road and encamped on Soap Creek. Turned our cattle out to grass for the first time. Corn 75 cents a bushel.

April 22-Traveled twelve miles passed through Dodge's Point and encamped at the ford of Charity River. Corn $1.00 a bushel.

Rainy and miserable, stayed at Charity River three days to graze cattle. Grass very thin and dry. No corn.

April 24- Traveled 21 miles, passed through Garden Grove and encamped on a branch of Grand River, all Mormons, the women dressed in Bloomer costume.

April 26- Traveled 16 miles, very cool, rainy and sleeting, cool enough for us to drive all day with our overcoats on. No corn, grass on uplands no better than it was when we started from home.

April 29- Traveled 15 miles and encamped on another branch of the Grand River at Johnson's. Corn $2.00 a bushel. Did not buy any.

May 1- Traveled 18 miles, crossed eastern Ishnabotny, forded and passed through Indian town inhabited by Mormons and encamped on the prairie, fine weather and good roads.

May 3- Traveled 15 miles, ferried our wagons and swam our cattle across Western Ishnabotny and overtook Bristow and Newingham wagons on Silver Creek. Seen several Indians. Bought 4 ton of Prairie hay for $2.50 ton. Paid $2.00 pasture for our cattle.

May 14- Crossing the Missouri River on the ferry was $8.50. Had to lay by on account that it was so windy that the rest of the party could not cross. Plenty of Indians of the Ottoe tribe. Friendly.

May 17- Traveled 20 miles and crossed Salt River; the water tastes a little saltish. Good roads. Two Pawnee Indians camped with us and slept in our tent.

May 19- Wood and water very scarce, had to burn weeds to cook with and carry water a half-mile.

May 20- Camped at the Platte River, shallow and wide, sandy, water hardly fit to drink. A caravan of 100 Pawnee Indians on a hunting party camped close to us.

Passed through a deserted Indian village and got plenty of wood. This village has been evacuated since the hard winter of 1848-49 when their ponies all died off. They formed a square with them and there were 63 piles of bones bleached perfectly white. Met some Cheyenne that were going out to kill as many Pawnee as they could.

May 26- Traveled 20 miles, passed through Fort Kearney and encamped two miles this side. Fort Kearney is beautifully situated on the Platte bottom about two miles from the river. It has four or five good-looking frame houses two stories high and several sod houses, which look very well, two or three of them were 50 or 60 feet long. The troops all are decently dressed and the captain appears to be very much of a gentleman.

May 28-Crossing the Platte River, which was two miles wide. Very hard on the men and teams. From six inches to four feet deep and the sand is continually rolling from under the wheels, which keeps the wagon rocking.

May 31- Lay by on account of sickness. Absolom Newinghan very bad with cholera, nearly half the company down with diarrhea, some very bad. Very poor water to drink and exceedingly warm weather.

June 1- Absolom Newinghan died half past two o'clock.

June 2- Josephine Bristow very sick, died at half past four. Many very sick.

John's diary goes on to describe the country, those who were sick and died. Passed by Chimney Rock and Scotts Bluff.

June 16- Camped near Fort Laramie. Traveled through the Black Hills where the roads were very bad. Grass very poor.

June 23- Passed the upper Platte ferry at noon and started across what is called the desert, which is 30 miles. No grass or water except for alkali, until you arrive at Willow Springs.

June 25- Traveled 21 miles and encamped on Sweetwater River, near Independence rock.

Here, John's diary suddenly ended. He himself had taken ill with the cholera, the dreaded killer of the emigrants. He died August 23, 1852 and was buried in a grave along the Oregon Trail near the present city of La Grande, Oregon. His coffin was made from the sideboards taken off his wagon that he had driven so far. He never realized his dream and destination that he had hoped for. John was born Aug. 13, 1830 and he had never married.

Soon after the family arrived at the Willamette Valley their final destination, Gilmore's wife Elizabeth died. The ordeal of the long hard journey, the grief of losing her son and the hardships and hazards of the trip attributed to her untimely death.

Settling near the present city of Eugene, Oregon Gilmore became involved in community affairs. A large man in stature, (six feet four inches), he was a powerful civic leader and a Minister. He served as a member of the Oregon Legislature during the years of the Civil War. Several of his sons joined the Union Army serving in the Civil War. When the war was over they returned to Oregon.

Before long William T. Callison the second son of Gilmore married Rebecca Linder whose family had also emigrated from the east and traveled the Oregon Trail. William went into farming near Eugene for fourteen years. Rebecca's health was failing and she needed to live in a dryer climate. William had a friend in the Fall River valley that had written letters telling William what a wonderful valley it was. In the spring of 1866 William saddled his horse and decided to take a look at this wonderful country for himself.

The Achumawi Indians in the Fall River Valley were restless. There had been raids on the ranches and farms. Livestock were stolen and the settlers were fearful. A military camp was set up near the forks of the Pit River at Lockhart Ferry and the soldiers were known as the 'Pit River Rangers'.

General Crook who considered himself a famous Indian fighter was sent from Fort Jones to command a post at Lockhart Ferry at Fall River. This was only a temporary military camp. Soon a full-fledged military post would be built and named after General Crook.

Even with the Indian uprisings William T. Callison decided this was where he needed to move his family. The Soldiers at Fort Crook would give them some security.

There were a few bold settlers along the streams, but most of the country was unclaimed, just waiting for homesteaders to stake their claims. Grass was growing high as their stirrups and an ideal land for raising cattle. Prairie chicken was seen in great numbers everywhere. Wild game was abundant for the taking to feed you family. The country exceeded all the expectations that William had.

This is the place that William T. Callison had dreamed of. He hastily rode back to Oregon to bring his family on the long journey back to California.

Two stout wagons were made ready and again packed with their worldly possessions. William drove one wagon and Rebecca drove the other. The two oldest of their six children, Charity and John followed on their horses driving the family's herd of twenty cattle.

The trip was 300 miles of mountainous, wilderness country. They traveled across the Siskiyou Mountains, past Mt. Shasta and into the Fall River Valley.

The Callison family arrived in the beautiful valley in October of 1866. Their friends the Riggs family offered to let the Callison family stay with them. However, William wanted to find a suitable home for his family on his own.

Winter was fast approaching and the Indians were still quite unsettled. The Indian problem was more severe in the Modoc nation near Fort Bidwell, so some of the soldiers had been sent from Fort Crook to Fort Bidwell. This left some empty housing at Fort Crook within the stockade. The Callison family was more than happy to occupy the empty home.

The Fort had twenty log buildings situated around a triangle extending from West to East and joined by picket fences. A tall pine tree in the middle stripped of its branches served as a flagpole where the flag was flown from sunrise to sunset. The boundary was a mile in any direction from the flagpole. The parade ground was of sufficient size for the soldiers to perform their drills. The area was surround by a stockade of twelve-foot tall logs with the bark on them and set upright in a trench. The buildings consisted of quarters for the Officers, Physician and the Privates. There was a hospital, mess hall, barracks, blacksmith shop, store, guardhouse and homes and a stable for 200 head of horses. Other necessary buildings also were within the walls of the stockade. The grass was abundant in the valley and it was a mild winter. The cattle and horses that Callison's brought with them from Oregon were able to graze the surrounding area the entire the winter.

When the family left the safety of the Fort and homesteaded along the river the Indians were still unpredictable. At night the family would take their blankets and sleep in the fields among the tall grass and weeds for fear that the Indians would burn them out during the night. The Hat Creek Indians planned a rendezvous with the Fall River Indians and they planned on a raid and burning out the settlers. The Hat Creek Indians did not show up so the Fall River Indians did not go through with the plans.

The next spring William T. filed a homestead on some property. He built a house, barn and other necessary farm buildings. He then filed on and made two payments on a tract of hay and swampland, which lay adjacent to his home property. Two and a half years later William T. became sick and met with an untimely death at the age of 37. He left his wife with two sons and three daughters to raise. Charity, Katherine, Lucy, William Logan and John were left to help their mother run the ranch.

Rebecca could not make the payments so the land reverted back to the State of California. Shortly thereafter J.F. Bowman acquired title to the property and added it to his ranch. This land later became known as part of the George Brown Ranch. William had also been negotiating on some land in Big Valley.

William Logan Callison was the third of the five children. He was but a young lad of eight years of age. Those months spent within the boundary of the Fort left a lifelong imprint on the youngster's life. He loved to watch the soldiers on horseback doing their maneuvers about the parade ground. He spent hours at the stable that housed so many horses and he thrilled at the bugle calls at sunrise and sunset.

When he was 24 years old he married Katie Brown. Her family had homesteaded near the town of Glenburn. Along the Fall River, William raised cattle and farmed for the rest of his life. The children of William and Katie were Mabel, Merton, Ferd and Nellie.

Merton was born in a log cabin west of Burgetville, (now known as Glenburn) near the base of Soldier Mountain, on August 7, 1890. Just a short way down the road was the town of Swasey that also had a store, post office and flourmill. Burgettville was the first town in Fall River Valley; established in 1869. It was located on Fall River a couple of miles south of Fort Crook. A story is related about Bill Burgett, the fonder of Burgettville. It is said that Burgett found that it was illegal to sell liquor within a mile of a military reservation, so he paced off the exact distance form the Fort Crook boundary and there he established his store and blacksmith shop. Burgett built his toll bridge across the river in 1864.

One of the most memorable things in young Merton's list of memories was when he was a small boy and the Wild West Show came to Redding. His parents took him to see the main attraction, which was Buffalo Bill. He always remembered him as a man with flowing white hair and beard. He treasured the memory of shaking hands with him.

The Callison family. Back L-R: Merton, Mabel, Ferd.
Front L-R: William Logan, Katherine and Nellie

Merton and Ferd both went to Mr. Wilson's Preparatory School in Adin to be teachers.

After Merton finished his course at Mr. Wilson's school in Adin he had to go to Susanville to get his teaching credential. He had a little old motorcycle to make the seventy-mile trip on a very bad dirt road. His motorcycle gave out part way through the trip and he had to walk and push his vehicle the rest of the way.

Ferd taught for three years at Surprise Valley in a one-room schoolhouse for $70.00 a month. He then decided to go to San Francisco where he enrolled in Medical School. He became a very successful Doctor, owning his own hospital. Ferd married Viola Harms and they never had any children.

Mabel married Robert Summers and they owned the Fall River Mercantile Store. They had four children, Ella, Claire, Floyd and Robert. Nellie became a schoolteacher at Dunsmuir and she married Peter Flood, they had no children. Nellie had an extensive collection of Indian baskets that she had acquired through her travels. She donated them all to the Fort Crook Museum.

Merton married Wanda Lee. She was the second child of the ten children born to William and Lillian Lee. The Lee family owned a large ranch north-east of McArthur and their roots began in the Fall River Valley in 1899 when they had moved from Bieber.

On June 23, 1917 Merton hitched his team of horses to his buggy and set out for his wedding. Arrangements had been made for him to pick up his bride to be and her mother and drive the twenty miles to Bieber for the ceremony. When they arrived at their destination, Merton tied his team to the hitching post in front of Tom Dunlap's mercantile store. The local merchant was also the Deputy County Clerk of Lassen County. Tom Dunlap issued them a marriage license and they then went in search of the local Justice of the Peace. Bernard Bassett the local blacksmith also held this title. Merton ask Bassett to perform the ceremony. The blacksmith was engaged in shoeing a horse and said he would do the honors as soon as he finished his job. In due time the Judge appeared at the appointed place and the wedding proceeded as scheduled. After the ceremony the bride and groom along with the brides mother made the trip back to the Lee residence where they spent the night.

Merton and Wanda had three children, Walter born in 1919, Lenora in

Walter Callison, Most Beautiful Baby Contest winner at the 1920 Intermountain Fair at McArthur, California

1921, and Roselee in 1928. The Inter-Mountain Fair that made its beginning in 1919 had started a "most beautiful baby contest." At the 1920 fair, tiny Walter Callison along with Bob Bruce was named the winners of that event.

Not all of the Indians were hostile toward the white settlers. In fact some of the homesteaders took Indian women for their wives. Such was the case of John Taylor. He took sick and would not eat. Mrs. Taylor became quite upset and went to some of her white friends for consultation. She said, "I know not what the matter with my man, he no eat. I do everything for him, I cook up cricket and grasshopper and big green worm, cook it all up for him good and he still no eat."

Merton became a very important person in the history of Fall River Valley. He taught for several years at the Pittville, Pine Grove and Rocky Comfort Schools. He taught in the Fall River Valley for nearly twenty years.

In 1920 Merton was appointed Justice of the Peace. A position he held until 1945. Along with his farming, ranching and teaching he was a very busy man. He enjoyed his job as judge and was known as the "Judge with a heart".

As judge one of his duties was to prosecute poachers of wild game. One man who had a family of starving children had to find something for them to eat. He made a long walk from his car and finally found a deer that he shot to feed his family. After carrying the deer through the rocks back to his car, he met up with the game warden patiently waiting for him. The game warden confiscated the deer and hauled the lawbreaker to Judge Callison. The Judge held court on the glassed in front porch of his home on the ranch. The Game Warden went on about his business and left the culprit for the Judge to deal with. As soon as the government official was out of sight the Judge said, "take this deer home and feed your family.

Many times the Sheriff, Oscar Kenyon would take a lawbreaker out into the hay field to meet up with the Judge. Late at night a knock would be heard at the door and some young couple would want to get married immediately. It was never known when to serve dinner at the Callison ranch, as there was usually someone to see the Judge.

During the time of Prohibition many bootleggers with their stills were established in the hills surrounding Fall River Valley. With that and the construction of the Pit 1 Tunnel and the local Conservation Corp Camps a period of lawlessness was raging in the area. When the bootleggers were caught the lawmen confiscated a twenty-gallon keg of their moonshine and took it with the culprit to the prominent Judge. After making his judgement Judge Callison would pour the contents of the kegs out on the ground. The house being uphill from the pig pen and the chicken yard the booze would run down the hill on the frozen ground. The pigs and the chickens thought this to be quite a treat and would drink to their hearts desire. The pigs would wobble about and squeal with delight and the chickens cackled wildly and staggered around. Walter, Lenore and Roselee thought this was the funniest thing they ever saw and always enjoyed the show.

Another thing that the Callison siblings' thought was hilarious was their mother's driving. It wasn't that she was a bad driver, but she did have some problems. One time when she came home from a grocery-shopping trip she was going to park the car in the garage. There was a slight incline into the garage and you had to gun the motor a little to make it into the building. Wanda gunned it just a little too much and she drove the car right through the front wall. She didn't hesitate a bit, but just drove the car around the circle and back into the garage door just as if nothing ever happened. Maybe she thought no one saw her and would never suspect what happened, but the children were watching.

The cattle from the Callison Ranch along the Fall River had to be driven to the railroad at Bartle. George Brown and Callison would drive their cattle the first night to the Whipple place. Whipple would add his cattle he wanted to sell to the herd and the three ranchers would head them towards their destination. The second night of the cattle drive they would camp at Bear Flat then the next day they would drive the cattle on to Bartle. At times the snow was so deep at Bartle that only the second story of the two-story hotel was visible. The horses had to break a trail for the cattle to get through the deep snow. The cattle would then be shipped to San Francisco to the feed yards and slaughter plants.

The 1930's seemed to be the hardest on the cattle industry. In 1933 the Callison's sold their steers out of the feed lot for $3.85 per hundred pounds. Poorer quality sold for as low as two cents a pound. The cattle drives had to be made on the appointed day for delivery or the rancher would not get paid. Rain, snow or blizzards the drive had to be made.

Marketing of livestock and produce from Big Valley and Fall River Valley was routed through Fall River, Montgomery Creek, Anderson and Red Bluff. Often times the cattle had to swim the rivers on their way to market. Several of the ranches in Fall River Valley were a stop for the herds being driven from Big Valley. The Albaugh and Knoch ranches were some of these stopping places. The cattle would be fed hay or pastured on these ranches and the cowboys were fed their meals and rolled their bedrolls out in the bunkhouse or barn. In payment for this service many times the cattlemen left behind a few head of cattle. This is the way some of the ranchers got a start in the cattle business. By 1903 the railroad was finished at Madeline and this was a much shorter drive for the cattle from Big Valley.

On November 10, 1931 the Golden Spike was driven at the railroad station in Nubieber joining the Great Northern and Western Pacific Railroads. This gave the ranchers of Big Valley a front door approach to far away markets.

The Cattlemen's Association was established to help control the grazing of huge bands of sheep that were trailed up from the Sacramento Valley. Sheepmen would start heading their sheep northward early in the spring, grazing and camping along the way. When they would reach the lush grasslands of Fall River and Big Valley they would spend the summer until it was time to herd them back South again to their winter feeding grounds.

Cattle production in the InterMountain area increased tremendously. In order to meet this threat of the Sheep invasion on their pastures a plan of leasing large tracts of land for cattle grazing came into use. Lumber companies mainly owned much of it being in high mountain meadows.

The Taylor Grazing Act, which preceded the U. S. Forest Service, came into effect in 1934 and began to control the grazing of the ranchers.

Merton Callison was one of the first Directors of the California Cattlemen's Association after it was established. He was director for nine years in that organization. He suggested that Albert Albaugh replace him when he resigned. In 1952, while the men were attending their meetings at the State Cattlemen's Convention the wives decided to organize their own organization, known as the Cow Belles. Elizabeth Albaugh and Wanda Callison were among the charter members of the InterMountain CowBelles and were instrumental in starting that organization. Wanda was honored at CowBelle of the Year in 1974.

Walter, Lenora and Roselee attended elementary school at Glenburn. They had to walk several miles to go to the one room schoolhouse. There were about fifteen students in the school, which were all eight grades. The children took turns doing the janitor work and

Merton Callison, Mable (Callison) Summers, Ferd Callison and Nellie (Callison) Flood

were paid $3.00 a month for the chore. Some of their teachers were Mr. House, Lydia Joiner, Miss Soderman, Miss Shields, Mrs. Gronwald and Zereda Jentzen.

After elementary school all three of the Callison children went to Fall River to High School. After graduation Walter went to a Sacramento business college for two years. In 1939 he went to work in the Bank of America in Alturas for a couple of years before returning to the family ranch at Fall River where he went into business with his Father.

Walter and Norma Bruce were married in 1944 in Reno, Nevada. They were secretly married for several months before they even told their parents. Norma stayed at home and helped her parent's, the Joe Bruce's, on their ranch and Walter was working with his folks. They finally started ranching on their own and bought a place where they raised their three sons, Robert, Richard and Russell and daughter Marilyn.

From the mid 1940s to 1972, Walter and Norma carried on the tradition, as the fourth generation, of Callison's to work the ranch on the banks of Fall River. During those years they made many changes and improvements to the property. They also built up the size of the cattle herd.

During their years on the ranch Norma helped to organize the InterMountain CowBelles and served as president for three and one-half years. Walter was on the first committee to start the InterMountain Cattlemen's Feeder Sale and was chairman of that sale for several years. Both of them worked hard to better the livestock industry. After thirty years of ranching, Walter and Norma sold their ranch and retired in 1973. They have also been members of the McArthur Grange for the past sixty years.

Lenora went to Sacramento Junior College and Chico State College to become a teacher. She taught at Mt. Shasta and McArthur then moved to San Jose. She married Frank Lang in 1952 who was a real estate developer and a manufacturing jeweler. He passed away in 1976. She retired in 1982 after thirty-five years of teaching Home Economics and lives at Windsor, Ca.

Roselee graduated at a time when there was a teacher's shortage and went immediately into a teaching position at Castella, California. She

Rosalee, Wanda, Merton, Walter, and Lenora in 1980 at F.M. Callison's 90th birthday

only taught one year then went to Sacramento Junior College. She married Bill Ross an Architect in 1944, and they have two children, Wayne and Linda. She and her husband still live in Santa Rosa where she has retired as a clerical worker for the school district.

Merton Callison was a valuable asset to his community of the Fall River Valley. As a rancher, teacher, Justice of the Peace and Historian. He wrote many articles about local history and lectured many places about the stories he remembered. One of his favorites was of when an elderly gentlemen came to town to visit. He checked in to the local hotel and he had never seen electric lights. The attendant at the hotel turned the strange thing on for him, but forgot to tell him how to turn it off. When the gentleman wanted to go to sleep it was glaring in his eyes. He blew on it but it would not go out. He put his sock over it, but soon the sock started to smoke and smolder. Finally he just grabbed the thing and tore it from the twisted wiring and threw it out the window. That settled that.

Merton died in 1986 at the age of 95. Wanda had passed away in 1985 at the age of 90. They had been married over 67 years.

Walter feels that he and Norma saw some of the best years for the livestock industry. Starting in with his father in 1942 then buying his own ranch kept them very busy. The ranches joined each other and made a sizable spread. He eventually was running around 300 cows and got into feeding around 400 yearlings.

They sold out when times were good and cattle were still a good price. He feels sorry for those in the cattle industry today. They have really a tough row to hoe. There is no profit in ranching anymore and the government regulations on the ranges and every other aspect is really hard on the cattle ranchers.

The sixth generation of the Callison family that immigrated to California by the Oregon Trail can be proud of their heritage and the fortitude of those hardy pioneers. They can be proud of their Great Grandfather that would not let a family starve and gave them back the deer meat.

Merton Callison, "the judge with a heart," will long be remembered.

June 4, 2000

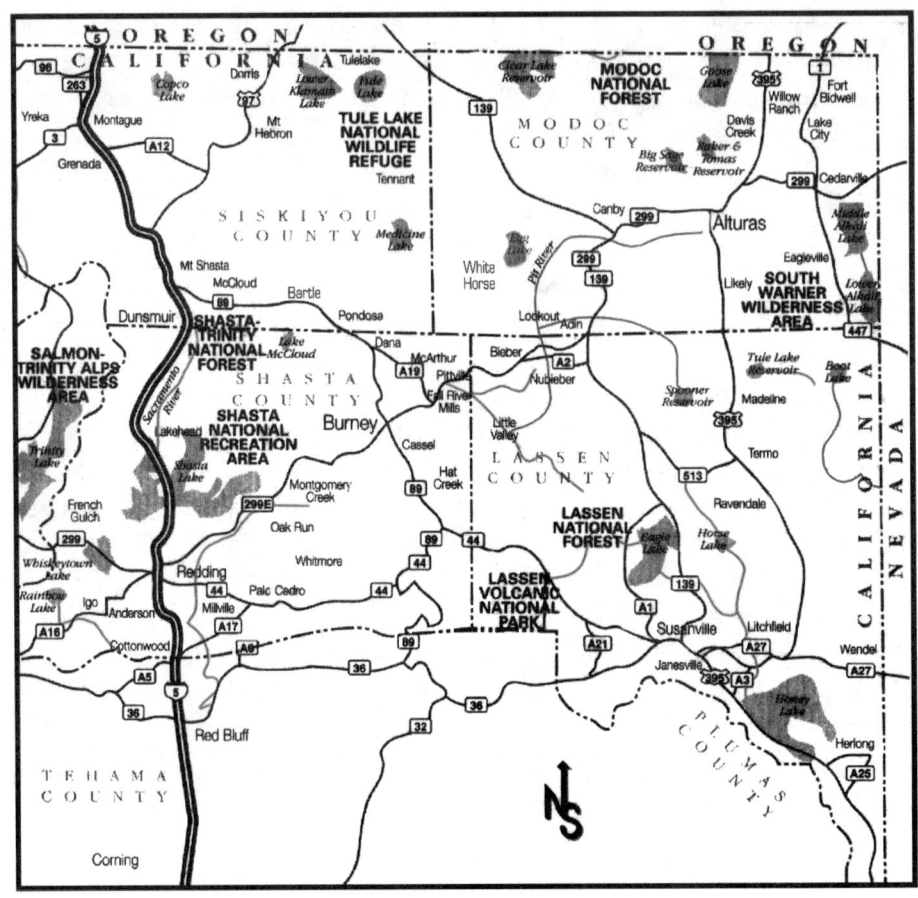

This map covers most of the area where these stories take place.

The Smell Of Sagebrush

As they say, a rolling stone gathers no moss, and this certainly is true of Boyd Moffitt of Yerington, Nevada.

Born in 1917 in California he has worked on ranches, cowboyed with the best of them and left a wide trail behind him. This salty character can tell the stories of the days gone by, but most of them are told in poems he has written about his life experiences. A book of his poetry, "Some Good, Some Bad and Some Indifferent", was published in 1995.

Boyd started writing poetry in 1958 and has a collection of 158 verses. He gave his daughter a collection of his writings and she had 73 of them published in his book. Each poem tells a story of ranches he worked on, people he met or a part of his life. Boyd's poetry intertwines with facts of his life to tell his story. He only has his poetry to remember his travels and the life he led as a young man. In 1936 someone pried open the trunk of his car and stole his entire collection of cowboy pictures, bridles, spurs and memorabilia.

In 1912, the team of horses that Perry Moffitt was driving ran away with him. Running blindly they ran over the bank throwing Perry out of the Surrey breaking his back. He was lucky to survive and was left a partial cripple the rest of his life. He and his wife Mayme were the parents of four children, Muriel, Daryl, Leland and Boyd. Another boy died when he was three years old.

In the small town of Hammonton, on Rag Hill near Marysville, California is where Boyd was born. His Dad worked on the gold dredges. The great depression hit the family hard in 1929. Perry was laid off along with hundreds of other men. The Moffitt's distant relatives and closest friends, the Joe Stevensons, lived in Big Valley near the small settlement of Lookout. Joe was sure Perry could find work in the hayfields on the local ranches.

Perry soon found work on the Louis Kramer ranch driving teams in the hay field. Even though he was handicapped it did not effect his skill with a team of horses. His sons were anxious to help carry their share of the load. Even though Boyd was only twelve years old he felt he could do the job of a man. Mr. Kramer let him drive the old horse, called Sleepy, to drag the hay nets out of the barn where they were stacking the loose hay. Boyd was proud of his work and his pay was that he could eat in the cookhouse with the rest of the men.

The Moffitt family was camping right out the front yard gate of the big Kramer ranch house. When the haying season was over Perry loaded his family up in their old car and went back to Marysville to the gold fields. The children had to go back to school. Perry and Mayme bought a small grocery store.

Hammonton was a small company town and when it was decided there might be gold under the town all of the houses were sold and moved away. The huge gold dredge's plowed right through the streets of the once thriving little village. All that was left were piles of gravel and tailings that the gold had been mined from.

MY DAD

'Twas on the second of January
In the year of 1957
The angels came to my father's place and carried him off to
Heaven.

He was the most gentle father
That a person ever had
And when they took him away up there
It made me feel so mighty sad.

Now my dad was a partial cripple
All due to a broken back
But I never knew him to complain
And I never knew him to slack.

He'd tackle any job there was
No matter if he was halt and lame
Ad all the hard work he accomplished
Would put an able man to shame.

He was the most upright honest fellow
That ever drew a breath
E was that way from the day he was born
And still that way at his death.

He never made a great name for himself
Such as Rockefeller, Astor or Ford
But if honesty and virtue were money
He would have swept them all overboard.

He was might good to us children
And my mother he treated like a queen
He very seldom said a harsh word to us
And he was never cruel or mean.

He would meet each day with a laugh and a smile
And be that way the whole day through
Somewhere up there in the Great Beyond
God is mighty proud of the dad that we knew.

I can never remember him spanking us
For I don't think spanking he did approve
But when he told us to do something and meant it
We figured pretty well it was our turn to move.

When god created my father
He looked at him with a joy to behold
He thought to himself, 'I can never do better,'
So right there and then He destroyed the mold.

Now if I could pattern my life after someone
I think nothing would be more fine
Than to pattern my life after him
That wonderful dad of mine.

Boyd Moffitt

Boyd Moffitt, July 4, 1938, taken at Cottonwood, California

When Boyd finished the eighth grade he could not wait to get back to Modoc County. He longed for the smell of sagebrush and he couldn't smell any sagebrush there. Going back north he again stayed with the Stevenson family until he found work. He was only 14 but an ambitious young man could find something to do. After arriving in Big Valley his first job was at the Cox & Clarke Ranch as chore boy.

Si Elliott who was a famous bronc rider was working there and breaking colts for the company. Boyd was a little guy and Si always called him "Button". Si would ride a colt a couple of times and call for Boyd to come ride him. "Hey Button, come get on this horse". "No Thank You", was Boyd's reply. "If you don't get on him on your own, I'll throw you on," were Si's exact words. Boyd had no choice but to get on and then is when he started his days as a cowboy under the careful guidance of one of the best.

There was always plenty of riding on the Cox and Clarke ranch as it was a big outfit. There were hundreds of cattle to work and lots of hay to put up. Even during haying time the cowboys had a special job. Young teams of horses were hitched to the mowing machines and rakes in the huge swamplands of grass. Cowboys were mounted at all times to catch the run-a-way teams, which dumped their drivers and were running wildly across the land. The machines were bouncing uncontrollably behind them, scaring the horses even more. It was quite a show and a pretty wild ride to get them stopped.

REMINISCING

I motored up to my old stomping grounds
In the northeast country of California state
In the county of Modoc
That to me still is great.

And as I rode around Big Valley
My mind started wandering back
To my youthful years of ranch life
And the days I spent in an old line-shack.

At fourteen I went to work as a chore boy
Up there on the old C.W.C.*
Fed some stock, milked a cow or two
Or whatever there happened to be.

At sixteen, I graduated to 'cowboy'
And was put out on the Pit River, the south branch
Out there in a cabin all alone
About ten miles from the ranch.

There were about 300 head of steers
That I had to overlook
And if I didn't want to go hungry
I had to learn to cook.

I ate a lot of burned or uncooked grub
Before I got it right
But before I got the hang of biscuits
I knew I had been in a fight.

Then you had to start from scratch
If you wanted anything to eat
Nothing came in packages, like today
That all you have to do is heat.

I stayed there for a year or so
And learned to ride a pretty good saddle
Then I got itchy feet and went
To where they had some wild- eyed cattle.

I had a couple of high ridin' cousins
That didn't have an ounce of fear
And we cut, ear-marked and branded the calves
Of those cows who could run like deer.

We would bring in unbroke horses
From out of the Indian Mountains
And some of those old nags
Sure got me to doubtin'.

Doubtin' whether I could ride these broncs
For they sure looked big and rough
But I sure was going to give it a try
'Cause I was young and tough.

Well, we gentled them up a little
Then we picked out what we would need
Some we turned back to the mountains
The old and crippled were sold for chicken feed.

Now, I'm going to tell you something
Something that is hard to believe
But I'm not telling you some 'windy'
And I ain't one to deceive.

We brought in a bunch of broncs one time
And put them in a corral we had there
Darned if there wasn't and antelope
That wouldn't leave a black mare.

I had always heard that an antelope wouldn't jump
But we found out that was a lie
For when we got after him with our ropes
Over that six-foot fence he did fly.

He got a running start at that fence
And over the top he did sail
It wasn't but a few seconds all we could see
Was the white flag of his tail.

But I guess everything has an ending
Old Uncle Sam saw to that
For he sent us each a letter of greeting
And told us not to scat.

So there my reminiscing ended
And no more did I let it roam
I mounted my four-wheel nag
And came on back to Nevada and home.

*{C.W. Clark Company}

Boyd Moffitt

Boyd and his cousin who was his best friend, Cheese (Melvin) Stevenson worked a lot of places together and were lifelong friends. There was always work on ranches doing something, but mainly in haying season there was a big demand for good teamsters. In 1936 Boyd was working on the Lawrence Weigand ranch, then he made his rounds of the Frank Studley, Joe Stevenson, Louis Kramer, Bill Kramer, Jim Thompson and Ed Albaugh ranches. When a job was finished at one place you just moved on to the next.

One of his jobs was for Ferd Chace. He was hired to milk twenty-five cows by hand morning and night. When he took the job he knew that Mr. Chace was a hard man to work for. Cheese bet him fifty cents that he would not last three weeks. Even though Mr. Chace had a large house with four empty bedrooms upstairs he would not let the hired man sleep in the house. He had to sleep in a loft above the milk barn. Boyd only had one thin blanket and the nights got colder. He found some barley sacks and covered his bed with those to keep warm.

Pay was $25.00 a month with room and board, (such as it was). Boyd was only to milk the cows and take care of them, but soon Chace started adding on other jobs such as picking the apples and pears. Boyd was getting unhappy but he was going to win that bet from Cheese. Mr. Chace returned from a hunting trip and told the young man he didn't see where he had done a thing while he was gone. Mr. Chace said he could get anyone for $15.00 a month and they would do twice the work that Boyd did. The young man told him he had better look for somebody and Boyd quit his job on the twenty-second day of his employment. He had won his fifty cents from Cheese, as he stayed one day longer than his three weeks.

In 1937 Boyd hired on as a buckaroo at the Bognuda ranch in Little Valley, California. There were wild times in Little Valley, with a rodeo almost every night with competition among the cowboys from that ranch and the Dixie Valley Ranch. Lil and Clover Bognuda became some of Boyd's best friends. Lil had been offered $500.00 to do an exhibition bronc ride at the Reno Rodeo. She had to decline, as she really had not been feeling too well. She soon was admitted to the TB Sanitarium to be healed from that disease. She recovered completely and soon was back in the saddle again.

THE LITTLE VALLEY RANCH

As I sit here alone tonight
My mind is never free
Of thought of that Little Valley Ranch
And what it meant to me.

It was there, along in the thirties,
Where Clover, Lil and I
Would ride our old cow ponies
To where the mountains meet the sky.

Now, they were daughters of the owner
While I was just a hand
Though you wouldn't know by looking
But what I was one of the clan.

I resembled Old Ned, they tell me,
From my head clear down to my toes
Short, bowlegged and stocky
And that ever prominent nose.

Old Ned was born in Switzerland
Along about 1883
Came to this country as a boy
To this good old land of the free.

He was a man of distinction
His name was one of renown
If a neighbor needed a helping hand
There Old Ned could be found.

We were all so happy together
There on the old NB
Until a greetings I got
Then it was the army for me.

After three long years I returned there
Thinking it would be the same
But I sure was fiddle-footed
And I took off again.

For several years I wandered around
Working at this or that
Be it a service station or a store
Or skinning a D4 "Cat".

I've traveled over the country
But nothing I ever did see
Could compare with Little valley
Back there at the old NB.

Now, as I sit here in this old arm chair
My mind, how it doth stray
To that ranch back in the mountains
Where I would love to return someday.

Boyd Moffitt

In 1941 he moved on to the Bill Kramer ranch at Lookout where he found his home away from home. He thought Mr. Kramer was the greatest man there ever was to work for. Six guys were working at the Kramer ranch and they all slept upstairs in the house. It was cold up there, but not nearly as cold as the hayloft in the Chace barn. Bill's son in law Cyril Mamath was also working on the ranch. The hay had been put up in loose stacks, as was all the hay in the Big Valley. In 1931 Cyril and Albert Joiner bought the first tractor and baler to ever be brought into the valley. This began to change the farming practices in the Big Valley.

THAT OLD RANCH HOUSE

I well remember the old ranch house
That stood there on the W.K.
It was built for a pretty big family
Which was normal for that golden day.

There was one bedroom on the bottom
And three on the upper deck
When things became icy
We'd triple up, by heck.

The big rock fireplace in the living room
Threw out a lot of heat
For a fire made from yellow pine wood
Was mighty hard to beat.

But after the fire went out
And the heat no longer came up the stairs
It got pretty darned cold
Even with lots of covers and "Long John" underwear.

The dining room was connected to the kitchen
And we spent most of our idle time in there
Playing cards and other games
While someone braided a rope made of hair.

Then there might be a leppy calf or bummer lamb
That we brought in from the icy chills
We took darned good care of them
For they helped to pay the bills.

The old wood range over by the wall
Used to fire my wrath
When I stooped over too far
While taking my Saturday night bath.

It may have been a Home Comfort
Or a Wedgwood, they both were pips
But when you stooped too far
You were branded across both hips.

It was the meeting place for all
No matter the time of day
It made no difference who or what you were
You had to eat before you went on you way.

But if you rode up with intentions to eat
And left your horse tied up outside
You better not let the boss catch you
Or he sure as Hell would have your hide.

First you take care of your horse
Before you sit down to eat
If he isn't taken care of
You may go out the door, but not on your feet.

Boyd Moffitt

It was 1944 and the war was on, Boyd knew he was going to be drafted so he joined the Army and was sent to Fort Ord for one year. He was then sent to Mt. Rainer for the ski troops to test ski equipment. The boots they had to wear were not sufficient and his toes were frostbitten. The frostbite was so severe that they discharged him, and he returned to Northern California. There was a job at the Corporation Ranch in Likely, Ca. where Charlie Demick was the foreman. Boyd went there and worked as a buckaroo out on the Madeline Plains riding herd on the cattle.

Another move found him at the Herlong Army Depot where he settled down for four years. In this country he could smell all the sagebrush he wanted. Eating in the cafeteria had its drawbacks and he got a bad case of ptomaine poisoning. He thought this was an omen to move on, again.

Another incident caused Boyd to lose the sight in his left eye. While feeding cattle he cut a baleing wire from the hay bale and it flew up and put his eye out.

It was time again to move on. and he headed out to see some new country and he landed in Bridgeport, Ca. Here he worked for the Hunewill Circle H Land and Livestock, which was a cow ranch and dude outfit. As a wrangler he took care of forty dudes. Meeting up with the cook Betty, their romance led to their marriage in 1948.

After their son Lance was born Boyd thought he had better move on to a job where there was more security and benefits than just that of a wandering cowboy.

In 1952 the couple moved to Yerington, Nevada where Boyd went to work at the Anaconda Copper Mine. This establishment employed around 500 men running three shifts a day. Boyd worked his way up to Foreman and was highly respected in that capacity. The ore was loaded onto railroad cars and sent to Butte, Montana for the final processing. Boyd worked in the Anaconda mine for 25 years until it closed in 1978.

Boyd and his first wife were divorced in 1956. He later married Bea and they had two more children Janice and Tom. His new wife was a schoolteacher and Boyd likes to joke that she thought she could teach him something, but she thought wrong. Bea died in 1998 just before their forty-second anniversary.

ROUND-UP TIME IN CLOVER VALLEY

Oh, I'd like to be in Clover valley
When they round-up in the fall
I'd like to see the horses running
And listen to the cattle bawl.

I'd like to hear the creak of my saddle
As I get astride in the early morn
And as my cayuse goes to buckin'
To reach wildly for the horn.

Just to hear the bit-chains tinkling
As he swings his head to and fro
Just to hear my bat-wings swishing
As out through the timber I go.

Just to hear an old cow bawling
With never a stop no a lull
Wondering if she' lost her calf
Or if she is looking for a bull.

I will help her if she's lost her calf
For no doubt he' out there all alone
But should it be a bull she's looking for
Well, then she is strictly on her own.

Just to watch my dog as he trots along
And of you, dear Lord, I beg
Don't let all the pine trees die

Upon which he has lifted his leg.

Just to hear my spurs a jinglin'
As they are bound there on my feet
I'll tell you boys, I'd be in heaven
'Cause, for me, this life can't be beat.

All this I had a few years ago
When I was a single buck
But now that I'm hitched and have some kids
I reckon with Anaconda I'm stuck.

But this job may not last forever
This job in this hot dusty mill
And if it should end before I do
I'll head right back over the hill.

Back there to those evergreen mountains
Back to where the waters run down from the snow
Unroll my "turkey" in the old bunk house
And from that range no more will go.

For that is sure the life, boys
For a feller such as I
To be out with the horses and cattle
Out where the mountains seem to meet the sky.

Boyd Moffitt

Blessed with his three children and eight grandchildren and lots of good friends Boyd feels like Yerington, Nevada is just the right place for him. His daily ritual of morning coffee with his cronies at the local donut shop, lunch with the Senior citizens and taking a ride on his bicycle keeps him active. He takes a weekly jaunt in his pickup to Smith Valley to see the sights and blow the carbon out of his vehicle. Boyd use to recite his poetry every once in a while at the Senior Citizens, in schools or wherever he was in demand. But now he and the guys just reminisce over their morning coffee and tell tales that are "Some Good, Some Bad and Some Indifferent."

RODEO DAZE

I started out making the shows
Several years ago
Figured I could make some dough
In some old rodeo.

I started in at ropin'
It seemed the simplest thing
I caught my calf and dogged him
But I had forgotten my piggin' string.

So of course the judge waved his flag
I knew that it meant no time"
And when that show had ended
I hadn't made a dime.

I then tried the saddle broncs
I'll tell you boys, they were rough
And after my falls didn't get any easier
I knew it was too damned tough.

They told me that to win any money
An eleven-second ride was a must
But I didn't win any money in that
Cause I watched the last few seconds from the dust.

I then tried my hand at bull-dogging
But I was such a little cuss,
The steer would take me right along with him
And not raise any fuss.

But one time I did get one down
(I guess he must have fell)
But he quickly threw me off
And left like a bat out of hell.

So I soon quit the rodeos
God, how my folks did laugh
When I went back to my gentle cow horse
And roping the milk cow's calf.

But let them laugh as they want to
For that rough stock brought too much pain
And I'll leave it to those who like it
And never go rodeoin' again.

Boyd Moffitt

July 11, 2000

"A Family Affair"

Floriano Roberti was born in Switzerland in 1865 and came to the United States when he was fourteen years old. He found a job working as a milker for another Swiss family that lived at Loyalton, California. He had known Martina Guidici in Giornico, Ticino, Switzerland before he immigrated to the United States. Martina later came to America to marry Alex Guidici, but he decided he wanted to marry her blonde sister, Sophia instead.

Martina later married Floriano Roberti in 1889. As many of the Swiss families did, they settled in the Sierra Valley near Loyalton.

Floriano was a hard worker and saved his money so he could buy a ranch in Sierra Valley. The Roberti's had seven children, Alfred was born in 1890, then Flori, Lizzie, Paul, Celestina, Joseph and Rena.

The children drove a buggy to attend the Island School then later the Fox Springs School. One day at Fox Springs during a thunder and lightning storm a bolt of lightning hit the flagpole on top of the schoolhouse. It traveled down the flagpole and a ball of fire came in the back door of the school, rolled right down the center isle of the schoolroom and went out the front door. The wide-eyed children watched it in amazement.

The one-room schools were every few miles throughout the valley. When they ran out of students in an area they just pulled the school to another location with teams of horses.

Times were hard and Floriano and Martina lost their farm in Sierra Valley. They moved to Reno in the Hunter Creek area for a time where they owned a dairy. To make a living they sold milk from their cart, delivering from door to door. Both of these pioneers were very hard workers and lived through some rough times. Floriano lived to be 90 years old.

During World War I Floriano wanted to keep his boys out of the war, so he started buying ranches through out the valley to be able to keep them home. If sons were needed to work on farms and ranches they did not have to go to war.

There were nine families in the Sierra Valley from Switzerland. When the Guidici, Ramelli, Dotta and Roberti families all got together for a picnic there were enough to have two complete baseball teams. Each family had seven children.

In January 1920 Alfred, Floriano and Martina's oldest son, married Josephine (Josie) Dotta. (Alfred went to school to the fifth grade and Josie finished the eighth grade.)

Josie was the daughter of Lodovico Dotta who came from Airollo, Ticino, Switzerland. Her mother Claudina (Ponci) came to America from Lugano, Ticino, Switzerland when a family from Sierra Valley paid her way.

There was a large hotel in Vinton where Claudina worked. She cooked, waited on tables, cleaned and made beds. In the evenings she was paid to dance with the men. She hated her job and would do anything to get away from the hotel.

One night Mr. Dotta came in for a meal. While she was waiting on his table he slipped her a note asking her to come to his ranch, not just as a cook, but as his wife. She put the note into her apron pocket and later that evening she read it. Mr. Dotta was thirty-five years older than she was, but he was a very highly thought of gentleman in the community.

He had quite a large dairy employing several milkers, but he did not have a cook for them. Claudina wanted out of the hotel so bad she would do anything. This did not seem to be too bad of an offer. Anything was better than the job she had. Mr. Dotta was such a nice man that she could not refuse him. In 1898 they were married. They had seven children, Josephine (Josie), Renoldo, Anita, Vic, Eva, Frank and Thelma.

For a time Alfred was the owner of the General Mercantile Store in Vinton. He was too trusting of his customers and had too many accounts on the books. It was hard to say no to people when they needed credit, so it was just easier to sell out.

Josie and Alfred had two children, Elia born in 1920 and Elmer born in 1925. Both went to the Island School like their father did. They both started milking cows when they were five years old. When they were very small and Josie had to do the milking she would put a blanket in the middle of an old tire and set the babies in that so they could not crawl around and get under the cow's feet and get hurt.

Both of the Roberti children grew up knowing only hard work. The family milked quite a few cows to make their living and everyone had to help. Elmer laughs and said when he got out of the eighth grade he got a milk bucket and milk stool. From then on it was the school of hard work and ranching. Neither Elmer nor Elia were allowed to go on to high school.

Elmer and Elia did most of the milking of the 50 cows by hand. In 1944 they bought their first milking machine. They sold milk to

Josephine Roberti, 1940

neighbors and separated the rest sending the cream on the train to Tomales Bay Creamery in San Francisco. Without refrigeration the cream would sour with the lids boiling over, but still the creamery was able to make butter out of it. Later they were classified as a Grade A Dairy. They sold whole milk in Quincy and all over the valley to local neighbors who would bring their own containers. Before that they sold milk to Crystal and Crescent Creameries in Reno, Nevada and Feather River Dairy in Quincy.

Josie hired cooks to help with the cooking for the hay crews. At that time she fed the men three huge meals a day and they bunked on the ranch. One of the cooks that she hired was a girl named Helen Wily from the Loyalton.

Helen's family had come from Fallon, Nevada after they lost their place during the depression. Her father's first wife had died leaving him with three small children. He later remarried and had three more daughters of which Helen was the youngest.

Helen only worked at the Roberti ranch for two weeks. Josie fired her so she went back to the Loyalton Hospital where she was working for eighty cents and hour for a Red Cross program. That was long enough for Elmer to decide this was the girl he was going to marry. After high school Helen went to pre-nurses training for one year at Santa Rosa Jr. College.

In 1941 Elia married Bruce Miles, a farmer. He was the first man to bring a tractor to Sierra Valley to mow hay. They had three children, John, Virginia and Pamela. Bruce passed away in 1986. Elia still lives on her ranch near Loyalton.

By 1950 Elmer decided to go into the cow business. The family had a few Hereford stock cows, but he wanted to expand. He bought thirty-two bred Registered Angus cows and a bull from F.E. Bush at Cedarville, California. He paid $500.00 per head for the cows, which was a pretty good price for that time.

Times were still not easy. The winter of 1951-52 was known as the "big winter." The snow was so deep that they did not get out of the valley for six weeks. There was five foot of snow on the level and the fences were completely covered. There were drifts much higher than that. Elmer was feeding 150 cows around the barn and they kept the snow tramped down. He could not get to the purebred cows that were close to the county road. There was three days of constant blizzard and you could hardly see to the barn. The electricity was off for six weeks.

Elmer finally got his caterpillar started and was able to travel on top of the snow. He drove it out to the cows and they followed the cat tracks back to the barn where they could be fed.

When Elmer and Helen got married in 1954 she was nineteen and he was twenty-nine years old. She started right in helping to milk the sixty-five cows. They had mainly milking shorthorn as the Jersey and Holsteins could not stand the cold winters at the 5000-foot elevation.

Helen and Elmer had three sons, Jim in 1956, Rick in 1958 and Dave in 1960.

People use to visit and have potlucks and good times as a community. Grange was very important and there would be at least one hundred people at each monthly meeting. When television came to the valley the show "Bonanza" was on Wednesday nights, the same as Grange. The

Alfred Roberti, first Sierra Valley rancher to aerial spray sagebrush, 1957

Grange could not compete with such excitement. Soon the membership started to dwindle until now there are just a few that attends.

Alfred was proud that he was the first to use airplanes to spray sagebrush to kill and control it to enable them to plant more productive crops.

Alfred died in 1957 at the age of 68 years, leaving Josie, Elmer and Helen to run the ranch. Josie still did the cooking for the hay crew and the hired help. All of the family ate their noon meal at her house, which always delighted the three young Roberti boys. They liked haying time with all the young men that spent time there and all the good food.

Josie lived on the ranch right up to the day of her death in 1989 at the age of 90. She did the work as long as she could and did not shirk her duty.

When Josie became unable to cook for the family and crew the job fell into the able hands of Helen. Still to this day there is a sign in her kitchen that says "FREE LUNCH". This is the time the men all get together and discuss the working of the ranch and the day's activities. Each one has their own job, but still discuss with each other their plans and what is going on. This is probably what holds the family and the ranch together. As Rick says, "Mom is the glue that holds things together by having us all to lunch every day". Not only are the family there, but the hired men during the haying season. It is not unusual to have nine or ten for lunch. Others drop in at that time as they know that is when they can catch the men to discuss business.

Helen's kitchen is also where she keeps things going. The telephone calls from hay buyers or other business matters keeps her jumping. She can radio to any of the men on the ranch to help with any situation that is at hand.

When Alfred died the ranch consisted of 1440 acres. Floriano had lost the home ranch during hard times in 1920, but Josie had bought it back

During the depression all of the farmers were getting kicked off of their ranches. They could not pay the 8% to 10% interest the government was charging.

Josie wrote a letter to President Franklin D. Roosevelt and told him that she couldn't make it on the ranch and explained how the government was foreclosing on all of the ranches in the area. She had a registered letter from the Federal Land Bank at the post office in Loyalton, but she would not go pick it up. Finally the Federal Land

Bank sent someone out to the ranch to ask her why she refused to accept the letter. She knew what it was and wanted nothing to do with it.

Two days later the Federal Land Bank in Susanville received notice that President Roosevelt had put a moratorium on the foreclosing of the ranches and it was to stop immediately. Josie always thought that her letter was responsible for this action. She was a scrapper and liked to keep everyone in line. She even liked to go to the bank and hoped that they had made a mistake so she could argue with them

Elmer and Helen's sons wanted to stay on the ranch, and they had to expand to accommodate them. The Roberti's started buying neighboring ranches and farms that were selling out and now the total acreage is 5040. In 1962 they purchased the Marvin Humphrey ranch, in 1972 they bought the Ede place, in 1983 the Wiley place and in 1991 the Gabrielsons. None of these places had homes on them; so after the boys were married they all had to build houses on the home ranch near their parents.

The dairy herd was phased out and the ranch now runs 450 mother cows, which are mainly Angus. Rick went to Artificial Insemination school and started improving the herd. He did some crossbreeding with the Gelbvieh, a breed of cattle from Germany.

At the beginning when Elmer bought his first purebred cows they began crossing with some Hereford. Rick did not like black cows because he could not tell one from the other when he was little. He was so excited when they had a white faced bull calf born. He wanted his dad to keep it for a bull. Elmer convinced him that they could not do that, as he would sire purple calves. Little Rick believed his father and never ask again. Now it is a family joke.

The ranch presently consists of 1700 acres alfalfa and 700 acres of irrigated meadow. The rest is pasture for their cattle. They sell 4000 to 5000 ton of hay each year. Selling mainly dairy quality alfalfa hay, but they will sell to anyone that needs it. Horse, cow, sheep, rabbit and goat ranchers are all treated the same. Large or small, the Roberti's are there to satisfy their customers.

Dave and Jim run the hay operation and the sprinkler irrigation. Six pivots are on the ranch and the largest one irrigates two hundred acres. These two brothers also do all the mechanical work keeping all the equipment running. Jim is the partner that takes care of all the spraying of crops and weeds. He is the one that thought the big baler to make the ton bales was a good investment. He was right; it is just the thing for the hay that is sold to the dairies. Rick is the pump and windmill man.

The water for the ranch comes from Frenchman Reservoir and large wells. The Roberti ranch does have a Forest Service permit on the Plumas Forest but it has been cut drastically from what it was in years past. It is only from June 15 to September 15 and they have to haul the cattle twenty-five miles to utilize this permit.

The dairy hay is a baled in one ton bale and three twine bales are also baled for the smaller customers.

The cows with Fall calves on them go to Marysville, Ca. to spend the winter months on pasture. The Spring calving cows are kept at home and calved out there in January and February.

It takes two and a half tons of hay to feed one cow through the long winter months in Sierra Valley.

The Roberti's sent their feeder cattle to the Harris Ranch for twelve years. Now they are sold to local buyers. At times they have tried the video sale.

The Roberti ranch is unique in that all of the family still works together. Each son has his own job, and they do it well

Rick and Elmer run the cattle operation. After Rick started to Artificial Inseminate he began to upgrade the herd quite a bit. At one time they took a bull to Reno where he sold on the stage at the Nugget Bull Sale. They were selling a few bulls to local people and using some themselves. The herd of purebred Angus was now built up to around two hundred cows. They were producing more and more good bulls.

Rick had a hard time pricing the bulls to his friends and neighbors. He was embarrassed to ask what he thought they were worth. The idea of a bull sale at the ranch became reality in 1994. At the first sale they offered about thirty-five bulls at a silent auction. They did the silent auction for three years, but with more bulls, the paper work was mounding.

People would wait and not bid until the last minute on the bull they wanted. When it was time to close the bidding they were still writing their names on the bidding boards. At that time bulls were just run in the barnyard pens for viewing.

By 1997 around ninety black bulls were ready for the sale. It was decided to put up a tent, add more pens and hire an auctioneer. That job was put in the capable hands of Bill Lefty. The sale consists of one-third Gelbvieh-Angus cross and two-thirds purebred Angus. In 1999 the eighteen-month-old bulls averaged $1,900 and the yearling bulls averaged $1,600.

The Roberti family "outstanding in their field." Dave, Jane, Rick, Carolyn, Helen, Elmer, Rose, Jim. Front: Katy, Weston, Jenny and Ben

Other than the auctioneer the sale is completely run by the family and their hired man Doug Morris. Doug has been a steady hand on the ranch for eight years and he is so reliable and faithful that they think of him as one of the family.

By not hiring a lot of extra people they do not have as much invested and can sell their bulls a little cheaper to the cattleman. Last year they had sixty registered buyers and one hundred and twenty-five were served lunch.

Rick thinks that if you hire a sale manager you lose control. Honest and dependability is what the Roberti's are known for and that is the way they want to keep it. They do not run the price of their bulls up.

Satisfaction is guaranteed with the Roberti bulls for one year of breeding. If the buyer is not happy with the bull he will be replaced within that year.

Their ringmen are the representatives from the Angus Journal, California Cattlemen Magazine, Western Livestock Journal and the Cowman Magazine. Rick's wife Carolyn and Dave's wife Jane are the clerks.

The quality of these cattle has proven themselves several times. For ten years the Roberti heifers have been sold at the Red Bluff Heifer sale. They have had champions several years and always place in the top sellers. One year they won every class that they entered. They usually sell open heifers but a couple times they have sold bred heifers.

Many of the people come to the Roberti Bull Sale for a social outing and a good barbecue lunch. Helen cooks for days preparing the food for the event. The daughter-in-laws help her and again it is a family affair. Helen and Elmer like to invite old friends just to come visit and eat even if they have no use for a bull at all.

Rick and his wife Carolyn have two children, Weston and Katie. Carolyn takes care of all the cattle registrations. Carolyn was raised in Garden Grove, California. She had moved to the Lucky Hereford Ranch in Loyalton before she met Rick.

Dave and his wife Jane take care of all the bookkeeping and pay all the bills. Dave met Jane at a Young Farmers and Ranchers Farm Bureau meeting. She was raised at Sonoma, California.

Jim and his wife Rose have two children, Jenny and Ben. Rose was raised on a farm in Wisconsin along with her ten brothers and sisters. Jim and Rose were Pen Pals through their church.

The daughter-in-laws cook for the men on Mondays so Helen can take some time for her other obligations. Helen has been the Secretary of the local Farm Bureau for thirty-nine years.

Rick is enthusiastic about the AI program that he has implemented on the cattle herd. He watches the EPD's (Expected Progeny Difference), for low birth weight and high gaining cattle. Several of the bulls he uses go back to Traveler, an exceptional foundation bull in the Angus breeding.

The ranch has sent 41 steers to the Harris Feedlot for a test trial and carcass evaluation. This is the only way they can compare and evaluate the carcass and to get proven records on their cattle. Rick thinks that soon ultrasound will take over in testing the rib eye and quality of the animals. With that, another aspect of higher technology will be a part of the livestock industry.

Last winter Elmer got mauled by a cow which slowed him up quite a bit. Lying around was not for him. He was so anxious to get back to irrigating that he could hardly stand it. He can't even imagine such a thing as retirement. Like Alfred and Josie he will work on the ranch until he can no longer pull his boots on in the morning.

The Roberti Ranch is looking forward to their sixth annual bull sale on September 9, 2000. The sale is held right on the ranch eight miles north of Loyalton in the beautiful Sierra Valley. The sale in September will be held in the new sale barn they built this year. The barn will house the equipment in the winter after the sale is over.

Ninety bulls will be sold of which sixty are Black Angus that are sired by the breed greats such as N Bar Emulation EXT, Sitz Traveler 8180, Rito Max and their Senior Herdsire, BCC Westwind Twister. Twenty-five composite bulls, which are mostly Black Angus and Gelbvieh will go on the auction block also.

A few select females will also be offered. Of this group there will be open and bred females with some registered and the rest from the commercial herd.

These bulls are raised at a 5000-foot elevation and not pampered nor halter broken. What is for sale is honest to goodness well-conditioned bulls that are ready to go to work.

The fifth generation of the Roberti family are now showing their 4-H steers at the local fair and helping with chores on the ranch. A legacy that goes on and one that they are all proud of is their ranch and family association.

If hard work makes people happy then the Roberti family must indeed be a happy bunch.

August 13, 2000

The Rancher And The School Marm

Henry and Anna Anklin were ranching near Cottonwood, California at the turn of the century where they were raising their four boys Richard, Albert, Bill and Raymond. In 1906 when Ray was only three years old their father died. He had been out riding for cattle and got his foot hung up in the stirrup; the horse drug him for some distance. He was left an invalid and died within the year from complications of this accident. Richard was only ten, but this left him the man of the house. At that time many young boys were out earning their own way in the world at that age but not running ranches on their own.

The young ranchers ran the outfit as their father had for a few years then started making changes.

The boys thought maybe it would be a good idea if they went into the sheep business. They purchased 1000 head of sheep in Cottonwood from Mr. Hendrix. They herded them over 100 miles through the lava beds near the Geissner ranch at Hat Creek, taking them to summer range at Hayden Hill in Lassen County. They were anxious to get their sheep to the pasture first as there were many bands being moved to the high country for the summer time. They walked all the way from Cottonwood with their band of sheep, which was only a half a day ahead of the band behind them. There were six more bands coming up the trail and the first ones there got the best feed. You had to keep on the move so as not to mix the sheep and if you stopped the others would pass you by. The Anklin boys were young and ambitious and were not going to let another band pass them. It took a week to make the drive with the sheep.Ray was only ten years old and they were camping out with the sheep, the four boys spread their sleeping bags out to surround the flock at night. Ray was asleep in his sleeping bag with his dog on the foot of it. All of a sudden there was quite a ruckus and a coyote attacked the dog right there on Ray's bed. It nearly scared the young shepherd half to death.

That Fall when it was time to move the sheep home it was already snowing in the high country. They brought the sheep down past the Parks ranch at Willow Creek and when they were strung out Ray was trying to count them. He would put a rock from one pocket to another each time he counted one hundred head. He came up a hundred head short, but decided he couldn't have missed that many. The snow was getting deep and they knew they had better get moving. They headed back to the lower country again walking their sheep all the way. When they got back to Cottonwood, they did find they were missing one hundred head and they had to go back to Hayden Hill where they found the missing sheep. One more time the boys walked the many miles back to Cottonwood.

This was before the days of the Forest Service controlling the range and Hayden Hill was wide-open grazing land. The Homestead Act was in force at that time, but later the Taylor Grazing Act was implemented to do away with that. The Taylor Grazing was later taken over by the Bureau Of Land Management.

The boys decided they needed to move north with their cattle and soon started looking for a place. First they summered their cattle at Montgomery Creek, but the bears and cougars scared the boys and killed the cattle. In 1914 when Ray was eleven, he and another boy were left at cow camp to tend to the cattle for the summer. One night a cougar was on top of their tent where he had dragged the last of a deer he was having for his nighttime meal.

When the Anklin boys drove their 300 head of cattle up to Montgomery Creek in the spring they had to swim them across the Pit River. First they swam the cattle, then unsaddled their horses and put the saddles and gear in a rowboat and swam the horses across. The river was about 100 yards wide near where it drained into the Sacramento River.

The boys had made a few trips to Bieber in Big Valley with their old Model A Ford and decided that was good cattle country. That Fall the young boys rented a ranch near Pumpkin Center in Big Valley from Tony Avila and moved the cattle up there.

Anna Anklin came to Big Valley with her sons some times, but she preferred to stay in the lower country where later she remarried. From then on the boys were completely on their own

Richard decided to rent the Avila place for five years where they cared for their cattle and put up the hay. They did not stay in the sheep business very long, as they had all the work they could handle with the cattle, haying and feeding the cattle in the winter.

By this time the Anklin brothers decided they should buy a ranch. They found one further north at Rattlesnake Butte near Canby and drove the cattle there. These four young boys were hard workers and were good businessmen. Their cattle were mixed breeds, just whatever they could buy. Their saddle horses were not too fancy, but they got the job done.

The boys bought the Kelley ranch that Frank McArthur had owned. They paid $2.50 an acre for the 1500-acre ranch. When the title was cleared at the courthouse the boys were surprised that at one time their Grandfather had owned the same ranch.

In 1910 the Modoc County ranchers started to construct the dam for the Big Sage Reservoir in Devils Garden. With horses, mules and Fresno Scrapers to drag the dirt many men worked for twelve years to finish it in 1922. The Fresno Scrapers would bounce around on the rocks so bad that it would almost beat a man to death to work them very long. With muscle, sweat and determination the job was completed and the reservoir is in use today. As Ray said, "those men had a job to do and they did it. They did not just sit around and do a lot of paper work and never do any work like they do today." The Big Sage holds 77,000-acre feet of water and is thirty-five feet deep and thirty-five miles around it.

A lot of the ranchers went broke as the taxes were raised because of the reservoir. They couldn't pay their taxes, but some kept refinancing until they finally made it.

When the Anklin boys came to Modoc County in 1919 there was a lot of grass for the cattle to feed on. There were just a few Juniper trees around, but soon they started to sprout up along the fence lines. The Junipers that are seen today standing in a row along the fences are the result of birds eating the berries and as they sat on the fence rails they deposited the seeds. The Junipers began to invade the hills and valleys and now are a large problem to the stockman. They take all the water and no grass can grow near them.

Ray decided to let his brothers run the ranch and he went out and found another job. He went to work for Vincent Caldwell for awhile on his ranch, then he went to work at the Ballard sawmill for $3.00 a day with room and board. When Ray was seventeen he was offered a job at the Potter Ranch in Blacks Canyon for $60.00 a month, which was about the same money, he was more of a farmer boy than a lumberman, so he took the job. This is the same ranch that was once owned by the famed

Miller & Lux, then in 1936 it was sold to Mr. Bacon.

Tom Ivory was the ranch boss and his brother John Ivory was the cow boss. Ray worked the cattle with John and they ran the cattle twenty miles from the ranch at Horse Camp. Potter ran 1000 head of cattle and he rented the Witcher place, Edgar Pope's and pasture at Stone Coal Valley.

Tom and Lil Ivory were raising their nephew Buster Ivory. Ray enjoyed caring for the youngster when the Ivory's had to be gone. He enjoyed Buster riding with him and having a good time together.

The cowboys worked seven days a week, but if they needed a day off, they could take it. There was no set payday; you just drew money when you needed it. There was no place to spend it anyhow.

Dorothy (Dean) Anklin, two years-old

Everywhere you went you had to go horseback. They would drive cattle to Alturas, to ship them on the railroad then they spent the night. They paid thirty-five cents for a meal, four-bits for a bed and four-bits to feed their horse. The next day they rode back to the ranch. At that time the Sheriff did the brand inspecting.

One time Ray was sent to the Spaulding ranch to check on the cattle. It was snowing hard and he got lost. He kept riding and when he ran into his own horse tracks in the snow he knew he was in trouble. He knew he was going to have to find a place to spend the night. He changed directions and luckily he ran into a fence, he followed that until he came to the Bill Bitz place. There was a barn and hay for his horse and the house. It was the law of the land if you were lost or needed to spend the night you were welcome to make yourself at home. Making a pot of coffee and finding some food was very welcome to the lost cowboy. You just left things as you found them and move on at daylight.

Another time John Ivory and Ray took off with a bunch of cattle to Boles Meadows. It was 20 degrees below zero. Again they were lost, but Ray had a little compass and they got the cattle turned in the right direction. At 40 degrees below zero they were driving cattle to the Cal Pines ranch where there was hay to feed them. It didn't matter the weather or how cold it was, if the cattle had to be moved the job had to be done. In those days, the cattle had to be driven to the feed, as the hay could not be hauled to the cattle as it is today.

When Ray first came to Canby it was just a spot in the road. There was a blacksmith shop with a gas pump, Stewart's general store, the post office and the big house that had served as a stage stop. There were a lot of small ranches in the area with fences everywhere.

There was always excitement with a dance close by every Saturday night. There were several dance halls and taverns in the area where the "Happy 5" dance band played.

In 1929 Tom and Clara Chambers ran the hot springs where they had a beautiful home with rooms to rent, bathhouses, a confectionery store and a nice dance hall. One night when they were going to have a dance someone decided to make some extra coffee early in the day. They put it in a five-gallon milk can and set it in the hot spring to keep it hot. When it was time to get the can out Richard Anklin was helping. He slipped on the slippery board and fell into the scalding water up to his waist. The other men pulled him out instantly, but the damage was already done. He died within a few days from the burns, leaving his wife and four little girls.

On August 23, 1929 three days before school started the stage brought the new schoolteacher to town. Dorothy Dean was only nineteen years old and had been on the stage all day from Redding. Fresh from the Sacramento Valley she thought she was in the Wild West. Mr. Stewart, the clerk of the school board had promised to get her a place to stay but he had forgotten. There was no hotel or boarding house for her to stay in.

It was just six o'clock and suppertime. Dorothy was scared to death, tired and hungry, but when she found out that Mr. Stewart had forgotten to find her a place she was also angry. He took her over to the home of Annie Hughes who sometimes rented out rooms. Mrs. Hughes told her she could stay a week, but she had better find a place after that. Dorothy won their hearts and her stay was for two years, the entire time that she taught at the one room Arlington school.

Canby School 1929-30. Back: Gordon Caldwell, Charlie Hughes, Bud Caldwell.
2nd from Back L-R: Amelia Hughes, Jane Caldwell, Lodena Torreson, Loretta White.
3rd from Back L-R: Kathy Caldwell, Buster Ivory, Ross White, Nelda Sherer;
Front: Tiny Torreson and unknown

Never having to deal with outdoor plumbing, coal oil lamps, building fires in wood stoves and packing water, the new little schoolmarm had a lot to learn. She had only seen a one room school house one time before when she had gone to a Halloween party near Red Bluff. This was different. Her first day of school would be in a couple of days with twenty-one students and she had no materials and no program. It was her first job and she would just have to wing it.

Dorothy was lucky to even find a job, as there were ten teachers for every teaching job in the state. Because her roommate's aunt was on the school board in Modoc County, Dorothy was offered the teaching position at Eagleville. The teacher there had decided to quit her job and take a teaching job in Reno. She didn't get the job in Reno so she decided she wanted the Eagleville teaching position back. That left Dorothy without a school. The job at Canby was open and they had eight teachers before who had quit. It was a pretty tough school with a bad reputation. At $1,400 for the year it was the highest paying position in the county. The teacher also had to be the janitor, haul the wood, be fire builder, and haul the drinking water in a bucket from the outside pump.

The school did have a good library. When you went in the back door the library was on one side and the cloakroom on the other. The children left their lunches in the cloakroom until cold weather set in, then they would freeze before lunchtime. The Caldwell children always brought their dog to school and they would even pack a lunch for him.

Being a young teacher Dorothy had a lot of pranks played on her. One of her top pranksters was young Buster Ivory. He was only in the first grade, but he had a few tricks up his sleeve. Miss Dean always started class by reaching in her drawer and grabbing her ruler and she slapped it on the desk.

One sunny afternoon as Buster was riding his horse home from school he saw a lazy old Gopher Snake basking in the sun. He caught the snake and took it back to school where he put it in the teacher's desk drawer. The next morning when she reached in for the ruler and grabbed the snake she screamed and reared backward in her chair tipping it over with her feet in the air. She knew in an instant that it was Buster that played the prank.

Later in her teaching career a young boy pulled a knife on her. She hit him over the head with the book she had in her hand and certainly got his attention. She never had a bit of trouble with that student again.

Dorothy was born in Sacramento, California on December 6, 1909. Her mother died shortly after her birth. She and her father lived with her Grandparents until he remarried several years later. After high school graduation Dorothy moved to Chico where she went to teachers college for three years. She was in the last class that could graduate with only three years of college.

Dorothy had lived a very protected life and her family just could not stand for her to move to the Wild West. School went along fine and she enjoyed her students. The small town of Canby was very friendly and the young men all wanted to meet the new schoolteacher. One of the young men that came calling was Ray Anklin. One night he just happened by to visit the Hughes family.

They started seeing each other and it must have been somewhat serious because Dorothy bought a wedding dress at Helm's Department Store in Alturas and carefully laid it away in her hope chest.

Ray and Dorothy Anklin, June 18, 1932, Sacramento, California

Back: Lois, Dorothy, Ray. Front: John, Pinky and Eleanor

Miss Dean taught at the Canby school for two years then her family talked her into coming back to Sacramento to teach. It was difficult for a teacher to stay too long at a one-room school as she had the same students year after year. When she went to Sacramento she taught the fifth grade one year then a split second and third grades at the Hagenwood School. In that class she had fifty-two students without any help.

After teaching two years in Sacramento Ray proposed. The young couple were married at her Grandmothers house in Sacramento, June 18, 1932.

Ray had leased a place in Canby and moved his bride to his ranch. It was isolated out in the country and she did not drive a car. It was very lonely for her, especially when her husband was gone a lot riding for cattle. At one time she rode for cattle with Ray. He told her, "she rode like a sack of potatoes." He should have bitten his tongue, because she told him "I will take care of the house and the children and you can do your own work and that is that".

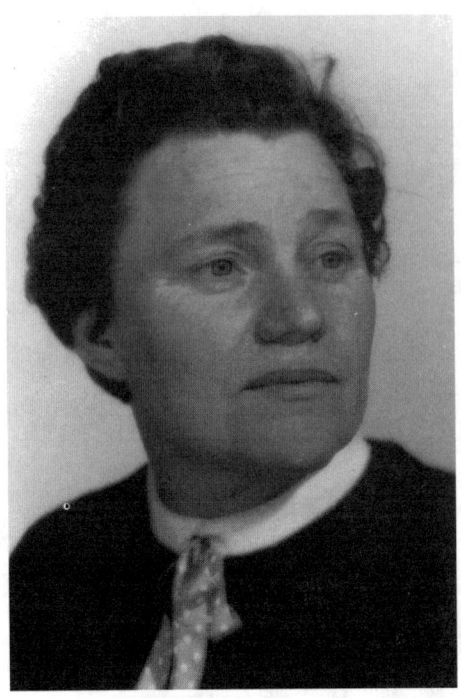

Dorothy Anklin,
Modoc County school teacher

Dorothy did try to help out one more time while driving a derrick to stack hay. As she said, "I was to pull something up, then pull something down when the men hollered. I did the wrong thing at the wrong time because I couldn't tell what they were hollering. And they just up and fired me." That was just fine with her.

Ray and Dorothy both filed on homesteads. It cost $60.00 to file and they had to live on it three years for seven months out of the year. You had five years to prove up on the land. Each of them filed on 640 acres and Ray would sleep on the homestead at night to fill the obligations, while working the other ranch during the day. After the Taylor Grazing Act was implemented that ended the Homestead Act.

In 1934 Ray and Dorothy bought the Hughes ranch in Canby and moved to the two-story house in town on St. Patrick's Day. It was the worst blizzard of the year. The Anklin's ran the ranch and raised their children there. Lois was born in 1936, Eleanor in 1939, John in 1941 and Richard (Pinky) in 1942. When the youngest boy was born, his hair was just as pink as could be. He acquired the nickname and has carried it his entire life.

Dorothy went back to teaching in 1946 at Alturas where she taught mostly third grade until she retired in 1973.

The Anklin's had sold their ranch in Canby in 1967 and moved to a smaller house near by. Ray still kept active and liked to play cards at the Canby Hotel to pass the time.

Ray told of the good years of deer hunting in Modoc County. There use to be a lot of big bucks and not so many hunters. The roads were not that good and hunters had to walk to find the deer not drive their vehicles

Dorothy and Ray's 50th Anniversary, 1982

all over the woods. The mountain lions have taken their toll on the deer population and very few big bucks are seen today.

Many Indians worked for Ray in the hay fields and they were good people. One of the Indians had a problem of drinking too much when he got his paycheck. His wife told Ray not to pay him until they needed to buy groceries. Ray told the man what his wife had said, and he said, "O.K. but that don't sound very Democratic".

Another of the Indians that worked for Ray like to go to Washington DC and demonstrate at the Whitehouse. While on one of these excursions the man died. His friends brought him home in a rented trailer. The Indian burial ceremony was held near Canby at his home and he was taken up the hill in a rickety old wagon. He was buried with all of his guns and other possessions along side of him. Ray thought that was not very Democratic either to bury all those nice guns.

Ray had a stroke while playing cards at the Canby Hotel in 1982. He was never quite the same again, but still enjoyed life.

Ray passed away in 1992 at the age of 89 years. He had never gotten over the loss of their twenty-year-old son John who died in a car wreck.

Dorothy still keeps active with her family and other activities. She has dozens of scrapbooks with family momentous and memories of her days of teaching.

Maybe the little Schoolmarm from Sacramento rode a horse like a sack of potatoes, but she left her mark on the hundreds of students whose lives she touched. She is dearly loved and respected by all.

October 3, 2000

A Time To Remember

Seventeen year old Richard (Dick) Haynes came from Buffalo, Missouri in 1869 by train. When he arrived at Redding, California there was nothing but a manzanita thicket and two buildings; a warehouse and a cookhouse. He was out of food and money. When he arrived at the cookhouse he was offered two jobs, peeling potatoes and washing dishes for fifty cents a day. It was just what he needed; he would receive his meals and sleep in the warehouse. He was looking for his sister Rachael and her husband Billie Eiler who had come out west with their ox team during the Civil War. They had left Iowa because Billie did not believe in fighting. It took them a full year to make the trip. They stopped over in Nevada where they found a cabin to spend the winter. The cabin caught fire and their youngest daughter was trapped inside. In the spring the devastated family had to move on leaving the lonely little grave on the hillside. They traveled over the mountains into California where they settled east of Redding at Cow Creek.

When Dick finally found their whereabouts he rode the stage over the bumpy dirt road to the small town of Millville, looking for them. From there he walked up Cow Creek where he found his sister and family. Staying with them he found a job working for a man that was building roads. At that time individuals hired hand labor built all the roads; after they were built the county took them over.

With pick and shovel and a wheelbarrow Dick started working building roads. He helped build the road up Bullskin Hill which was later named Oak Run road.

Dick got tired of cooking in a frying pan over an open campfire so he thought he would move on. He decided he wanted to see the ocean and he moved to the coast. There he went to work splitting rails out of the redwood trees. It was so cold and foggy that he never saw the sun the entire time he was there. That was not for him. He met a man that was going to Virginia City to work in the mines in Nevada and traveled along with him.

It was the time of the Modoc Indian War and on the way through Fall River Valley on the Glenburn plains they saw some Indians all dressed in their feathers and battle gear with their war paint on. Dick and his friend just pulled their oxen over to the side of the road and waited while the Indians just rode on by. Later they found out that this band of Indians were on their way to the Lava Beds to meet up with Captain Jack.

That night they camped at Fall River Mills. The stars were shining and Dick kicked his boots off and went to bed. The next morning on the tenth of May there was six inches of snow covering everything. His boots were full of snow. Dick noticed that his friend had carefully tucked his boots under his blankets. An Indian lady kindly let him dry his boots at her wickiup fire so he could get them on. They continued their journey to Nevada and when they camped in the Madeline Plains one evening, a panther became their camp companion for the night. The two men kept a fire of sagebrush burning all night while the panther kept his distance.

The Knoch Family at Carbon, California. Grandparents of Bessie (Haynes) Bosworth, Clara (Haynes), Mary (Murrer), Fred Knoch, Dee Knoch, Helena Knoch, Lillie (Brockman) and Anna (Rieger)

Fred and Helena Knoch at their home at Carbon, California

Before they reached their destination they stopped at Carson City, Nevada. In the letters Dick wrote to his sister he told that he could get a job running logs down the Carson River for the mines for $2.50 a day, but he couldn't swim and would be wet and cold all the time. He found a job on a ranch doing chores in Carson City for fifty cents a day, it was less pay, but he would have a warm bed and hot meals.

After a year Dick moved back to the Fall River Valley and went to work for Knoch and Murcken building a road down the Pit River Canyon. It was so steep going down into the canyon that they put a rope around Dick and lowered him down the cliffs to do the work. Mr. Winter had started the road, but he never got very far when he turned it over to Knoch and Murcken.

There was a trail at the bottom of the canyon along the Pit River from Carbon to Fall River Mills, which was an eight-mile trip. In 1859 Mr. Winter and Mr. Miller built a toll bridge across Pit River on the road. They were unable to finish the road and contracted to Knoch and Murcken to finish it for the price of $3,000. They hired a crew of Indian and white men for fifty cents a day and it was built with pick, shovel and wheelbarrow. Horses were used to move the large trees and rocks. Mr. Winter went broke and was unable to pay for the construction job, so Knoch and Murcken had to turn this into a toll road in hopes of recovering

Haynes Sawmill at the head of Goose Creek near Goose Valley

some of their expenses. The charge was .25 cents for horse and rider and .75 cents for a wagon with four horses. Even at that it would be a long time before they ever saw a profit.

Knoch's daughter Clara was fourteen years old and was helping her mother cook for the men over an open campfire. The camp moved to where the men were working as they moved down the trail. That is where Dick Haynes met his future bride. Clara was fishing in the Pit River and caught a big sturgeon that almost pulled her into the water. He was close by and saw she was is trouble. He grabbed her around the waist to save her. Not long after that they were married on December 6, 1884 just after her fifteenth birthday and he was twenty-three.

Dick had homesteaded a piece of land on Hat Creek near the Carbon Ranch where he had built a cabin; (this is now the Hat Creek Park on Highway 299 between Fall River and Burney.) This was the first wedding in the Knoch family and with all the neighbors pitching in it was a very festive occasion. As her dowry Clara's parents gave her the string of dairy cows that she had been milking

The newlyweds moved into his cabin on the homestead across Hat Creek. The couple lived there four years where their first two children

The Haynes family: Dick, Clara, Bessie, Fred, Etta.
In front: Annie, Eva, Alvin and Birdie. 1901 at Goose Valley

were born; Rosa in 1885 and Etta in 1888. Rosa lived only a few months when she died of the measles. They buried her there under a big Oak tree.

Dick Haynes explored opportunities in the surrounding country, searching for ways to turn his abilities and skills into a paying industry that would serve his needs and that of his neighbors as well.

He knew that people in the area would need lumber and he believed a small sawmill would be profitable to the whole country. Dick Haynes traded his homestead bordering the Carbon Ranch to Clara's Uncle, Dick Murcken for a place on Goose Creek. This place was ten miles north of Burney at the foot of Bunch Grass Mountain. This was just what Dick Haynes needed to develop his plans and Dick Murcken was glad to add a few more acres to his Carbon ranch.

The Goose Creek ranch was situated in a small valley at the head of Goose Creek where there were springs, swamps and bog holes as well as wild grassland and timbered areas. Dick moved his family into this beautiful spot and began the work of making a home and a productive ranch. He drained all the land possible and built a corduroy road of logs across the swamp. There were many improvements he wanted for the benefit and comfort of his family. They lived in a two-room log cabin; one room had a board floor and the other a dirt floor. There was a room above where the children climbed a ladder to crawl through a hole for a sleeping loft.

After moving to Goose Creek ten more children were born. Fred in1890; Alvin 1892; Eva, 1894; Johanna, 1896; Birdie, 1898; Bessie, 1900; Sidney, 1904; Gladys, 1907; Alice, 1909; and Leland, 1912. The children loved their home there and called it "Echo Dell", as the mountains would echo back to their hollers.

Burney and the surrounding settlements were desperately in need of lumber. Dick Haynes knew this was the opportunity he had been waiting for. His father-in-law Fred Knoch knew of a small mill at Nelson Point in Plumas County, which was available. That fall after the haying was done Fred and his son Dee went to Plumas County with two four-horse teams and wagons and brought the mill back to Goose Creek. Billy Eiler found a Pelton water wheel and a truck to haul it. With the help of his family, friends and neighbors, Dick built what was known as a "Muley" mill, the first of its kind in Shasta County.

Dick Haynes and his Indian friends, Samson Grant and Jack Hunt dug a ditch by hand to bring the water down from Goose Creek to run through

Haynes homestead at Goose Creek

the 250 foot flume they built to run the Pelton water wheel which powered the sawmill.

The neighbors, many of which were Indians helped to run the mill and they also fell and skidded the logs to the mill with their teams of horses. Everyone who worked at the mill was paid in lumber. Dick paid for the mill as well as supplying a needed commodity to the community, which gave him a real sense of accomplishment. Good clear lumber sold for $10.00 per thousand. In those days timber was plentiful and Dick only cut the best. Some of the Indian neighbors that worked at the mill were Jack Hunt, and his son Cleveland and Samson and Sullivan Grant. They all took their pay in lumber. This enabled the Indian families to build their homes before Dick built one for his own family.

The Indians idolized Dick Haynes; they always spoke of him by saying, "my good friend, Dick Haynes". The Indians had good houses that were finished outside but never on the inside. They also had good log barns. They raised gardens and wild hay for their horses and cows. Their children went to school at the Bunker Hill school with the Haynes children. Bessie was always chosen to help the Indian children with their work at the chalkboard and they loved her as they did her father.

Herman Lonquist, also a homesteader, and a good carpenter built a lovely home for his family. In 1892, Dick hired Herman to build a large two-story house for his family. He paid Herman in enough lumber for a house and a barn and besides that he gave him $75.00 in cash.

Dick built a dairy-house with a water-powered box-churn for Clara. He brought water to the dairy and his home in a wooden flume. Clara did the work of a dozen people. She operated a small dairy, milking thirty cows. She set the milk in large tin pans after each milking then skimmed the cream off every night and morning. She then churned the butter and packed it for market. She raised chickens, pigs and a large garden besides, all her regular household duties. The children helped their mother, as they grew older. At night, she sewed to make the family clothing. Clara's clothesline was an advertisement for the Fall River Milling Company. Each undergarment that she made for the children was stamped with that insignia from the flour sacks that they were sewn from. On top of this she had a new baby every two years, for a total of twelve children.

The store in Burney took all of her butter and eggs in trade for the things she must buy. She usually had more credit at the store than she could use up.

The big garden fed the large family year around and there was enough to share with the Indians. Root vegetables and potatoes were stored in pits, first covered with hay and then a layer of dirt to keep them from freezing. Cabbage was turned upside down, wrapped in the outside leaves and stored in a trench filled with dirt. Onions and garlic were hung to dry. A barrel of sauerkraut was always made in the fall and stored in a cool place where it would last until spring. The hogs were butchered and smoked to provide them with hams and bacon. When Clara and Dick made their yearly trip to Fall River Mills to visit her family and get flour they brought enough back for the Indians. They also shared meat with them at hog butchering time. The Haynes family worked hard, but they ate and lived well.

The Indians were good, honest people and were hard workers. They liked the white people and would do anything for them. They would work at any job that Dick had. Anytime they needed money they would come to him and he would get his old pouch out of his pocket and always managed to dig some money out of the bottom of it so they could go to the grocery store and get their supplies.

The children went to the Bunker Hill school. It was the first school that was ever built in Burney Valley. The school was later moved closer to Goose Valley to what they called Chicken Flat. Even later on it was again put on skids and moved on into Goose Valley. The schools were moved to where the children were. This little brown schoolhouse only had room for ten or twelve kids.

Goose Creek was five miles up the hill from Goose Valley. The children had to walk down the canyon to Goose Valley to school. When Bessie first started school she was so small that her little legs would not carry her that far so her older brother Fred would carry her on his shoulders.

The older brothers and sisters walked that canyon for nine years. At one time a Panther stalked the children when they walked home from school. The oldest girl would walk backwards while the others held the hem of her dress to guide her. Their father told them if a panther ever was stalking them, they should turn and face him, as he would not attack as long as you were looking him in the eye. This was really difficult for the little girls to do, and they were very relieved when one of the Indians that worked for their father came along and scared the panther off. He told the girls to tell their father that he would not be at work the next day, that he was going to hunt the panther. He did kill him and the animal measured eight feet long from his nose to the tip of his tail.

Some of the Indian neighbors, friends and employees of the Haynes.

Selena LaMar, her Indian name was Sunset. Her father was a medicine man.
She taught Indian customs at the Mt. Lassen National Park

Old Gunsmith. Selena LaMar's grandfather

Piute Hooch named after a Pinto horse, Hat Creek Indian

Hat Creek Indian Chief Buckskin Jack

Short Charlie Snook

Dr. Liue, Burney Indian

Chuck Brown, Hat Creek Indian, father of Dave, Eric and Holiday

Old Shavehead Bob was mean and in a lot of massacres. He joined up with Captain Jack

Burney Valley Pete. Lived up Goose Creek and worked in Haynes Sawmill

In 1900 Dick Haynes contacted Typhoid Fever. The closest doctor was Dr. Cadwalder in Fall River Mills. It took him all day to drive his horse and buggy down to see Dick then drive back. An old lady that lived up the creek had a son who died of Typhoid and she took the blankets down and hung them in the creek to wash the germs out. She caused an epidemic all the way down the creek where the people used the water for drinking.

Bessie was a tiny baby and the eighth of twelve children. Clara had all she could handle. The neighbors were very good to come over to help, and the Hays brothers took turns and came to set with Dick at night so Clara could get some rest.

The children started working as soon as they were old enough. The older boys worked on the ranch and the smaller ones helped to hoe and pull weeds in the garden. The older girls helped with the cooking, housework and the caring of the smaller children.

The country schools had to have at least seven children to hold a school and keep a teacher. At times when a school district was short of students, the Haynes family would loan out one or more of their children to help out those school districts. One winter Clara had no school age children at home at all.

Birdie and Johanna practically grew up at Billy Eiler's at Cow Creek. There they only had a mile to walk to school. They sent Bessie down when she was six, but she was so little that all she did was set in the corner and cry all the time so they sent her home. Eva went to school at Oak Run with the Hunt family, as they needed an extra student there. Later she and Leland went to live with Dee Knoch and went to the Beaver Creek School.

Traveling was quite an adventure as you could only travel about twenty miles a day with a team and wagon. That is why so many of the first towns that were settled are twenty miles apart, as that is only as far as the pioneers could make it in a day. 1916 was the first time Bessie went to Redding when she was sixteen years old. It took three days when the family went down to see the Circus. Other than that the trip was made once a year for needed supplies.

In 1907 Dick Haynes bought a ranch at the foot of Hatchet Mountain from Litterall. It was a beautiful place of 1000 acres of good meadow and two homes, and a barn that would stable thirty-two horses. Other buildings included the blacksmith shop, a large chicken house and woodshed. The big house had three big bedrooms upstairs, one for the boys, one for the girls and the one for the overnight guests. When there were guests the girls would go out on the porch roof from their bedroom window and slide down a pole so they did not have to go through the visitor's bedroom. Down stairs was the parents bedroom, a huge living room, big dining room, parlor and kitchen with a porch all the way around the back of the house. The water was abundant and a lot of good timber was on the ranch. Richard thought that the price of $10.00 an acre was a fair price.

The ranch had been a stage stop for all the freight teams, cattle drive's and stage coaches when the Litteralls owned it. Travelers continued to stay there at the Haynes ranch. They had special corrals built for the cattle drives. Billy Woods and Pete Hook were the main people that drove cattle out of that country. Billy Woods worked for the Minch Meat Company out of Red Bluff and he would go around the valley and buy up cattle to drive down to Redding to butcher shops. Some were shipped to San Francisco to the packing houses there. Pete Hook bought cattle for his own butcher shop in Redding.

Cattle that came from the higher country of Big Valley had a longer drive and made several stops on the trail traveling southwest. Many of the ranchers put up the cattle and cowboys along the trail. From Big Valley their first stop was at Albaugh's near Pittville. Then on to Dee Knoch's at Fall River, then over the hill to Dave Doyle's at Hat Creek and on to the Haynes ranch past Burney. They then had to cross over Hatchet Mountain to Montgomery Creek where they stopped at the Spear's place, then on to Billy Eiler's at Cow Creek next on to Churn Creek at Charlie Lambs. The cattle could only be driven ten or twelve miles a day. Usually the herds of cattle were only about one hundred to one hundred and fifty with three to five cowboys driving them. Sometimes if the cattle had come out of Big Valley and gotten as far as the Haynes ranch, the Big Valley cowboys would turn around and go home as this was about half way. Then the Haynes boys would drive the cattle on to Redding.

The winter of 1916 was really severe. Seventeen feet of snow had fallen on Hatchet Mountain. It would snow, then rain and settle it, freeze, then snow again. They went twenty-eight days without mail. Finally Herman Giessner walked across the mountain on snowshoes and packed the letter mail back.

There was seven foot of snow on the level at the Haynes ranch. Clara was afraid the roof of the house was going to cave in so she had all the children get up there with shovels and shovel the snow off. The barn roof

Richard and Clara Haynes

was also in danger, but they used a different technique for that. They threw long cables over the roof with a team of horses hitched to each end. Driving the horses back and forth in a seesaw fashion the snow was cut into large chunks that could be removed more easily.

The cattle drives going south usually came through about Christmas time. All the cattle had come into the Haynes ranch and were waiting for a chance to cross over Hatchet Mountain. The cattle were fed there, but they were getting short of feed because there were so many cattle. The mountain was a frozen block of snow but something had to be done. Alvin went into Burney and hired all the available men that could handle a pick and shovel and they shoveled a trail across Hatchet Mountain. Cutting the snow into huge blocks and prying it out of the trail they cleared a trail just wide enough for one cow to travel. At that time the snow had settled down to seven feet deep so the men could walk above the cows.. The cattle were trailed out single file with the men walking above them pushing them along with a prod pole to cross over Hatchet Mountain until they got to Montgomery Creek where there was not so much snow. The Haynes cattle came along behind them traveling to pastures at Oak Run on the Hunt Ranch. Nearly 600 head of cattle traveled one by one over that trail.

One of the reasons Dick decided to leave Goose Creek was because they were pretty isolated and there were no men traveling by. He had all those daughters he wanted to find a good husband for and there was not much of a chance at Goose Creek.

In 1941, the 57th Wedding Anniversary of Richard and Clara Haynes. Their children back row: Etta Hufford, Fred Haynes, Alvin Haynes, Eva Giessner, Sidney Haynes, Birdie Bidwell, Bessie Bosworth, Leland Hanes. Front Row: Richard and Clara Haynes and her father Fred Knoch

The first to marry was Etta who married Ed Hufford. He was the first Government hired ranger and he was living on Hatchet Mountain in a small shack. Dick told him he should move to the ranch with them and not live up there all by himself. When he moved on to Hat Creek to work he lived with the Wilcox family. He was the first person to catch trout in the lower lakes and transport them by packhorse and plant them in all the small lakes in the 1000 Lakes area of Mt. Lassen. It was said that Mr. Haynes gave Ed Hufford a sack of potatoes to marry his daughter.

Dick and Clara were proud that their daughters married well. Eva married Otto Giessner who was a rancher at Hat Creek, Birdie married Mac Bidwell who owned one of the best ranches at Hat Creek, Annie married Herman Giessner who ran a creamery at Hat Creek. Bessie married Wallace Bosworth who was from a ranching family at Cayton Valley.

Wallace started taking cattle from Cayton Valley to Flournoy, Ca. when he was only seventeen years old. They drove the 500 head past the Haynes ranch to their winter pasture.

Bessie met Wallace at a dance and they were married in 1924. They went to Redding and were married in the hotel there. When they went

Bessie Bosworth on her 100th birthday, May 29, 2000, with her sons Robert and Bruce

downstairs the next morning there was the whole crew of men that she had been cooking for all summer on her fathers ranch. They stayed at Cayton Valley for several years where he worked with his family on the ranch. Their first son Robert was born in 1927 then Wallace Jr. (Bruce) in 1929.

Wallace and Bessie would take the cattle to Red Bluff in the wintertime. The first year they stayed at Flournoy, east of Red Bluff caring for the cattle. They lived in a little shack that would not even make a good buckaroo camp. Bessie cut up old cardboard cartons to fill the cracks in the walls and floor to make it as warm as she could.

The boys would go to school wherever it was handy, sometimes they would be at Hat Creek or Burney in better weather, then move with the cattle to the cow camps. They did go to school at Proberta for three years then Wallace and Bessie bought a home in Red Bluff where they finally made a permanent home.

Each year they would travel back and forth with the cattle, summering them in the mountains around Cayton Valley then to the lower valley in the wintertime.

Later after being married Wallace and Bessie ran sheep. In the summer driving the sheep to Cayton Valley took about three weeks from the lower country. They ran sheep there until the bears ran them out. They had 3000 ewes that they wintered around Red Bluff and later they trailed them to Hayden Hill in Lassen County for the summer months. During the war the sheep business was thriving. The Army needed the wool to make uniforms so the wool price was good. The military also fed a lot of mutton to their troops.

Dick was born June 9, 1852 in Missouri and died at his beloved ranch June 11, 1947 at the age of 96. His motto, *"If you cannot speak well of a man, do not mention his name at all."*

Clara was born at Nelson Point, Ca. in Plumas County November 22, 1869. She passed away on November 30, 1954.

Clara deeded the Haynes ranch to all of her children after her husband's death. Alvin was the manager until he died from injuries from a tractor accident.

Bessie and her sister Eva did a lot of traveling. They toured Canada, Alaska, Hawaii, New Zealand and Australia. Some times they would take Bessie's grandson with them as their tour guide.

Three daughters of Dick and Clara Haynes celebrated their 100th birthday. Eva, Birdie and Bessie all passed that birthday. Bessie who celebrated her birthday on May 30, 2000 is proud of her heritage and likes to tell the story of times to remember.

The heritage that Dick and Clara Haynes proudly left their children was their belief,

"The joy of working and living a successful life."

October 9, 2000

About the Author

Glorianne Weigand and her husband Stan are fourth generation Cattle Ranchers on the 101 Ranch at Adin, California. High in the mountain country of Northeastern California they ride the range, put up the hay, feed cattle in the wintertime and calve them out in the spring. They are one of the few true ranch families that still do a lot of things the way their ancestors did. Calves are still roped at branding time with all the neighbors pitching in to help each other. Gathering cattle and working together where neighbors help each other is the main social life in this ranching community.

Glorianne has written for a livestock monthly newspaper for nine years and has compiled her historical feature articles into her series of books. Living the ranch life and working with cattle gives her an insight to the stories that these Pioneers have to share.

Wagons West is her seventh book in six years. Each book contains up to eighteen different true short stories of pioneer families with over one hundred wonderful old photographs.

101 Ranch

Glorianne Weigand
Star Rt. 2 Box 31
Adin, CA 96006
530.299.3465
www.dustytrails101.com
Email: weigand@hdo.net

Qty	Title	Price Each	Total
	"Dusty Trails"	12.95	
	"More Dusty Trails"	14.95	
	"Dusty Trails Again"	14.95	
	A Mare Among The Geldings	14.95	
	Circle The Wagons	17.95	
	Wagons West	17.95	

7.25% Sales Tax _____

Postage & Handling per book $2.00
(Maximum $5.00)

Total _____

Customer Name _____

Address _____

_____

Phone _____